The Mystery of the Silver Salver
is Kathy's fourth book in the
Woodford Mystery series.

Kathy Morgan lives on the Wiltshire/ Dorset
border, and is involved in the world of
antiques.
She worked for many years as a school
librarian, and also had an equestrian hoofcare
business. Now Kathy is enjoying having the
time to write about some of her experiences,
and uses her imagination for the rest!

Sadly many of the things she has seen and
heard will never make it into print.

Kathy Morgan's
Woodford Mystery Series:

The Limner's Art
The Bronze Lady
Death By Etui
The Mystery of the Silver Salver
Deadly Philately

Also by Kathy Morgan:
Silver Betrayal
Snowflake, the Cat Who Was Afraid of Heights

The
Mystery of the
Silver Salver

by Kathy Morgan

Copyright September 2017 Stormybracken Publishing Kathy Morgan.

Printed by KDP

2nd edition 2021

For Barry 'Basher' Beaumont, with whom I shared many hours sitting on the back of the van at antiques fairs, discussing Life and eating bacon sandwiches. I avoided his cigar smoke; he complained about the state of my boots.

Although my name is on the cover, a large number of people have contributed to this book. A few special mentions for Bob, Mum, Fiona, Lydia, Martin, Nova and Annette - you have all been wonderful, thank you.

My facebook, twitter and Words friends - thank you for keeping my brain ticking over during the writing process, and answering my random questions!

My photograph is also on the cover, thanks to *Photography by Louisa Jane* who came and spent some time with me and my horses one glorious sunny evening, and worked miracles with the results. Snowflake wasn't so keen!

The photograph of me and Storm was taken by Bob!

Thank you Charlton Chilcott-Legg for the wonderful image of a silver salver on the front cover, and a map of Woodford!

Silver Salver

The word 'salver' originates from the Latin 'salva' and roughly translates to 'Safe & Sound' (we could either study German or Latin at my school. I chose German, so please excuse this attempt!). Food tasters were employed to check whether the food intended for Very Important People had been poisoned, and then if they suffered no ill-effects would place the tested, and therefore presumed safe, food onto the salver for the intended consumer.

A salver is typically a tray without handles, and can be in the form of a plate or platter. They regularly feature in period dramas, usually carried by a butler to present the master of the house with his post at breakfast, or by a maid offering cocktails to the guests at a party.

Silver or silver plate salvers are also a popular choice for trophies, and are easy to engrave with the name of the sport or company. One exception to this is the trophy presented to the Ladies' Singles Tennis Champion at Wimbledon for all the photographs and celebrations. That salver is retained by the All England Lawn Tennis and Croquet Club in their museum, and the champion is given a 14 inch replica of the trophy, engraved with the champions' names. The original trophy is very ornate, measures 18.75 inches in diameter, and is known as the Venus Rosewater Dish. It is not named after five-time winner Venus Williams, but it is a copy of an antique stored in the Louvre museum in Paris. A rosewater dish was an integral part of the English tradition, where after a meal the people would wash their hands under a stream of rosewater (and those of you who have read *Death By Etui* will know all about the modern day benefits and uses of rosewater!) which was poured into the dishes.

Silver is a precious metal, and was first mined over five thousand years ago, in the part of the world now known as Turkey. Around seven hundred years ago in Britain, the decision was made to introduce a system of hallmarks to prove that the gold, silver and platinum items conformed to a designated standard. In the modern day United Kingdom this is done by one of the four Assay Offices: Birmingham, Edinburgh, London and Sheffield, and only if the item is legally hallmarked can it be described and sold as silver, unless it weighs less than 7.78 grammes, in which case the item is probably too small to accommodate a hallmark. In 1999 the UK law was changed to conform to European law, and lowered the accepted standard of silver, which enabled a much wider selection of items to be legally described as silver.

A silver hallmark is made up of at least three different marks: a maker's mark, for example an item made by the silversmith Hester Bateman would be stamped with her initials HB; a purity grade, for example 950 grade, or 925 grade; and the Assay Office which has tested and graded the item as silver, for example the three towered castle for Edinburgh. Originally the hallmarks were made by hand, using a stamp and a hammer, but these days lasers are usually used.

Character list in alphabetical order:

Adrian Edwards – antiques dealer
Alison Isaac – equestrian coach, sister of Jennifer, daughter of Peter
Amadna – chef at The Ship Inn
Barry Johnson – works at Williamson Antiques
Bertram Kemp – co-owner of Kemp and Holmes Antiques Auctioneers and Valuers
Caroline Bartlett – daughter of Lisa Bartlett
Christine Black – ex-wife of Paul
Cliff Williamson – owner of Williamson Antiques, husband of Rebecca Williamson
Crispin Keogh – works at Kemp and Holmes Antiques Auctioneers and Valuers
Dafydd Jenkins – silver dealer
Daniel Bartlett – Black's Auction House employee, cousin of Caroline Bartlett, son of Gemma
Gemma Isaac – co-owner of The Woodford Tearooms, sister of Lisa, mother of Daniel and Nathan
Hazel Wilkinson – antiques dealer
Heather Stanwick – daughter of Kim and Robin
Hugh Jones - silversmith
Ian McClure – policeman
Jason Chapillon – works at Kemp and Holmes Antiques Auctioneers and Valuers
Jennifer Isaac – equine vet, girlfriend of Paul Black, sister of Alison, daughter of Peter
John Robson – antiques dealer
John Thomas - policeman
Linda Beecham – antiques dealer
Lisa Bartlett – co-owner of The Woodford Tearooms, mother of Caroline, aunt of Daniel Bartlett
Lydia Black – daughter of Paul and Christine Black
Kim Stanwick – married to Robin, mother of Heather

Madeleine Powell – manager of Woodford Riding Club

Natasha Holmes – co-owner of Kemp and Holmes Antiques Auctioneers and Valuers

Nathan Bartlett – son of Gemma, brother of Daniel

Nicola Stacey – works at Williamson Antiques

Patty Coxon – Detective Sergeant

Paul Black – owner of Black's Auction House

Peter Isaac – equine vet, father of Jennifer and Alison Isaac

Rebecca Martin – works at Black's auctions

Robin Morton – antiques dealer

Sarah Handley – owner of The Ship Inn

Simon Maxwell-Lewis – antiques dealer

Stanley Simmons – auctioneer at Swanwick Auctioneers

Tanya Gordon – works at Swanwick Auctioneers

Tom Higston – barman at The Ship Inn

Tristram Bridger – Woodford shop owner

Veronica Bank – Woodford resident

WOODFORD
By Charlton Chilcott-Legg

Chapter 1

Monday 1st August 2016, 11.30am

'I heard that he has spent the last five years creaming off the best of the silver they sent to him to be repaired. I always thought there was something dodgy about him. *I* never trusted him with any of my stock,' said the pale faced antiques dealer, his greasy black hair falling over his forehead into his eyes.

Rebecca Martin decided she had heard enough from the man, who seemed to have only dropped into Black's Auction House to waste her time with malicious gossip. The antiques trade press were reporting that the body of a well-known silversmith had been discovered a few days earlier, and dealers like this one were doing their bit to assist the investigation by sharing their versions of events with each other. Opening the front door she managed to manoeuvre him out with soothing promises that she would ensure her boss, Paul Black, took a look at the two Japanese bronze vases the man had brought in to be entered for the next Oriental antiques sale. She watched with relief as he slunk off down the brick-paved driveway towards the High Street, no doubt ready to spread his unpleasant opinions with someone else.

It was a baking hot and sunny day in the town of Woodford, in Brackenshire, and the reception area, which also served as her office, was marginally cooler than the outdoor temperature. The whole of the south-west of England was engulfed in a heatwave which was set to last for several more days, if the weather forecasters could be believed.

Closing the door firmly behind the man, Rebecca went to the fridge, in the small kitchen area at the back of the office. Tempted to climb inside to cool down, she settled for leaning in and slowly picking out an ice cold bottle of mineral water.

Returning to her desk, she began to sort through the lists of items still waiting to be collected and paid for by the purchasers from an auction three weeks earlier. She winced as she heard the noise of a fierce argument in full battle, forcing its way through the solid door and walls of her boss's office.

A blast of the hot summer air as someone opened the front door startled her, and her face flushed even more with embarrassment at being caught listening to the dispute.

'Was that Adrian Edwards I just saw leaving? He was walking down the High Street with that awful Veronica Bank and another older lady.' Cliff Williamson, Rebecca's ex-husband, stood in the doorway, his question barely leaving his lips before he was looking in horror towards the sound of the shouting coming from behind the closed door in front of him. 'Good grief, who on earth is in there with Paul?'

Cliff was a well-built man, but even his six foot two inch frame wasn't enough of a barrier to prevent the heat from outside rushing in.

'Hi Cliff, you made me jump! Please shut the door, you are letting what little cool air there is in here escape.'

'Oh, yes, of course, sorry.' Cliff busied himself with closing the door firmly behind him, before turning to his ex-wife. 'What a racket! Is he OK?'

As always when he saw her, which was several times a week because of the nature of their individual jobs, and the fact they had three teenage children together, he could kick himself for breaking up their marriage. In his eyes Rebecca was the perfect image of a woman: five foot eight inches tall, with a gorgeous curvaceous figure, dark brown eyes and long black curly hair. Although, he reflected, her hair was much shorter now than when they were married, only brushing the bottom of her shoulders instead of reaching to the small of her back.

Rebecca nodded towards Paul's office. 'Christine went in there a couple of minutes ago. The argument started just before you came in.' She glanced at Cliff. 'It feels just like old times, listening to those two argue like that, doesn't it?'

Cliff grimaced. 'Horrible. And I bet I know what it is about. It will be over a woman, just as it used to be all those years ago.'

Rebecca looked at Cliff in amazement. 'Really? Another woman? Why on earth would Christine be upset about Paul's liaisons after all this time?'

She stood up and locked the front door, turning the 'OPEN' sign to 'CLOSED'. Beckoning for Cliff to follow her, Rebecca began to walk down the corridor which ran alongside Paul Black's office.

'They have been divorced for years, and Christine has definitely moved on, as has Paul. I can't bear to listen to any more of that, and it doesn't sound as though they are going to calm down soon. I feel as though I am eavesdropping, and I don't like it. Come on, it is both cooler and quieter over in the warehouse. You can tell me what you know in there.'

Together they walked in silence the short distance between the administrative offices and the auction house's sales rooms. Once they were both ensconced in a corner of the warehouse, surrounded by display cabinets containing hundreds of thousands of pounds worth of silver items, Cliff checked that none of the other Black's employees were within earshot. He ran a hand over the top of his short auburn hair, a sign Rebecca recognised and it made her suspicious.

'Christine came round to see me, last night.'

Rebecca kept quiet, although she wanted to ask why her best friend was having secret meetings in the evening with her ex-husband at his flat. An unwelcome thought flitted through her mind that this was what Paul was angry about.

Seeing the look on her face, Cliff guessed the conclusion she had jumped to, and he quickly tried to explain 'Oh, no, nothing happened between us. I mean, er, you know, me and Christine, no, no, nothing is going on. I wouldn't. *She* wouldn't. We wouldn't. I promise.'

The expression on Cliff's face was similar to the one she was used to seeing on their children's faces when one of them was accused of doing something they hadn't that Rebecca began to laugh.

'Alright, calm down. I believe you. Anyway, it is none of my business who you sleep with now, Cliff, remember? Just as my love life is none of yours. Although having said that, you and my best friend together is not a great image. I know you weren't happy when you thought Paul was making a move on me.' She winked at him, trying to encourage him to relax a little too. It worked, and Cliff began his explanation again.

'Right, yes, of course, no I wasn't happy about that. Anyway, Christine wanted my advice about something completely different. She had some news to break to Paul, and was worried that he wouldn't take it very well.'

Rebecca chuckled 'Well, she was right there! What on earth did you tell her to do? It doesn't sound as though it was very successful.'

Cliff ran his hand over his hair again, and looked around for somewhere to sit amongst all the items prepared for the next auction. He spotted a comfortable-looking sofa covered in a strong William Morris print, and sank his body down onto it, breathing a sigh of defeat. Rebecca watched as he leaned back and put his hands over his face, as if he was hiding the part he had played in the storm currently raging in the office of his best friend.

'To be honest Rebecca, by the time Christine came to see me the damage had already been done. I promise you, this has nothing to do with me; Christine just wanted a sounding board, you know, someone to bounce a few ideas around with.'

'So, why didn't she come to see me? What is it that only you could help her with?'

'I don't think she came to me because she thought I was the only one who could help; Christine knew I would understand Paul's feelings on the subject, that is all. Lydia has decided to leave school now that she has finished her GCSEs, which I don't think Paul is going to be too worried about' Rebecca nodded in agreement as Cliff continued 'and will start work as a trainee at Kemp and Holmes Antiques Auctioneers and Valuers.'

Rebecca looked at Cliff in disbelief. She suddenly realised her mouth was open, and closed it quickly. Slowly, she spoke as she worked out the implications of the news. 'Paul's sixteen-year-old daughter is going to be working closely with Natasha Holmes? And Christine is happy about this? Good grief, I am not surprised Paul is reacting the way he is!'

'I know, I know. I couldn't believe my ears when Christine told me. Apparently Lydia had already applied for the post, and been called for an interview, before her mother knew anything about it. But what could Christine do? Lydia is rebelling against her father in the most effective way she knows how, and she is fully aware of the consequences of her actions. Christine was hoping Lydia wouldn't get the job, but it looks as though Natasha doesn't have any qualms about the situation. Which is typical of that woman. It wouldn't surprise me if she has employed Lydia precisely to upset Paul.'

Rebecca joined him on the sofa. 'What a mess,' was all she could think of to say.

They sat side-by-side for a few moments in silence, contemplating the tricky situation their friends were in. Cliff took Rebecca's hand and said 'I really hope that none of my kids despise me enough to try to hurt me like this. I know I have given all of you plenty of reasons to do so.'

Rebecca squeezed his hand and said 'Yes, you have, but you have been doing your best to make up for your behaviour. Paul really hasn't made much of an effort with his children over the years. He never tries to see things from their point of view, or spend time with them doing what they want to do. I can't see Paul running either of his children all over Brackenshire for swimming or riding lessons, or helping them to set up for music gigs, as you do. Don't worry about our children; you are doing a good job as their dad, and they all love you to pieces.'

Cliff wiped his eyes with his free hand. 'I really have become a soppy wuss in the last few months,' he laughed. 'Thank you Rebecca, I do hope you are right.'

Rebecca unclasped her hand from his and asked 'Is that why you came up to Black's? To warn Paul about Lydia's plans? Or have you heard any more about Hugh Jones' death? You were right, by the way, it was that ghastly Adrian Edwards in here, trying to make out he knew all along that Hugh was not to be trusted, and that he had never used Hugh's silversmith skills in the past. The chances of a man like that having anything worthy of Hugh's attention is laughable, I had to get rid of him as quickly as I could.'

'I thought I recognised his greasy black hair. He was with that awful woman Veronica Bank, and an older lady who I did not recognise. Adrian lied if he told you he didn't work with Hugh. Adrian is one of the top silver dealers in this country, and Hugh was one of the best silversmiths. They worked closely together, and I know that Adrian was one of Hugh's best customers. Don't you remember all the rumours about Hugh's disappearance in the first place were linked to some deal he and Adrian had about a salver? Adrian came and found me while I was having breakfast in the tearooms, and specifically asked me if I had seen Hugh. I wasn't aware Hugh was missing until that day. Adrian said he wanted everyone in the trade to work together and shut Hugh's silversmith business down.'

'Oh yes, I had forgotten about that, no wonder Adrian is trying to distance himself from any connection with Hugh now that his body has been found. I had no idea that Adrian deals in quality antiques. I find that hard to believe, but then I suppose I have only ever met him once here at Black's, he usually buys from us online. He is always buying the crap stuff, you know, the silver which is split and full of dints. He doesn't come into the antiques centre does he?'

'No, I always thought it was because the stuff we have in there isn't good enough for him. I am surprised he is the one buying up all the crap from here. I suppose he buys it at below-scrap prices and then sends it to the melt.'

'Well, whatever he is doing, he is one of the worst rumour-mongerers I know, and that is saying something working here!'

'I know; the trade is full of the gossip. Isn't it a sad situation about Hugh Jones though, whatever the true story? I haven't heard any more genuine details; only what is said in the paper and all the versions the general dealers have been coming in with. Although, I have been waiting for our pet undercover policeman to turn up at any moment. He is never far away when there is trouble in the antiques world.'

'You mean Robin Morton? Yes, he is noticeable by his absence isn't he?'

Cliff nodded. 'As for this Lydia business, I am going to do my best not to get any further involved than I already am. I came to see you, actually. Rebecca, I have to tell you some more bad news: Simon Maxwell-Lewis has been released from prison.'

Chapter 2

Monday 1st August 2016, 11.30am

'How the hell could you let this happen?'

'Me? This isn't my fault, Paul. You have brought this on yourself.'

'Oh, yes, that's right, blame me. Everything is always my fault isn't it?'

Christine sighed, and tried not to let her voice rise to match his. 'This isn't about blame or fault.'

'No? What is it about then? No daughter of mine is going to breathe the same air as that bitch. Managing Director, my arse. Managing the Director more like. You know she is only MD because she lets that idiot do perverted things to her?'

'Oh, Paul, stop it. You don't know that any of those rumours about Natasha Holmes and Bertram Kemp are true. If you ask me, they are typical of the sort of rubbish men make up about women they are scared of, and women make up about women they are jealous of. I notice you don't object to Lydia working with Bertram Kemp, who, if these assertions of yours are true, is equally if not more guilty of being morally bent?'

'Well I didn't ask you. Everybody knows about those two. Why else would someone like him go into business with someone like her? I do not want Lydia to be exposed to that sort of way of working. And this *is* about fault. If you hadn't made such a fuss about custody when we first broke up then none of this would have happened. Anyway, Lydia could have come to work for me if she wanted to go into auctioneering. Why didn't she come and ask me for a job?'

'Now hang on a minute, I admit I was angry and upset when you cheated on me while we were married, and there was no way I wanted my babies to grow up thinking your bit of skirt was more of a mummy to them than I was, but you broke the custody agreements we had by not seeing your children when you should have done far more times. And let's not forget when you built your house next door you made no provisions for them. If you were so desperate to see your children why did you not give them their own bedrooms? You have had years to put right any wrongs you think I may have instigated. And, another thing, Lydia did ask you for a job at Black's, but you turned her down.'

'Two years ago!' said Paul, ignoring Christine's points about his part in the break-down of their custody agreements, and about his cottage and the deliberate lack of bedroom space for his children. 'You cannot blame me for not wanting to have a fourteen year old tampering with the computer system of my business. She could have screwed around with all sorts of confidential customer records and financial information. Hardly the image I want to project of a professional auction house. And it would have smacked of nepotism.'

'At the time she asked you, Lydia knew far more about computers and the internet than anyone who was working here, and you needed help. She was very upset when you rejected her. She is reliable and trustworthy, and she would have been an asset to you. She told me there was no way she would ever ask you for a job again. And as for nepotism, I don't know how you dare bring that up as an argument when you are only here because your father set this company up.'

'I got to where I am today because I grafted and worked and studied. My dad did not just hand me the company, and I won't let my children think they can simply walk into a job here.'

Christine held her hands up in surrender. 'I am sorry, you are quite right, you have earned your position here. All I am saying is, that you have had plenty of opportunities to put right the wrongs we *both* exacted on our children years ago, and this time you are going to have to take responsibility for the fact that your daughter has deliberately chosen to go and work for Natasha Holmes, even though she knows it will upset you.'

Paul stopped pacing and looked over at his ex-wife, who was sitting on the chaise lounge in the corner of his office, her smooth blonde hair defying the heated atmosphere, and maintaining its normal straight neatness. She had positioned herself there in an attempt to calm the situation, and hoped that Paul would copy her body language and also sit down. So far her actions had only resulted in causing Paul to build himself up into even more of a rage. He felt as though he was the only one in the room who could see the seriousness of the situation. In his opinion she was behaving like an unfeeling ex-wife instead of a caring mother.

In contrast to Christine's pale complexion, Paul's was turning an unpleasant shade of crimson, and his glasses were steaming up. His six foot frame was topped by slightly too long floppy brown hair, and he loomed over her as he shouted 'Don't you mean "because" she knows it will upset me? You know perfectly well that Lydia has never shown any interest in the auction business, or in antiques, and is only doing this because I wouldn't pay for her to go and fritter her life away on a Gap Year in a couple of years' time after she had completed her 'A' level courses. Well if she wanted my attention then she has it now!'

Christine closed her eyes and attempted to stay calm, although she was finding it hard, because he was right to some extent. Lydia had told her that she only applied for the apprenticeship at Kemp and Holmes because the job description specifically mentioned working directly with Natasha Holmes, and Lydia knew how much her father despised the woman. Christine decided it would be better to keep quiet about that piece of information.

Standing up, she said 'Look, Paul, whatever has gone on in the past is now history. We have to deal with the present, and that means accepting that Lydia will be taking up a position at Kemp and Holmes, in Swanwick, next week. Whatever her motivation, our daughter has applied for and been given a job there, and we *both* need to accept that. I suggest that you congratulate her …' Christine gave Paul a steely glare when he began to explode again, causing him to swallow his anger and purse his lips in an effort to keep the words from spewing out, and her voice hardened as she continued '… by sending her a text message. That way you can at least be seen to be behaving like the adult in this situation, if, as you believe, she is behaving like a child. And as for this other nonsense about Natasha Holmes' morals, which I think is all a load of made-up nonsense, then you will just have to trust that your daughter takes after her mother, and not her father.'

Paul watched open mouthed as Christine swept out of his office. She closed the door a little harder than she intended, and stood outside for a few seconds while she attempted to regulate her breathing. She had been taken by surprise at the level of emotion which had swamped her usual serenity. During the breakdown of their marriage, and for several years afterwards, Christine had dropped as low as she thought a person could go. Her health suffered to the point where the thought of committing suicide seemed to be a solution to her overwhelming problems.

One day she found the inner-strength and then the courage to begin the long climb back up to health, and for several years she had thought she was home and dry. But the past few minutes had rattled her, and she was upset that those old feelings of frustration and anger had so easily resurfaced, and with such force. She was cross that she and Paul had resorted to their old pattern of hurling insults and accusations at each other.

With tears threatening to blind her vision, Christine made it to the front door, temporarily held up by the fact that Rebecca had locked it earlier, and then she was out into the blast of heat bouncing off the driveway. Quickly she walked out to the road, and down the High Street, to the estate agents where she worked. She forced herself to move back into professional mode. Christine greeted her colleagues, hoping they wouldn't notice she had been upset a few minutes earlier, before settling down behind her desk and focusing on her work.

Meanwhile Rebecca and Cliff's little chat had been interrupted by the rest of Black's staff returning from their lunch break. They had spent it almost opposite the former chapel which now housed Black's Auction House, sitting in relative coolness under the trees on The Green, near the village pond, eating ice creams. The tranquillity of the warehouse was replaced with the noise and energy of rested and revived workers, as they enthusiastically began the afternoon's jobs.

Cliff decided to go straight back to his antiques centre for the afternoon, and give his friend a chance to calm down, leaving Rebecca to tentatively make her way back to her desk. She was relieved to hear the shouting had stopped, and guessed that one or both of the warring couple had left through the now unlocked front door. By the time Paul opened his office door again Rebecca was engrossed in calculating and making payments to the vendors from the recent general auction.

'If anyone needs me, I'll be in The Ship Inn,' he said, as he walked past her. Rebecca had a suspicion he had been crying.

Chapter 3

Monday 1st August 2016, 12 noon

Paul didn't have far to walk, because his auction house was situated at the top of the High Street where it joins the Brackendon Road off to the west, and The Ship Inn was diagonally opposite, to the left. The pub backed onto The Green, a large piece of common land covering approximately twelve acres, where the cricket club played their matches in the summer months, and the town held its annual Woodford Summer Fete. It was also the site of the Woodford Flea Market, a recent venture between Cliff Williamson and The Ship Inn's landlady, Sarah Handley, and one which already had a loyal following.

Paul's mind was in turmoil as he crossed the Brackendon Road without checking for oncoming traffic, and he was brought to an abrupt halt by a horse and rider who narrowly avoided running him over. The horse stretched out its head to touch him as he walked out in front of them, making him jump.

'Sorry, sorry!' he apologised to the rider, and then did a double-take. 'Jennifer?'

Jennifer Isaac, Paul's girlfriend and local equine vet, looked down at him with concern. 'Are you alright, Paul?'

'Yes, yes, it's nothing. I'll tell you about it later.' Despite his anger and frustration Paul admired Jennifer's shapely legs at his eye level, which were clad in navy blue with a wide fluorescent pink stripe running down their length. 'Who is this?' he asked, patting the black muzzle which was gently nudging his arm.

'This is Baby!'

'Baby?'

'Yes, well her real name is French Spinner, but when her owners bought her years ago she was the youngest of their horses, so they nicknamed her Baby, and it has stuck. Isn't she gorgeous?'

Paul wasn't particularly interested in horses. As far as he was concerned one end bit and the other end kicked, but he had to admit that this horse was a friendly soul. 'Mmmh, lovely. Where are you going?'

'Oh, only around the block for an hour. We left the stables and came up on the Trailway. We have just checked out the bridleway which runs around the back of this line of buildings where your auction house is. Baby and I enjoyed being able to have a long canter, so we'll be doing that regularly from now on. Now we will continue down this short section of Brackendon Road, rejoin the Trailway, and then back to the stables. Are you sure you are OK?' her brown eyes were full of concern.

Paul smiled; he felt a lot better for seeing Jennifer. 'Honestly, I'm fine. You go on and enjoy your ride.'

He gave the horse a pat on her neck, and stood back as Jennifer and Baby continued walking down the road.

Neither of them noticed the leather clad motorcyclist who had been taking photos of them with his mobile phone. He waited until Jennifer and Baby were a distance away, before climbing on board his motorbike and riding down the road behind them.

Reaching the door to the pub without further incident, Paul walked in and was welcomed by the barman, Tom Higston.

'Afternoon, Paul. Boozy pint, or vitamin C boost?'

Paul smiled, acknowledging Tom's familiarity with his usual choices. 'After the morning I have had a whisky would be my preference, rather than a beer, but I had better settle for an orange juice, please mate.'

'Anything to eat?'

Paul focused on the Specials board, realising if he didn't have some lunch now he wouldn't have time to eat again before six o'clock that evening. 'Yes, please, I'll have a beef salad. Thanks, Tom. I'll be in the snug.'

Paul carried his drink through to the snug, where the Victorian grate contained a dried flower arrangement, and settled his jeans-clad backside down on a section of the old velvet covered benches which ran around the walls. He began to brood over the morning's interaction with his ex-wife.

'Hello, Paul' Sarah Handley called into the snug on her way past. 'Oh, you don't look too happy!' She stopped, her hands full of the used plates discarded by happy diners.

'I'm not,' grunted Paul.

'Hang on a minute, I'll pop these to the kitchen and come back.'

Sarah returned, less than a minute later. Recently widowed, Sarah's plump figure had undergone a transformation and she had dropped a couple of dress sizes. Paul thought she looked a bit thin, but knew better than to comment.

Sarah asked 'What has happened?'

27

Paul shook his head. 'My daughter is going to work for Natasha Holmes.' Seeing Sarah's puzzled expression he explained 'You know, Natasha Holmes, of Kemp and Holmes Antiques Auctioneers and Valuers in Swanwick.'

Sarah perched on one of the stools opposite Paul. 'Yes, I know who Natasha Holmes is. I just can't think why it is such a bad thing for Lydia to go and train alongside one of the best auctioneers of antiques in the county. No offence.'

Paul couldn't look Sarah in the eyes, and instead found his hands fascinating to study as he linked his fingers together, and repeatedly flexed and unflexed them.

'Because Natasha hates my guts, that's why. She has only given Lydia a job to pay me back.'

'For what?'

'For breaking her heart.'

'Really? You and Natasha? I didn't know that. When?'

'Oh, ages ago. Probably before you and Mike moved here.'

'And you think she has held a grudge for all of these years, and is taking her revenge by giving your daughter the chance to learn the family business in a successful auction house, and providing her with the opportunity to see a wide range and variety of antiques? Well, Paul, Natasha Holmes is clearly a vindictive woman whose romantic aspirations were squashed and stamped on by you. It must be more than twelve years since Mike and I moved here, so just how long ago, exactly, was it that you and Natasha were rolling around between the sheets? And how many months or years did this intense romance last?'

Paul looked sheepish. 'OK, OK, we only slept together once, probably about fourteen years ago. But Natasha was furious when she found out I was married, and she put a lot of energy into spreading nasty lies about me to anyone who would listen. For a few weeks the auction business was affected, and we lost a member of staff and several customers because of it.'

'Hang on a minute, Paul. Kemp and Holmes didn't even exist fourteen years ago. How could Natasha cause you so much trouble?'

'No, it didn't, but she was working for Slippery at the time. *She*' he said with a venomous tone 'only set that rival business up once she got her hands on Bertram Kemp and his wallet. God only knows what sexual favours she did for him, to persuade him to back her like that. I don't want any daughter of mine to learn how to prostitute herself to get what she wants from a man.'

Sarah was momentarily speechless at the misogyny coming from her friend's mouth. She briefly contemplated picking him up on several of his statements, but decided not to waste her energy, and standing up she began to walk out of the snug, muttering something about needing to work for a living.

'Wait, Sarah, I'm sorry, please, come back.' She turned around to see that Paul was also on his feet, and pleading with her to return. She sat down again on the stool, and waited for him to continue. 'Saying it all out loud like that makes it sound pretty improbable,' he admitted.

Sarah nodded.

'It is no secret that Natasha hates me. Why else would she employ my daughter, if not to get back at me in some way? Tell me that?'

Sarah shrugged, and said nothing, realising he had no interest in hearing that by employing his daughter it was possible that Natasha was trying to make amends.

29

'I mean, you wouldn't give the son or daughter of someone you hated a job here, in this pub, would you? You need your staff to be loyal and trustworthy, in the same way that I do.'

Sarah thought about it for a moment, and then said 'No, but then right at this minute I can't think of anyone I hate enough to behave towards in that way. You know, rather than stewing in your own hate-filled misery, convinced that a one-night stand with you over a decade ago could have such a strong effect on a woman, why don't you try to see things from a different perspective?'

Paul groaned 'You sound exactly like Christine!'

Sarah looked at him for a few moments, before saying quietly 'Is that such a bad thing? Your ex-wife has turned her life around, and is one of the happiest, well-balanced people I know.'

'Alright, alright. But Natasha Holmes certainly isn't in the same league as Christine. She is mad!'

'I doubt that very much, Paul. Somebody who is as bad as you seem to think she is could not have achieved the respect from other antiques dealers that she has. But, I can see how upset you are, so come on, and let us get some perspective on this. When you and Natasha had your fling, was it you who pursued Natasha?'

Paul nodded.

'And did you hide the fact that you were married to Christine from her?'

Again, Paul nodded.

'And did you make it clear you were only looking for a bit of nookie, or did you play her along and let her believe you were looking for a relationship?'

Silence.

'Did you make it clear before the event you were only interested in a one-night stand?'

'Oh come on Sarah, you know how it is. I didn't know I wouldn't want to see her again until after it happened. I tried to let her down gently by not calling her; I thought she would get the message. But instead she went berserk and started harassing me with phone calls, and turning up at work and even at my house. Christine went mad.' Paul shivered at the memory of the two women discovering the existence of the other for the first time.

Sarah had heard enough of Paul's pathetic attempts to justify his actions. With a steely tone she said 'So, it isn't surprising that a young woman in her early twenties who thinks she is being wooed by a single older man, who appears to want to spend all of his spare time with her, is devastated when he has sex with her once and then not only refuses to communicate with her, but turns out to have deceived her over his marital status?'

More silence.

Grudgingly Paul offered 'I suppose not.'

'Now we have cleared that up, shall I start to unpick your offensive statements about women in business?'

Paul looked up shame-faced 'Oh Sarah, I didn't mean to imply that you … I mean, you are different, obviously!'

'I am glad you think so. And what about Gemma Isaac and Lisa Bartlett? Do you think the only reason they have been so successful with the tearooms is because they manipulated some poor unsuspecting chap into stumping up the finances to run their business by giving him a blow job or letting him touch their boobs? And what about your Jennifer? Has she only qualified as an equine veterinary surgeon because some man spanked her bottom? Didn't her own father get her the job with Woodford Vets? What does that say about their relationship?'

Paul looked crestfallen. Sarah's voice had risen, until she was talking so loudly that Tom Higston rushed into the snug to see what was going on. Hearing the end of her sentence he stopped short in the doorway, his face a picture of horror. Sarah turned to see the expression on Tom's face and collapsed with laughter on the bench next to Paul. It was infectious, and Paul also started giggling until tears were coursing down their cheeks.

Shaking his head, Tom left them to it.

When they eventually managed to take control of themselves, Paul said 'Of course, you are right Sarah. I think I owe Christine an apology too. Although I am still convinced that Lydia is going to work for Natasha because she knows it will upset me.'

'Well then, you need to show her you fully support her decision, don't you. After all, it is a great opportunity for her, if she chooses to take advantage of it.'

Paul nodded. 'That's what Christine said.'

'Wise woman.'

'Yes, she is. And I am sorry for all those things I said about how Natasha does business. I have believed it for so long, it will take a while for me to view her in a different light. Maybe I just need to accept that she is successful in this business because of her skills and knowledge as an antiques expert and as an auctioneer.'

Sarah raised her eyebrows. 'There really isn't any other explanation.'

Paul nodded. 'You are probably right. But, you know, I am not the only one who thinks she has used her feminine wiles to get to where she is today. As the saying goes, there is no smoke without fire.'

'What a load of rubbish, you have clearly never tried to light that bloody fire' she gestured towards the empty grate 'for the first time every autumn. Why do you think we keep it going twenty-four hours, seven days a week, over the winter?'

Chapter 4

Monday 1st August 2016, 2.00pm

Natasha Holmes held the door open for an elderly lady
who was leaving the building. She had not seen the
woman for several years, and smiled at her in
recognition, but the woman only muttered a 'thank
you' and kept her eyes on the path in front of her.
Natasha watched as she made her way carefully across
the car park towards a bright blue Nissan Micra, but
then opened the driver's door of the car next to it: a
charcoal grey Porsche 911. Natasha smiled at her own
mistaken assumption, and hoped that when she was
that age she too would have the guts to drive a car like
that.

As the sports car roared out through the brick archway
between two buildings, which formed the entrance to
Kemp and Holmes Antiques Auctioneers and Valuers,
Natasha walked into the large reception area. Her
immaculate short glossy straight black hair did not dare
to move from the bob into which she had styled and
positioned each strand. The four inch heels of her
silver sandals clicked with every stride across the stone
floor of the Victorian building; her long white skirt
swished revealing a glimpse of silver straps criss-
crossing up her tanned and toned legs; her green eyes

scanned the area to make sure everything and everyone was where they should be.

Natasha came to a halt at the curved reception desk, and waited while the auction house's administrative officer, Alex Howard, finished talking to a client on the telephone. She watched him as he politely explained that bedroom furniture bought in the 1980s did not qualify as 'antique', and he gave them the name of a more suitable place to dispose of their unwanted items.

Natasha nodded when he put the phone down. 'Well done, Alex. That lady who just left, what was she doing here?'

'Oh, she was a dear old thing wasn't she? Sadly hers is a familiar story: her husband died recently, and as she has no family left she was hoping to dispose of some of his things through one of our auctions. Crispin Keogh dealt with her, if you want to know the details.'

Natasha brushed the suggestion aside. 'No thank you. Any messages for me?'

Alex smiled. He liked working for her. She never allowed sentiment to get in the way of business. In his view she was an exacting taskmaster, but fair, and he approved of the example she set of ensuring her own work practices met the high standard expected from her staff. Some people only lasted a few weeks before leaving with relief to find different employment, but Alex was one of the members of staff who had been with Natasha since she and her business partner, Bertram Kemp, established their auction house six years earlier, and he had no plans to leave.

Once Alex had finished passing on all the messages which had come in since she left the building the previous Friday, Natasha continued on her way. As she walked past offices and workrooms she permitted the ghost of a smile to form on her bright MAC Ruby Woo red lips as she noted her employees hard at work.

Glancing up from the silver teapot he was appraising, Crispin Keogh, Kemp and Holmes' twenty-four-year-old trainee auctioneer, pushed his dirty-blond coloured hair out of his eyes and muttered 'Look busy!' to his new colleague, Jason Chapillon.

Jason risked a quick peek through the glass door of their office to see what Crispin was talking about, and watched as his new boss strode past.

'Well, she is a far better sight than Slippery!' he commented, causing Crispin to tut and roll his eyes.

'For goodness' sake don't say anything like that in front of her! Come on, we had better get this list finished before she starts chasing for it. Believe me; you do not want any hassle from Natasha.'

Jason looked as though he thought hassle from Natasha might be something to enjoy. 'Someone told me she used to be a pole dancer?' he asked hopefully, his brown eyes making it clear he wanted the rumours to be true.

Crispin stopped typing while he gave Jason's question some consideration. 'Could be,' he shrugged. 'I dare you to ask her,' he winked. 'And I'll have a bet with you this will be your first and last day working for Kemp and Holmes if you do.'

Jason laughed, but decided to follow his friend's advice and keep his thoughts to himself. The two men turned their attention back to the catalogue they were compiling for an auction of quality silver items later in the year. Jason was keen to make a good impression with his new employer. He enjoyed the research side of the job, and was in his element with this first assignment. But rumours of Natasha Holmes' past were rampant throughout the antiques trade, and he was curious to know which of the ones he had heard were true.

'Make sure you check that those hallmarks are genuine,' Crispin nodded to the silver tea service Jason was cataloguing.

'Too right mate, I don't want to end up dead in a ditch like Hugh Jones.'

'God, that whole incident sounded awful didn't it? Did you know him?'

Jason stretched his muscular arms above his head, while he thought about how much to reveal.

'Sort of. Hugh came to the auction rooms to do various deals with Slippery Stan, but I didn't know him other than to make the tea for everyone when he was there. Did you?'

Crispin shook his head; the movement of his floppy blond hair reminded Jason of a fringed lampshade. Jason preferred his own dark brown hair to be cropped short and under control.

'Not really, but I did meet him a few times. Nice chap. Scary to think he could have got things so wrong that someone killed him over it. I know there are people out there who think that violence is the best solution to a business disagreement, but I hope I never have to deal with any of them.'

Jason ran the palms of his hands over his head, and wondered how his friend could stand to have all those kinks and curls. 'There must be more to the story than we know about. I only heard that he stole a salver from one of the big silver boys, and killed himself once they found out, not that he was murdered. Slippery was very jumpy around the time Hugh was missing back in, um, I can't remember, when was it? March? April?'

Crispin shrugged. 'I don't know. I think I first heard he had disappeared in May, when Natasha had some

37

silver she wanted him to take a look at. She was in a foul mood for days when she couldn't get hold of him, and it was all she was talking about. She had Alex ringing Hugh's mobile every hour, and she was asking everybody who came in here if they had seen him. She was obsessed!'

Jason raised his eyebrows 'Was she? That does sound interesting. Do you think she is involved in his death?'

Crispin shook his head. 'No way. Natasha is totally straight. As is Bertram. Neither of them would countenance anything dodgy, I am sure of it.'

'I can't say the same about Slippery. He was definitely on edge and kept having to take his phone calls in private. I reckon he was involved in a scam in some way.'

'Oh? Now that wouldn't surprise me. Who knows what the real truth behind it all is? I haven't heard any rumours about Slippery being involved, but he is not one of the trustworthy members of the antiques trade. I was told that Hugh was the one who was faking the silver for the gang. Apparently he kept some back for himself and sold it at a huge profit, so they put a contract out on him to teach him a lesson.'

Jason gave a grim laugh. 'Well they certainly did that. Hugh Jones won't be stealing any silver from anyone ever again.'

Chapter 5

Monday 1st August 2016, 3.00pm

'Slippery' Stanley Simmons grunted as he attempted to brush flakes of pastry and unidentifiable meat products from his grey beard. Dropping a significant portion of the cheap pie down his front was just one of several things going wrong in his life that day. Tanya Gordon, his assistant, closed her eyes to prevent the familiar gagging-reflex from kicking in, and turned back to her computer. She had worked with Slippery since leaving school after taking GCSEs twenty years ago and was used to his ways, but in recent years his occasional anti-social behaviours were escalating. His sloppy eating habits, combined with farting whenever he wanted to, the nose-picking and wiping the successful result on the chairs, and the stench of unwashed clothes for several days at a time, were all increasing in their frequency.

When at sixteen Tanya first started work at Swanwick Auctioneers, Stanley was a rough-around-the-edges failed antiques dealer from London who had arrived in Swanwick the previous year with a chip on his shoulder, determined to exact his revenge on all the crooked and cheating dealers who, in his view, had caused the downfall of his own antiques business. Her interactions with him in those days had been limited to giggling with the other members of staff at his posturing and boasting, avoiding his intrusive and wandering hands, and having to listen to him whenever they had staff social events telling endless stories about what a tough-guy he had been during his London years.

Over time Stanley had progressed from general dogsbody to the main auctioneer, simply by outstaying everyone else as they left for pastures new, retired, or died from natural causes. Stanley preferred a different version of events; if he was to be believed he earned every one of the promotions by having something salacious on each of the Directors of the once prestigious auction house. He liked to tell everybody that he was knowledgeable, experienced, and honest. He was so busy decrying everyone else and singing his own praises, that he failed to learn from the mistakes he had made while trading as an antiques dealer which had led to the collapse of his antiques business.

Stanley could be classed as a successful auctioneer, because he earned a lot of money. In truth, he earned far more than he should have done, because he was prone to 'mis-placing' valuable items from job lots entered into the auction, and selling items off the books prior to the auctions to dealers with equally loose morals. If the genuine owners remembered to query what had happened to their belongings, which sometimes would only happen several months or even years later, and were able to provide the relevant paperwork, then Stanley would claim that the items had been lost. The original owners could never prove that he had pocketed the money, the auction house would reimburse them for a fraction of the value of the items, and Stanley would behave himself for a while. Until the next time.

Everyone except the directors knew what was going on, and even they had an idea of his dodgy practices, but none of them knew how to deal with him without scoring an own goal against the reputation of Swanwick Auctioneers. So long as Stanley kept the legitimate side of the auction business running at a decent level, no one wanted to risk being the whistle-blower. Instead the antiques dealers voted with their feet, and rarely put quality items into Swanwick Auctioneers. His nickname of 'Slippery Stanley' evolved over the years from whispered complaints behind closed doors to common knowledge, and much to his annoyance the name 'Slippery' replaced the one his parents gave him, at least amongst members of the antiques trade. He and his staff had to work harder every year to hunt for stock to put through the auction, relying on unsuspecting members of the public who were only too pleased to find a company who would clear their mother's /grandfather's /aunt's house for free.

Slippery could put on the charm when he needed to. He placed numerous full page advertisements in society magazines and up-market newspapers, and on the days he was meeting the unsuspecting members of the public who responded to them, he bullied his down-trodden wife into producing clean, ironed clothes for him to wear. Slippery would only meet prospective clients by appointment, so he could ensure he was correctly attired in flamboyant waistcoats with matching bow ties, and he would ostentatiously pull out a gold Patek Philippe pocket watch whenever he could manufacture an appropriate moment. He was careful to employ at least one member of staff, always well-spoken and attractive and usually well-connected, who could pander to the egos of the moneyed rich.

Those types of people expected to be treated as if they were the only person the auction house were dealing with. Slippery would use the chosen employee as a foil against which he could project the image of a very important antiques specialist, whose time was money. In this way he nearly always succeeded in having the effect of making the target end up feeling grateful to Slippery for deigning to give them the time of day.

The first spoke in Slippery's wheels that morning had been learning of the defection of the current patsy to a rival auctioneers. Jason Chapillon had lasted nine months with Swanwick Auctioneers, before decamping to Kemp and Holmes, who were based ten doors down the road.

'I am fed up of that bloody woman stealing my staff' he grumbled to Tanya. 'She should stick to stealing other women's husbands; that is what she is good at. I spend all that time and effort training 'em up only for that bitch to reap all the benefits. James Chapillon, huh, he is an ungrateful little sod. If it wasn't for me he wouldn't have a foot in the door with her. Oh, he'll regret it, you mark my words. She'll make him work much harder than I did, and for less money. Oh, he'll wish he'd stayed with me!'

Tanya pretended to ignore him, and kept her eyes on the computer screen in front of her, but his words triggered a thought process she had been trying to suppress for several years. Working for Swanwick Auctioneers hadn't always been this bad. In those early days when Tanya first left the confines of the school day, and joined the antiques trade, the auction house had been a place of excitement and possibility. Ditching her bright green Woodford School uniform, with its pink, yellow and white braid which edged the blazer and compulsory straw hat, Tanya had embraced

42

the world of scruffy jeans and T-shirts emblazoned with the names of her favourite bands. After more than a decade of predictable timetables and strict deadlines, the flexible world of last minute deals and anticipated high prices in auction was everything the television series *Lovejoy* had led her to believe the world of antiques would be.

Tanya reflected that for several years she had been working like a drudge. Tanya pushed her chair back and made her way out to the lavatories where she knew she could find some peace and quiet. As she pushed open the door she caught sight of herself in the full length mirror on the wall opposite, and momentarily halted. In front of her was a bored-looking middle-aged woman, dressed in a mish-mash of brown shapeless clothes, with brown hair in need of a good cut and style. Tanya thought she looked like a quiet mouse of an employee from the seventies; when the only career available to women was nursing or secretarial work.

It was the last straw. She didn't know when, or how, it had happened, but somehow Natasha Holmes had become a successful entrepreneur, in charge of her own working life and able to sleep with any man she chose, while Tanya, who was the same age as Natasha, was stuck in a dead-end job with no career prospects, a sexless nobody, who lived alone and could not remember the last time she went out on a date.

For goodness' sake, she and Natasha had even worked alongside each other at Swanwick Auctioneers before Natasha made her escape. How was it that Natasha had an amazing life while she, Tanya, lived a mundane and boring one? Where was the career? The social standing? And the handsome husband who would mow the lawn and take the rubbish out? Where were the two point four children?

As the years passed, Tanya's friends had gradually dropped away as they either moved from Brackenshire to follow high-powered careers, or became immersed in breast-feeding and school runs, and in a few cases both. She had nothing in common with any of her former classmates, some of whom had also moved from Woodford to live in Swanwick, so she regularly saw them when she went food shopping after work. She had no friends within the antiques trade, because the people she came into contact with tended be busy mothers juggling kids and the need to earn a living, or married/separated/divorced men who wanted to flirt with her, but nothing more. Somewhere during her twenties Tanya had lost her self-confidence and become a wage slave.

Turning on her heel she marched out, and back to her desk. As she picked up her work, Tanya resolved to find that excited teenager again; the one who had been enthusiastic about life, and who had woken up every day with a sense of anticipation.

She was sure that girl was still somewhere inside her.

Chapter 6

Monday 1st August 2016, 3.30pm

Natasha Holmes was employing all of her professional skill to keep calm as she listened to the furious client on the other end of the telephone line. After allowing the woman to list all of the things she thought were wrong with the way Natasha ran her company, Natasha ended the conversation with a succinct 'Well, at least we can both agree on something, and that is we never want to do business with each other again. Good bye.'

Natasha firmly pressed the red off button on the handset, before she speed dialled Alex on reception and asked him to add the woman's number and email address to the small list of blocked contacts.

A knock at the door preceded the short and bulky figure of her business partner, Bertram Kemp.

'Are you busy, Natasha?' he queried, his bald head reflecting the bright sunlight streaming through the picture window of her office.

Natasha leaned back in her chair, and felt the tension in her shoulders and head evaporate at the sight of the man she always thought of as a warm cuddly teddy bear. Her smile was a sight very few people witnessed, but Bertram always had that effect on her. She shrugged and nodded her head towards the telephone in front of her.

'One of those people who thinks we should be able to do magic for them, while they put no effort into the business arrangement. Thank goodness the world is not made up of people like her! She is now on our blocked list.'

Bertram smoothed his moustache with the thumb and forefinger of his left hand while he thought. 'That makes a grand total of three doesn't it? Not a bad number after six years in business. We must be doing something right.' He winked at Natasha as he walked over to the huge Parker Knoll green plush sofa which filled the wall space along one edge of Natasha's office, and sat down.

'How are the plans for the silver auction going? In the light of recent events I think we should both go through everything with a fine-toothed comb, rather than leave it to Crispin and, what's the new boy's name? James?'

Natasha leaned her elbows on her desk, resting her chin on her hands. 'No, he is called Jason. Jason Chapillon.'

'Ah, yes, Chapillon. I knew his uncle, Miles. He was one of the big characters in the antiques trade, and was a highly successful silver dealer. A really sad story. Shagger Chapillon used to travel all over the country in some type of bus, a Bedford I think, towing a massive trailer behind him. He had the morals of an alley cat, and always had at least two stunning girls with him whenever he stalled out. Have you heard about him?'

'No, never! What happened to him?' Natasha settled back into her chair. She loved hearing about antiques dealing in the seventies and eighties from Bertram, and was always teasing him about harking back to The Good Old Days.

'Shagger Chapillon used to turn up at every antiques fair going. I don't know if he actually had a bricks and mortar home, but if he did I can't imagine he spent many nights in it. He had an old coach thing he lived in, which was fully kitted out inside, and doubled up as the towing vehicle for the trailer in which he stored and displayed all of his stock.'

'It was probably a Blim bus.'

'That's it! A Bedford Blim bus. We used to call it the Pimpmobile. While the rest of us were driving Ford Transits and Toyota vans, and sleeping in the back amongst all of our stock, usually freezing cold, there was Shagger in his Pimpmobile having the time of his life. His trailer was also something special. When he was ready to start trading, which was usually about an hour after the rest of us had begun, he would open up one of the sides, and it was like something out of a fairground. The whole of the interior was lit up with coloured lights. He stored his stock inside the trailer, in cabinets, and once the entrance was open and the stairs had been pulled down, also complete with coloured lights under each step, it was like an Aladdin's cave. He always had music playing in the trailer, usually something by Stock, Aitken and Waterman, and he would stand on the steps dressed in a sharp suit, welcoming people inside. The girls would be in the trailer, dressed in impossibly high heels, short skirts and low-cut tops, and they would be the ones showing the buyers what was for sale in the cabinets, and taking the money. Wads and wads of notes were handed over in that trailer. Shagger would stay trading long after the rest of us had given up and gone home, and then he would close up the trailer, and drive on to the next antiques fair.'

'So if he spent all of his time selling at the markets, when did he have time to buy more stock?'

Bertram shrugged 'That was one of the big mysteries. His stock of silver items was phenomenal, and the items on his stand were always the best and most sought after. He never bought anything at the markets, we never saw him at any auctions or in antiques shops. In those days there was no selling over the internet, and like I said, he didn't seem to spend any time at a home or even a business address. But he looked as though he had stepped out of the London Stock Exchange, whilst living in this bus like a hippy.'

'So what happened to him in the end? You said it was a sad story.'

'Yes, he came to a violent end. As I heard it, one day on his way from one fair to another, he stopped at the Rownhams Services on the M27, and went inside. In the gents toilets a girl shot him in the head, and killed him. She calmly walked out of the services, and onto the bus, where another girl was waiting with the engine running. The pair of them drove off and continued along the motorway, east bound.'

'My God! Were they caught? They must have been pretty obvious, driving something unusual like that.'

'Don't forget that in the eighties a bus and trailer combo was not as unusual as they are now. That is not to say they were a common sight, but Shagger's were probably unique because of their internal layout, rather than how they looked from the outside. We didn't have all the cameras and mobile technology that we do today, and so tracking and tracing them wasn't as straight forward. But to answer your question, no, they were never caught. Nobody knows who they were, and although we all assumed it was a robbery, if his stock has been sold it was done very quietly. The bus and the trailer have never been seen again. I would love to know what happened to all of that silver.'

'Amazing,' Natasha shook her head. 'Mind you, if he went around like that I am surprised it didn't happen sooner.'

'Looking back I can't believe there weren't more muggings, but in those days everybody was doing well and it just wasn't an issue. Certainly after that we all began to take much better precautions. Even to this day I have an old police truncheon within easy reach in my car.'

'Isn't that illegal?'

'Mmmh, yes, but I always have a price label on it, so I can claim it is part of my antiques stock and then it is not against the law. Mind you, I don't carry it with me when I go to the toilet at a service station, so it wouldn't have made any difference to Shagger if he had one in his bus. Anyway, back to the present day thieves, we need to make sure we have our own protection in the form of vigilance.'

'Yes, don't worry, I am already on it, Bertram. Crispin and Jason are checking all the silver items as they come in, and then cataloguing them before providing me with a daily list. I will go over to their workroom and check it at the end of every day. Apparently someone brought in a fantastic silver tea set this morning, so I think our silver sale will be a good one.'

'Good, good. I thought you probably would have it all under control. This Hugh Jones business is very unsettling, not to mention bad for the trade. The dealers are suspicious of each other, and the public don't trust them either. Not good, not good at all. By the way, I have made a donation on our behalf to the fund which has been set up to help Hugh's wife and children. His poor wife is a lovely woman. It is a desperately sad situation for that family to find themselves in.'

'That was kind of you, Bertram. I can't imagine how she must be feeling. I don't think I ever met her?'

'She used to come with Hugh in the early days, before they had their children. You know, I can't believe the rumours about Hugh Jones' involvement with the faked silver can be true; I always found him to be honest and reliable, if a little slow at getting the work done. But then that is the price you pay for using a skilled craftsman; slow and right beats fast and wrong in my book.'

Natasha nodded 'I agree, I never had any reason to doubt his integrity either, even while I was still working at Swanwick Auctioneers and he used to come and do business with Slippery. I think there must be another explanation to the one, or ones I should say, we have heard so far. Do you remember those spoons we gave him to tidy up? The ones which came from the estate down in the New Forest? He was quick to point out that they were not genuine, and he explained the telltale signs which gave them away. I can't believe he would have done that if he was involved in any dodgy business. It would have been easy for him to give them back to us without pointing out what was wrong with them. Neither you nor I had spotted the problem.'

'Yes, I remember. He would also do additional work for no extra charge to items if it would improve their value, pointing out damage you and I both thought was part of the decoration. If he was as dishonest as the current gossip would have us believe he would have charged us for work he hadn't done, or was unnecessary, not the other way around. But, it is possible that he was honest with us because he knew we wouldn't put any work his way if he wasn't, and all the while he was happily dealing with the undesirable elements to our trade in a way they were happy with too.'

They both sat in silence, before Bertram slapped his hands on his thighs and stood up. 'Well, I'll leave you to your work. Just ask if you want a second opinion on any of that silver. You won't mind if I cast my eye over it now and again, will you?'

'Yes, of course, you go ahead, please do Bertram. I value your input. I have asked the boys to take extra notice of who brings what in, just in case there is any pattern which emerges.'

'Good idea, yes, well done. It isn't enough just to keep track for our records who the vendors are; we need to be alert to which individuals are associated with any items we are unhappy with. Smart thinking, Natasha.'

'Thank you. And if I am suspicious about anything I will bring it straight to you, so we can decide what to do about it together.'

Long after Bertram had closed the door, Natasha remained sitting in her chair looking after him, with the hint of a smile on her face. She loved the man for his gentle and considerate nature, and would do anything for him. These past few years working with him had been the best years of her life. Although in theory they were equal partners in the business, while Natasha grafted harder than Bertram on a daily basis, he was the one with the knowledge and experience which kept their business at the top of the antiques auction house table.

Bertram Kemp was a third generation antiques dealer, with both the reputation and the money many people, including Natasha, admired. When the directors of the international auctioneers which employed Natasha and

Bertram as antiques experts decided to sell a number of their provincial offices, including the one in Swanwick, Natasha immediately set to work persuading Bertram to go into partnership with her. She was sure that she had the energy and the ambition, but she needed his years of experience and contacts. He was easily flattered by her attention, and inspired by her enthusiasm. Faced with the prospect of redundancy at fifty-four-years old, no obvious job to walk into, and a wife of thirty years who made it clear he was not going to be allowed to stay at home all day, Bertram accepted Natasha's proposal. They took the plunge and bought the business together as equal partners.

Their actions caused small ripples throughout the local antiques trade, but almost resulted in a tidal wave in Bertram's personal life. For the next few months his marriage was on rocky ground as his wife was shocked out of her complacency towards her boring, dull, overweight and reliable husband. She frequently and fiercely questioned him about his uncharacteristic behaviour, and the reasons behind it. Bertram had always been one of the trustworthy foot soldiers within the antiques world; content to follow his father and grandfather by working for the same auction house they had done, but without their flair for creating fortunes in addition to his monthly wage packet.

His wife, Janice, was seven years younger than him, and they met when she was first employed by the auction house as a secretary at the age of sixteen. By the time she was seventeen they were engaged, and they married within a few months of their engagement. Janice relished the social standing which being Mrs Bertram Kemp gave her, and happily gave up her tedious job to become a full-time housewife. Two children later, Janice decided she did not need to put up with Bertram's fumbling any more, and put a stop to sex within their marriage.

Bertram loved his wife, and also basked in the attention she received from other men when she was by his side. He knew he was lucky that such a beautiful creature would agree to share her life with him, and so although he was sad, and frustrated, by her rejection of him in the bedroom, he was grateful she still wanted him in her life. He meekly accepted his solitary move into the fourth bedroom in their home, but lived in hope they could resume marital relations one day.

Meanwhile, Janice and her best friend's husband came to a twice-weekly arrangement in which they were both deeply satisfied; as was her best friend who was oblivious to their deception, but relieved not to have to have sex with her nice but boring husband five times a week. Twice a week was manageable.

For the next twenty years the Kemps continued to keep up appearances of a happily married couple, burying themselves in their children's social diaries and concerning themselves with their increasingly ageing parents' welfare.

Bertram's decision to rock their comfortable world by stepping out of the safety of middle management, and into the role of co-owner of a brand new auction house, was a shock to Janice. He had never demonstrated any signs of ambition before, despite her attempts to encourage him to apply for promotions within the international organisation, or even make a move to a rival one.

At first she was overjoyed when he tentatively mentioned his plans, believing that he was finally listening to her. But then she realised who he was going to be working closely with: Natasha Holmes, a gorgeous young woman who was clearly the driving force behind the partnership. The knowledge brought out a hitherto unknown jealous streak within Janice, and she refused to accept Bertram's denials that they were having an affair. Again Bertram shook her perfect world by continuing with the setting-up of the new company against her wishes, despite her threats to leave him, or, as was more likely, throw him out of the family home.

For a few weeks Janice wondered if maybe now was the time to finally end their marriage, but her best friend's husband refused to leave his wife. Janice was faced with the scary prospect of living on her own, and having to socialise without a partner by her side. In addition, she realised that their children were young adults who no longer relied on her to organise their diaries, or to act as an unpaid taxi service. She did not have a social life of her own, or any way to fill the hours in the day so Janice decided to quietly drop her opposition to Bertram's plans.

Janice wasn't the only person to suspect sex had a big part to play in Bertram's decision to form a business partnership with Natasha Holmes. Without exception everyone who knew them in the antiques trade assumed she was giving him sexual favours; why else would a man act out of character to promote a young woman?

Chapter 7

Monday 1st August 2016, 4.00pm

Natasha Holmes was well aware of the rumours concerning her relationship with Bertram, and which surrounded the origins of their joint business enterprise, but she knew that trying to prove their innocence was near impossible. She was a successful auctioneer, commanding high prices for quality goods in the auctions she presided over, and she was confident in her abilities. What other people thought of her personally was none of her business.

Natasha had been a quiet girl at school, someone the teachers struggled to write report cards for because she was so ordinary. 'Average' was a word frequently used to describe her academic, sporting, and artistic achievements.

But all of that changed when she went to university. The careers advisor at her school had spent many hours with the girl who appeared to have no ambitions or desires, and he secretly despaired of finding her the higher education course his employers expected him to locate for each of his clients.

Natasha was the only child of parents who were rich, and both of whom came from large tight-knit families who were local business and land owners. They worked seven days a week in their own business, and rarely had time for their only child who showed no aptitude for following in their footsteps. Natasha was brought up in a world where she was dragged along with her mother or father while they met with employees and business associates, most of whom were relatives, or with clients. She had to sit quietly in a corner of the room, or wait in the latest top-of-the-range high-spec vehicle her parents had bought, until it was time to move on to the next appointment.

Her friends were the children of her parents' friends and relatives, because outside of school they were the only other children she met. She had little in common with her cousins, second cousins, and in some cases aunts and uncles who were a similar age to her. In school she didn't fit into the cool kids' gangs which dominated the sports fields, the academic achievement tables, or the daily fashion contests which pushed the school uniform rules to their limits and beyond. Neither was she accepted by the geeky alternative crew who looked down their noses at the beautiful people, but who engaged in their own equally competitive desires to excel at activities outside of school hours.

None of this bothered the young Natasha in the slightest. She was content to be left alone, and occupied her time by reading anything and everything which came her way: children's books; 'young adult' books; thrillers; romances; trade magazines; science fiction; women's magazines; newspapers; fantasy books; graphic novels.

Her father tried but failed to love his little girl who he wanted to spoil like a princess, but who preferred to go unnoticed. Her mother exuded a mild air of frustration whenever she looked at or talked about Natasha, and often wondered aloud if she had been swapped at birth in the hospital. Natasha's mother was a stunning woman, with a curvaceous figure dressed to emphasise, and wore enough make-up to keep her natural facial features a well-disguised secret. She longed for her daughter to show an interest in her own appearance, even if it was a rebellious determination to style herself in the opposite to her mother's reflection. But Natasha mildly agreed to wear everything her mother chose for her, and have her hair and make-up as her mother suggested on the days she remembered to go into her daughter's bedroom before they were due to leave the house, and still Natasha looked unremarkable.

By the time Natasha was seventeen-years old her parents were worried that they would have to find her a position within one of their companies. This was despite sending her to one of the top local private schools which promised to provide a safe and secure environment within which the offspring of people who are somebody could network their way into high-earning careers whether or not they had a natural aptitude for academia. Everyone stayed at the school until they were eighteen or nineteen-years old, and then they were expected to either continue their studies in a college of further or higher education, or walk into a six-figure salaried job for a company owned by one of their own or someone else's relative.

Natasha's parents inhabited a dynamic world in which business breakfasts and power lunches were the norm, and everyone was always rushing to be somewhere else. Much of their success was achieved by force of personality, and that was something their daughter was sadly lacking. No daughter of theirs was going to be paid the minimum wage for quietly sitting behind a desk typing up someone else's correspondence or answering their phones, but neither did they want her heading up projects or teams within one of their companies; they didn't think she had it in her to make a success of anything, and failure was not an option. They had tentatively begun to think about arranging a marriage with a suitably driven and successful potential husband. There were a number of eligible young, and not so young, men under their employment, although sorting out how close the blood ties were was a major concern.

Meanwhile the teenage Natasha was blissfully drifting towards examinations which would signify the end of her time at school, sure that something would turn up afterwards. The careers advisor was determined to place Natasha somewhere, thus maintaining his unbroken record for the past three years of a beautifully designed graph detailing every student who completed their final academic year as either being employed, continuing their education, or taking a gap year. Two days before their final meeting he had been desperately scanning through his lists of previously successful placements when his eyes spotted the perfect destination for Natasha.

'A Fine Arts degree!' he told Natasha, in such a way she was unable to refuse. She nodded agreeably and the relevant paperwork was processed. After her predictably average exam results were revealed, she left her parents' home to live in an apartment her parents bought for her near the college, ready to begin the next stage in her life.

The transformation from quiet, agreeable, ordinary girl with an attitude of laissez-faire to spiky, aggressive, driven woman dressed in an armour of tailored suits and expensive make-up started that September, took several years to develop, and made her parents very proud.

Eighteen years later here she was: the leading antiques auctioneer and valuer for a high profile company; earning a salary of tens of thousands of pounds per annum, and even more in company perks; respected by others in her field; and with the sort of well-groomed looks and fashion sense which turned heads wherever she went. For several years her parents had been begging her to move in to the family business, with a view to Natasha eventually taking over their portion from them. But Natasha had no intention of giving up her hard-earned business reputation of which she was so proud, and return to the heavy shadows of her parents' personalities and familial ways of doing things.

Contrary to her former colleague Tanya Gordon's belief, Natasha did not think her life was perfect. The one area Natasha Holmes was not satisfied with was the gaping hole where a husband and children should be. After years of leading an exciting and sex-filled life, changing partners as regularly as the seasons, and feeling fulfilled and content, at thirty-six-years old she was becoming deafened by the ticking of her biological clock, and was beginning to panic that she would never meet a man strong enough to fulfil the long list of qualities she desired in a permanent partner. She despaired of all the men she considered to be suitable husband material, but who ran a mile when, as she saw it, they met a smart, clever and intelligent woman. Unfortunately she felt contempt for the men who declared they fancied her, sneered at those who wanted to marry her, and disdain for those who simply wanted to worship her.

Natasha was beginning to feel desperate.

Chapter 8

Monday 1st August 2016, 4.00pm

Nicola Stacey looked up as the front door to Williamson Antiques banged open with some force.

'Blimey, Paul, I think you could probably succeed in taking it off its hinges if you have another go.'

Paul Black stomped over to the cabinet where she was rearranging some of the jewellery, after a customer had bought a large Victorian sapphire necklace from the display. 'Sorry Nicola, I have had some bad news. Is your boss around here somewhere?'

'Oh really? No, sorry, he isn't. Cliff and Sarah Handley are having a meeting next door in the tearooms about the upcoming Woodford Flea Market.' She checked the Victorian mahogany fourteen inch drop-dial clock on the wall. 'They left here an hour ago so I don't imagine he will be much longer. Do you want to wait? I was just about to make myself a cuppa, and can get you a coffee or something if you don't mind keeping an eye on the place while I am upstairs? Unless there is anything I can do to help?'

'Thanks Nicola, but no, I don't think anyone can help. I really only wanted to see Cliff so that I could have a moan about something; I am sure he will understand. But yes, yes please, I'll have a cup of tea if you are making one anyway.'

Nicola carefully locked the glass cabinet doors and returned the key to the drawer behind the counter. Leaving Paul brooding on a walnut chaise longue, she bounced up the stairs to the flat which doubled as the company kitchen and bathroom, and Cliff Williamson's home. Within minutes Paul watched as the tall slim black girl came walking more carefully down the stairs with two mugs of tea.

'I don't mean this in a creepy way, Nicola, but you are looking very fit these days,' Paul accepted his drink, and moved over to make room for Nicola beside him.

'Well thank you Paul, I will accept your compliment in the spirit within which it was intended. Once upon a time that comment coming from you would have been totally creepy, but since you and Jennifer have hooked up together you are actually turning into a reasonable version of a human being.'

'Ah, you see, all I needed was the love a good woman.'

'Careful, I don't think you are totally rehabilitated if you are going to say things like that. Anyway, back to me. All of those months of Zumba, horse riding, and early morning boot camps are finally beginning to pay off. I am in better shape as I head towards my fortieth birthday than I was when I was a teenager.'

'Good grief, you are not forty-years old this year are you?'

'No, not for another couple of years. Imagine how "fit" I will look by then' she winked suggestively. 'Have you seen Sarah Handley? She has lost over three stone this year. What a transformation!'

'Yes, I popped into The Ship Inn for lunch, although I think she is looking a bit thin. For goodness' sake don't tell her I said that.'

Nicola laughed. 'I know what you mean. I think she is struggling to come to terms with life without her husband Mike, and isn't eating properly. But it is very early days. He only died seven months ago. So how is your rehabilitation going? Cliff said that you are nearly back up to your running speeds from before you were attacked.'

'Did he? No, I wouldn't say I was that close, at least not yet. But I suppose that I do now feel as though that time can't be too far away. Running has been an important part of my life for a long time, and Tony Cookson knew that when he assaulted me. His incarceration is permanent; mine was temporary. While I was recovering, Cliff was building up his times, so he is now even further ahead of me.'

Nicola nodded. 'Yes, Cliff is serious about his training now. Sarah and I have been trying to persuade him to join us at one of the Strong by Zumba sessions, but he is too much of a coward.' She looked at Paul, who almost choked on his tea.

'Don't you start picking on me! There is no way I am going to start shimmying and skipping around for an hour in the village hall.'

'Oh Paul, you have absolutely no idea what we do have you?'

A noise made them both look to see who had opened the front door.

'Cliff, thank goodness it is you. Your employee here was just about to make me put on one of her bright green bra tops and prance around to some loud music!'

Cliff laughed. 'You mean she has been trying the Zumba hard sell on you too? You know, mate, we ought to give it a go one day. If only to show these girls how to do it properly,' he winked at Nicola as he walked past them towards the stairs.

'You are on Cliff Williamson; your challenge has been accepted. No excuses. Tomorrow night, you and Paul can join us.'

'Oh, no, I can't tomorrow. Maybe next week. Excuse me, I have to put this away,' he waved the folder he was carrying at them, and ran up the white painted wooden stairs two at a time.

Nicola tilted her head to one side and looked at Paul, who hurriedly gulped down the last of his tea and stood up. 'I'll just go and wash this mug up,' he said, as he too disappeared up the stairs to the sound of Nicola laughing.

Chapter 9

Monday 1st August 2016, 6.30pm

Paul Black's girlfriend, Jennifer Isaac, was having a difficult telephone call with a client about a life or death decision. Jennifer had come to work for the Woodford Equine Veterinary Practice eight months earlier, when they suddenly found themselves short-staffed. Her father, Peter Isaac, had asked her to take a temporary post to cover while the injured veterinary surgeon, who was also the head of the practice, recovered from serious injuries inflicted by a frightened horse.

At that time Jennifer had been swamped by a ridiculously heavy work-load leaving her little or no time to have a life outside the hours she was expected to devote to the equine veterinary practice in her home county of Shropshire. Initially, the opportunity to go and work with her dad was not an appealing one. Jennifer was dedicated to the practice which employed her straight from university, and she believed that working long hours, and being called in on her days off, were all part of working in the 'real' world. But her dad's offer gave her the opportunity to evaluate her position within the Shropshire practice, and she realised that despite her commitment to their expectations, they were not prepared to show any loyalty towards her, or understanding of her needs. Jennifer took the plunge and handed in her notice, and followed her father's move to the south-west of England.

She struggled at first with the demands of a new job and a new location, exacerbated by the fact that the person she was covering for was a hard-working and well-liked vet who had been an integral part of the local equine community for over thirty years. But in a relatively short space of time, mainly thanks to her father's blossoming relationship with one of Woodford's popular residents, Gemma Isaac née Bartlett, co-owner of The Woodford Tearooms, Jennifer was finally able to enjoy a social life, and she too found love in the form of the local auctioneer, Paul Black.

But as blissful as her personal and working life appeared to be, the nature of her job meant that hard and sometimes traumatic decisions had to be made. After her ride out on Baby that lunchtime, her next appointment was to a horse who was suffering with laminitis. The owner was doing everything she could think of to manage the horse's health correctly by keeping him off the grass, and feeding him with a Laminitis Trust approved commercial horse feed. The farrier was one who came highly recommended by several other clients, and Jennifer had no concerns about his work. But still the horse's health was deteriorating rapidly rate. Jennifer had suggested that the owner could do some research on different nutritional support for the horse, but the owner had paid for advice from someone who claimed to be an equine nutritionist and, politely, refused to listen to what Jennifer had to say. After Jennifer left the stable yard the horse's condition had continued to worsen, and the owner was now desperately grabbing at straws, and wanted to know what Jennifer had been trying to tell her. It was much harder to explain by telephone than either face-to-face or via email, but Jennifer knew the next telephone call would be to ask her to euthanize the horse, and so she attempted to provide the information as simply and clearly as she could.

She could see her father leaning his tall, lean body against his truck, a gentle smile on his face as he took in the view of the beautiful Brackenshire countryside, and wished the owner had listened to her earlier on that day so that she too could gaze over the sun-drenched hills, fields and woods which made up the area known as Stormy Vale.

Peter let his mind wander. One year ago to the day, or rather night, Peter had been on duty when he was called out to a mare who was about to give birth. Recently divorced and in his early fifties, Peter had been at a crossroads in his life for a while, before circumstances steered him in the direction of swapping his well-earned status as partner in an equine veterinary practice in his home county of Shropshire, and moving both geographically and emotionally south, down to Brackenshire.

He was the vet on duty when the call came in about the mare in labour, having recently joined the Woodford Equine Veterinary Practice as a junior member of staff, and he was still finding his feet. His was a more laid-back approach than his new employer's in many ways, including preferring to see horses living out in herds, barefoot, and with as little veterinary involvement as possible. Peter's first visit of that night had been to a stable yard which was the antithesis of everything he wanted to see in a facility for horses; but his second visit had been his vision of an ideal set-up. He had arrived to find the whole family waiting quietly nearby, while the mare, Molly, and her companion, Maggie, sorted themselves out. Peter ended up drinking hot chocolate with the Stanwick family, while they let the mare give birth in peace, and now a year later he was watching the healthy young gelding playing 'stallions' with another new herd member.

'Peter! How lovely to see you. Would you like a cup of tea, or would you like to join me with a lager?' A smiling thin lady with short blonde hair appeared around the corner of one of the barns, her strappy T-shirt and shorts revealing sun-kissed skin; her socks, paddock boots and damp sweat marks making it clear this was no catwalk supermodel, but instead a horsey person who had just finished poo-picking. Kim Stanwick waved her own bottle of lager to emphasise her suggestion.

'Oh, well, as this is a birthday celebration, and I am not on duty any more, *and* my daughter can drive me home, I will join you with a bottle of lager, please.'

'Oh great, is Jennifer with you? Where is she?'

'She's sitting in the truck, talking to a client on her mobile. She shouldn't be too long.' Peter turned his attention back to the horses and pointed to the youngster. 'He has grown up into a fine fellow, hasn't he? What have you named him?'

'He is called JD, because we wanted to drink a whole bottle of Jack Daniels when we realised Molly was about to give birth. We only bought her a few months earlier, and had no idea she was pregnant. These Buy One Get One Free offers some horse dealers provide are not without their stresses.'

'Ha ha! So he is JD? Not Jack or Daniels?'

'Nope, he is always JD' said Kim, firmly.

67

'And I see you have gained another horse? Who is this?' Peter pointed at the big grey who had decided that watching the humans was more interesting than seeing who could stand on his hind legs the highest. As he was more than a foot taller than the youngster, it wasn't surprising he always won.

Kim handed Peter a cold green bottle, dripping with condensation. 'Ah, my husband's new boy. Meet Storm. He got jealous of all the fun Heather and I are having with Molly and Maggie, so he decided it was time he had his own horse again. Of course Heather is over the moon because she thinks when she grows taller her father will let her ride Storm.'

'Ah, the horsey parents' problem of when their children grow old enough to steal their horses! My ex-wife had that challenge with both of our daughters, and of course she kept being left with their ponies to ride instead.'

'Yes, I think we have that to come in the not-too-distant future. And of course having another horse here means that JD isn't always left on his own when Heather and I go out with the two mares,' Kim explained.

Peter put his lager down on the picnic table, and climbed through the post and rail fencing into the paddock to say hello to the two horses. The first to greet him was the big grey, who gently nudged him with his muzzle.

'Hello boy. What breed is he?'

'Irish Draught, of course! My husband wouldn't have any other breed.' Kim climbed over and joined Peter. 'His mother is one of the Swanwick line, you know, the stud Mrs Barker used to run up at Swanwick Manor. He is only five-years old, and so he still has plenty more growing to do. He is about sixteen hands and three inches now; goodness knows how big he will finally end up. Mrs Barker would not approve, because she was always insistent her horses kept within the breed standard.'

Peter laughed 'I have only recently met the lady, and I can imagine she would not be happy to hear such bad behaviour as growing too tall! So, let me get this straight, in the space of a year you have doubled the number of horses in your herd?'

Kim shrugged. 'You know what they say, you can never have too many horses! Anyway, your life has changed quite a bit in the last twelve months too hasn't it? Didn't you get married at the end of last year?'

'Yes I did. To my beautiful and wonderful wife, Gemma. It was one of the best days of my life when she agreed to marry me. Although the proposal itself was also one of the most nerve-wracking things I have ever done. Thank goodness she said "yes"! We had only known each other for a few months; in fact, we got together the day after I had been up here for this little one's birth.' He gestured towards the foal. 'So in a funny way, my family has doubled too since then, because I gained a couple of stepsons to add to my two daughters.'

'You are not planning to add any more to the family then?' Kim winked, as she took a swig from her bottle.

'Not in human terms!' laughed Peter. 'I think Gemma and I are both well past the stage of nappies and sleepless nights. But I would like a truck dog of my own. You know' he explained, seeing Kim's puzzled expression, 'a nice, friendly dog I can bring with me on my rounds. A new addition of the canine variety would be just the thing; although I often have my wife's dog and, or, Jennifer's dog with me.'

'Oh yes, Jennifer, is she still on the phone?'

They both peered over to the truck, where Jennifer was deep in the discussion.

Kim continued 'Jennifer is lovely. She has been out to see our horses a couple of times since she began working for you. Nothing serious, just routine vaccinations. And she was the one who vetted Storm for us when we wanted to buy him. She was very nervous about the fact we planned to have his shoes removed as soon as possible, because his previous owner claimed he couldn't possibly cope without them.'

'Yes, she wanted to come with me today to convince herself that everything was alright, and he was comfortable. It is taking Jennifer a little time to adjust to the idea that all horses can be healthy and barefoot, but not all owners can.'

'Ah, I don't imagine it will take too long, there are quite a few examples of comfortably working barefoot horses around here. Once Jennifer is convinced she will never be able to unlearn it. She is settling into Brackenshire life I hear, isn't she seeing Paul Black? The antiques auctioneer?'

Peter nodded. 'Yes, she is living with him now.'

'From what I hear from my cousins, who are antiques dealers, the antiques trade is a dangerous place to be at the moment. Wasn't Paul beaten up by another dealer a few months ago?'

Peter nodded 'Yes, he was. Jennifer was the first person on the scene, and she was the one who phoned the emergency services. But that was an isolated incident; I am sure nothing like that will ever happen again.'

Kim pulled a face. 'I don't know about that. My cousins were telling me about a man who was something to do with the mending of silver, and he was stabbed to death just a few weeks ago. I hope nothing like that is going to happen to Paul Black! Although, I should think Paul has had a few death threats in his time, you know, from cuckolded husbands.'

Peter rolled his eyes. 'Yes, I was concerned when Jennifer took up with him. His reputation in Woodford preceded him. But, she seems to know what she is doing. Or at least I hope she does. She has even agreed to marry him.'

'They are engaged! Really? Well good luck to her. I hope she finishes that phone call soon so we can toast their engagement properly. I remember Paul from my school days. He was a few years older than me. I hope for her sake he has changed his ways with regard to women.'

'Mmmh, yes, we are aware of his unsavoury history. But he does seem to be serious about building a life with Jennifer, and I don't think she is one to have the wool pulled over her eyes or "Stand By Her Man". Or at least I hope not.' Peter paused while he reflected that he had pretended to ignore numerous affairs his former wife, Jennifer's mother, had enjoyed while they were married. He desperately hoped his daughter would not follow in his footsteps. 'Anyway, Gemma tends to hear all of the gossip in the tearooms, so if Paul does start messing my daughter around he will have plenty of us to deal with.'

'Oh yes, I am sure. He was never very secretive about his dalliances. I always got the impression he enjoyed the notoriety more than the relationships themselves. I haven't seen him for years, so I hope he has grown up a lot since those days.'

Peter decided that silence was the best response. He wasn't convinced that Paul was the reformed character Jennifer believed him to be, but until there was evidence to the contrary he would give their relationship the support necessary from a father for a daughter.

Kim took a sip from her bottle, and continued 'But Jennifer seems to have her head screwed on, certainly when it comes to veterinary matters anyway. You must be very proud of her.'

'Oh, I am,' agreed Peter. 'I am proud of both of my daughters. The other one is a riding instructor, and she works with her mother up in Shropshire, so we don't get to see quite as much of her as I would like. Although all of that may be changing in the next few months, because she is considering taking up a position at the Woodford Riding Club.'

'Oh how exciting! Heather and I both ride there, so maybe she will be teaching us one day?'

'Oh, I expect so, if she decides to make the move. She is very traditional in her outlook though, so I don't know how well she would fit in with the way Madeleine has turned the place around.'

Kim nodded. 'I know what you mean. We would never go there before Madeline Powell took over. I'm afraid tight nosebands and gadgets to try to make up for riders' shortcomings are not our cup of tea. But since Madeleine transformed the place it has a very welcoming and relaxed feel to it.'

'Well, although my ex-wife and I were terrible as life partners, I hope we have brought our daughters up not to think that horses should be beaten into submission, so Alison doesn't have that kind of attitude, I am pleased to say. I would describe her as traditional in the sense of believing horses need shoes to do roadwork, and the only saddler you can trust is one with the words Master in the title, neither of which I have found to be true. Nothing may come of it, but I would love to have both of my daughters living close by again.'

'You seem to be very content with your life.'

'I am. I have a beautiful wife, two gorgeous daughters, and I get to spend my days like this,' Peter raised his bottle in a toast, before adding, 'well, not exactly like this. Not all horse owners are like you and your family, but I am seeing an increase in horses being managed in the way you do it.'

'Why do you think that is?' asked Kim. 'I have only learned because of the problems my husband's old horse, Wicky, had. We never would have dreamed of having barefoot horses, or buying up miles of electric tape to create tracks in our fields if it hadn't been for his health problems. Surely not everyone is as lucky as we are that his rehabilitation was successful, or that all horses managed in stables and with shoes get plagued by injury?'

'Oh no, of course not. There are plenty of examples of healthy shod horses galloping around the countryside, and stabling is an essential part of many people's management for their animals. But I think that as more examples of healthy barefoot horses are seen out and about at competitions and training clinics, then interest in how their owners have achieved it is growing. Similarly, people like you who have had problems with one or more horses, start as you mean to go on with your future horses, just as you are doing with young JD here. It doesn't mean that he is never going be injured, but my experience tells me that with your attitude towards the work he will be expected to do, and the lifestyle he will be growing up in, he is less likely to fall prey to the kinds of long-term damage which end many a horse's working life.'

'But there is so much to learn. How do people find out about it all?'

'How did you and your husband learn?'

Kim sighed. 'Mainly through trial and error. It is horrible feeling as though you are gambling with your horse's life. At times we had to be careful we were not experimenting with him. A friend mentioned an online forum, which turned out to be a godsend, and from there we made contact with people who had claimed they had rehabilitated their injured horses, and were now riding all over the country in different disciplines. Of course, anyone can claim anything online, so we contacted a few of them and asked if we could meet up. There were one or two who kept having last minute emergencies meaning they had to cancel our visit, so we stopped following their online exploits because we just didn't believe in them. We travelled to Devon and met a lady who both rehabilitates and hunts barefoot horses.'

'Oh I know who you mean! She is one of my go-to people when I am not sure about my facts. I have also referred a number of clients to her.'

'It is a small world, isn't it?'

'But a growing one,' Peter smiled. 'Who else have you met?'

'We drove up to North Wales and met another lady who does both endurance and dressage with her horses. Now we don't have to travel for hours to see working horses' hooves, and have gone from being the only barefoot people in the neighbourhood to having a small local group of barefoot friends. We ride out together and swap information. Although to be honest, we rarely discuss anything to do with the horses' feet any more, because none of us have any problems with them these days! We are more likely to be discussing training techniques and saddle fit than the state of our horses' hooves.'

'I notice you didn't mention any equine professionals in your list. Does that mean you didn't follow veterinary or farriery advice?'

'No!' Peter was a little taken aback by the vehemence with which Kim spoke. 'Our vet was a complete nightmare. She was against us doing anything which didn't involve remedial shoeing and box rest. But after a year of trying all of that and still having a lame horse at the end of it, whose condition had actually deteriorated during that time, and seeing all of these people who had healthy, happy, comfortably working horses by changing their diets and removing their shoes, we took the plunge and went against her advice.'

Peter was silent for a moment. 'Are you talking about my former boss?'

Kim nodded.

'I see. Well, she took a big risk employing me then, didn't she? Good for her.'

'I suppose so. She was always very nice, and convincing in her beliefs, but in the end we took the view that as she did not have any experience of successfully rehabilitating horses with injuries like Wicky's using barefoot protocols, she probably wasn't the best person to go to for help. Anyway, that is the past. What are your plans for the practice, now that you are in charge?'

'Ah, the fifty million dollar question. It has all happened so quickly that our plans are still up in the air. This time last year I had taken a big step back in career terms, and here I am in charge of my own veterinary business with plans for expansion. It is a dream come true, with nightmare overtones,' Peter laughed. 'The first thing we need to do is move into our new premises. We have found somewhere that will allow us to set up a small rehabilitation yard, which isn't possible where we are now. But finding the money to fund the staffing of it is going to be a major stumbling block, and so the rehab side of things is going to take a little while to establish.'

'How exciting! I am sure the local horse community will benefit from a facility like that. I can think of several horses who could do with help along those lines.'

'Yes, I am keen to get it off the ground as soon as possible, but the logistics still need working out. Right,' Peter checked his watch. 'I had better go and see if Jennifer needs any help to bring that phone call to a close. If Jennifer doesn't hang up soon she won't have time to have a proper look at your horses. I need to get a move on, and hurry home to my wife! Gemma has been working in the tearooms all day, and will be exhausted. She hasn't been feeling one hundred percent recently, so I don't want to be too late home.'

Chapter 10

Monday 1st August 2016, 8.00pm

When Jennifer pulled into the driveway of Gemma and Peter's home on Brackendon Road in Woodford, opposite The Green, she declined her father's offer of a quick after-work drink. She knew Paul would have her dinner ready for her, and wanted to have a quick shower to wash away the day's troubles first. She gave her dad a kiss on the cheek, and walked the short distance along the road to the cottage she shared with Paul, located behind Black's Auction House.

Peter watched her for a few moments, pleased that she seemed to have found her own soul mate, and made his way past the overhanging jasmine bushes around to the back door, to find his. Instead he was greeted enthusiastically by his wife's Staffie, Suzy, and his daughter's greyhound, Lucy, who spent more time with them than at Paul's cottage with Jennifer, and by the delicious smell of roast chicken.

'Hi, love!' he called, as he stripped off his work boots and overalls. 'Are you cooking a roast? I thought a barbeque or a salad would be a good idea in this weather; I was going to sort something out for us.'

Gemma appeared, her long curly blonde hair swept away from her face in a high ponytail. She was wiping her hands on her apron, and she stood on her tiptoes to give him a kiss on the cheek.

'Hello darling. I know, I am mad, but I really fancied a roast dinner this evening, so we have chicken, potatoes, Yorkshire puddings, calabrese, carrots, and peas. Or at least we will once you have picked some from the veggie patch. Here, take this bowl.'

'Have the tearooms been quiet today, then?'

Gemma nodded. 'A little, yes. A beautiful sunny day like this means the tourists and locals disappear down to the beaches, so all we have been left with is the antiques dealers who have come to view Black's next auction. Mind you, there have been enough of them to keep me busy. It seems that someone in the trade died a few weeks' ago, and since then I have heard three different versions of what happened to him. Oh, and another piece of gossip. Simon Maxwell-Lewis came in too, which is strange because he rarely came in before he went to prison for his part in the house burglaries and the damage to the antiques centre.'

'Did he? I suppose the tearooms are so close to his family home at Wellwood Farm there wouldn't have been any reason for him to come in to eat or drink anything. Former family home, I should say. But now that his mother no longer rents the farm it maybe that he doesn't have anywhere else to go. I wonder where he is living now?'

'I have no idea; nobody has said anything about his living arrangements. You could be right about why did not come into the tearooms, although Cliff Williamson lives next door, and he is always popping in for something to eat or drink.'

'True. But then Cliff doesn't live with his doting mother, like Simon used to.'

'No, or even with his wife and children any more. I wonder how long it will be before he finds someone new. Anyway, it was all a bit awkward when Simon did come in, because Cliff and Sarah were spread out over one of the tables planning their next flea market on The Green, and a couple of the antiques dealers whose property he destroyed in Williamson Antiques were at another table. I didn't see the exact moment he walked through the front door, but I heard the bell go and looked out through the serving window to see his back as he walked out again. Apparently he took one look at the other customers and decided not to stay. I do feel sorry for him, because he has served his time, and his behaviour last year did seem to be out of character, but I am also relieved that nothing kicked off in the tearooms today; I don't think I could have coped with it. How was your day? I hope it was trouble-free?'

Peter laughed 'I wouldn't describe it as trouble-free, but it was nothing as dramatic as yours by the sound of it; although Jennifer had a bit of a difficult time with a client this afternoon. They claimed to want her help, but didn't seem to understand that taking some time to listen to what Jennifer was saying would be more productive than employing a whole gamut of emotions. Poor Jennifer was inundated from the start of the appointment, through to phone calls, text messages, and then emails.'

'Really? What was the problem?'

'Simply, the woman was feeding her horse into a state of laminitis. She was clued up enough to recognise that her horse was not well, so she asked for our help. Jennifer went to see her and the horse this afternoon, and assessed the horse's condition and made recommendations for his treatment, which the woman did not want to follow for whatever reason. She then proceeded to blast Jennifer over a four hour period with tears, abuse, begging, and finally emotional blackmail.'

'What did she want Jennifer to do?'

'Well, that's the point, Jennifer had already given the woman all of the advice she could at that stage; it was up to the woman to take it and utilise it, but I think she wanted Jennifer to agree to doing things the way the woman wanted to instead, which was clearly not working as the horse's condition is deteriorating. Jennifer handled the woman really well by not allowing the communications to become side-tracked by whatever else was going on in the woman's life, and sticking to the welfare of the horse, so we just have to hope the woman acts on the information she has been given before it becomes a welfare case. Anyway, enough about that traumatic situation, and onto something lovely. Do you remember this time last year I was up all night with a family, watching while one of their mares gave birth to a dear little colt?'

'Oh yes, I remember,' Gemma winked, as the memories of how she and Peter finally took the next step in their relationship came flooding back.

Smiling, Peter continued 'I went back to visit them again this afternoon. In the space of a year they have doubled their herd, and now have four horses! All looking very happy and content, I am pleased to report. Jennifer came with me, so it was a good opportunity to further her education into natural horse-keeping once she could get away from the difficult client's demands. I just wish I had known all the things I now know about hoofcare, nutrition and saddle-fitting when Jennifer and Alison were growing up. Jennifer is well on her way to transforming her approach towards horses; and with any luck Alison will be moving down here soon and I can get to work re-educating my other daughter too. Don't worry, I'm going!' Gemma was making yappy hand shapes and looking pointedly at the empty bowl in his hands.

Peter wandered down the garden in his boxer shorts and polo shirt, bowl in hand, with the two dogs following him. 'This is what happens when you marry a chef!' he told them. 'Mad woman. She has been cooking for other people all day, and now she wants to cook a whole roast dinner for just two of us, in the middle of summer! Well, four of us, I suppose,' he said, as he looked at the two smiling doggy faces.

Gemma had moved to Woodford several years before Peter arrived in the town. She and her two sons chose to change location when her marriage broke down, along with the business she and her husband ran together. Theirs was an amicable break-up, as much as the ending of a shared life can be, and the cottage was the one she bought at the time. Gemma and Peter's was a whirlwind romance in one way, although it had started with a relatively slow courtship.

Peter was in his fifties, and Gemma a few years younger in her forties. They were both divorced after long marriages, with no other serious relationships in between, and both with grown-up children. Once they decided to be a couple, and move in together, they were in agreement that marriage was the next perfect step, and were legally husband and wife within weeks of Peter's romantic proposal.

Gemma owned and ran The Woodford Tearooms, which was next door to Williamson Antiques on the High Street, with her sister Lisa. Together with Lisa's daughter Caroline, they provided locals and visitors alike with early morning breakfasts, elevenses, lunches, and afternoon teas. The two sisters produced as much of the food as they could themselves, preferring to put together a dish from scratch than buy in from a wholesaler. The hours were long, and Gemma rarely cooked at home on a day, like today, when she had been at work from opening to closing. Often they ate leftovers from the tearooms, or Peter rustled something up if he wasn't working late, and when they could be bothered they popped across the road to The Ship Inn for their dinner. A full roast dinner on a Monday night was unheard of, and Peter wondered what had brought on this sudden desire.

Once he had hunted down enough vegetables, and placed most of them in the bowl, and only a few in his mouth, and given one small carrot to each of the dogs, he strolled back towards the cottage. Gemma was on the patio, sitting at the table she had laid earlier complete with linen napkins and a huge vase of flowers and foliage she had picked from the garden. Peter laid the bowl down, and sat next to her, taking her hand in his.

'Ah, this is the life,' he breathed. 'I am so lucky to have found you, and grateful that you agreed to be my wife. I love you, Gemma. You make my world whole.'

'Oh Peter, that is such a wonderful thing to say, thank you,' Gemma's eyes were filled with tears. 'And I love you, even though you make me cry.'

Together they hugged and kissed, before parting and sitting quietly side-by-side for a few minutes, peacefully soaking up the evening sun.

'One year ago today' Gemma winked at him, a mischievous look on her face.

'Happy One Year Anniversary' he winked back.

Chapter 11

Tuesday 2nd August 2016, 12 noon

Lisa Bartlett smiled as she watched the couple sitting at the table in one of the bay windows of The Woodford Tearooms. Paul Black and Jennifer Isaac were holding hands across the table, carefully avoiding the small vase of beautifully scented and colourful sweet peas in the centre of it. They were in the middle of an intense conversation; their low tones making it impossible for the people nearby to understand what they were saying.

'What are you smiling about?' Gemma carried two plates of pomegranate and feta salad over to a tray on the wide shelf which separated the kitchen from the customers, and peered through the window.

'Oh, I was just thinking that if even someone like Paul Black can find love, then there is hope for me too. Just look at him and Jennifer, they only have eyes for each other. I wish I had someone who wanted to sit with me like that.'

'Oh Lisa!' her sister tutted as she turned back to collect the two glasses of elderflower cordial, and added them to the tray. 'Stop thinking about it so much, and get on with enjoying your man-free life.'

'It's alright for you!' Lisa protested, as she walked around to the other side of the window, and prepared to take the tray over to the happy couple. 'You have found your perfect man. Even your not-so-perfect man wasn't bad. Yours had to be one of the most amicable divorces I have ever witnessed. You have a better relationship with your ex-husband than I have with any men in my life. My divorce was horrendous, my love-life is non-existent, and my trust in the males of the species has been torn apart. And you weren't even looking for love when Peter Isaac walked in here!' Lisa gestured towards the tearooms' front door, through which Gemma's future husband had walked almost seventeen months earlier. 'You are so lucky,' she grumbled, 'whereas I only seem to attract bullies and deceivers. Why can't I find True Love? It's not fair.'

Lisa delivered the food and drinks to the two love birds, and returned to the kitchen, ready to continue to pour out her misery to Gemma. As she opened her mouth to begin, Gemma stopped her by speaking first.

'So, let me get this straight.' Lisa came to an abrupt halt, taken aback by the fierce tone coming from her sister. She stared in shock at the woman in front of her standing with her arms folded across the flowery patterned uniform apron they both wore. 'You think that if you and Paul Black got together, the pair of you would be sitting in a café somewhere being lovey-dovey during your lunch-break?'

Lisa was stung to tears at the vehemence in her sister's voice, and found that a huge lump in her throat rendered her unable to answer.

'Well? Do you?' Gemma's blue eyes had taken on a cold steely look which matched her voice, as she waited for a reply. Her face, usually cheery with the merest hint of naughtiness about it, was covered in frown lines and looked anything but friendly. Keeping her voice low so their customers couldn't overhear her, Gemma continued 'Paul Black has numerous failed relationships behind him, including two broken marriages. He is well-known in Woodford as a serial heart-breaker, and since we moved here five years ago we have never seen him in a monogamous and loving relationship. Until, apparently, now with my stepdaughter, Jennifer. But the jury is still out on whether or not their relationship will last without breaking anybody's heart. What makes *you*' Lisa flinched at the emphasis 'think that could have been you sitting out there gazing lovingly into his eyes? Instead of comparing your life to everyone else's and finding it lacking in something, why don't you make the most of the good fortune you do have, Lisa?' Gemma began to tick off the points on her fingers 'One, you have two beautiful healthy children; two, you have your own health; three, you are responsible for your own happiness; four …'

The sound of the cowbell tinkling to signal the front door was opening made both sisters turn to see what the interruption was, and broke the rising tension before it could break them.

Lisa's heart sank even further at the sight of one of her exes, Robin Morton. Gemma threw her hands in the air, shaking her head, as she turned back to the salad she had been prepping, forcing Lisa to be the one to greet the man.

Quickly wiping her eyes with her fingers, whilst trying to regulate her breathing, and attempting to adopt a professional attitude, Lisa forced a smile and called through the serving window 'Robin. What can we do for you today?'

Robin Morton knew before he came through the tearooms' entrance that his welcome would not be friendly, and so he was grateful for Lisa's attempt to be civil, even if the effort she was making was clear for everyone to see.

85

'Hello Lisa. A mug of tea, and a cheese toastie please. Is it alright if I sit over here?' he indicated to a small table over to the right of the room, under a bright sunburst painting by one of the local Woodford artists who displayed their work in the tearooms.

Lisa nodded, and turned away to prepare his order, carefully avoiding her sister's eyes. Robin and Lisa had a brief love affair the year before, which Lisa ended as soon as she discovered he had lied about several aspects of his life. Although at the time Gemma had provided Lisa with a much-needed shoulder to cry on, now Lisa wondered if her sister was judging her, and thought she should have known what Robin was up to all along. Certainly Lisa had felt incredibly stupid at the time, but as more information emerged about Robin's life as an undercover policeman, everyone around her reassured her that it wasn't her fault she had been duped; it was the nature of his profession to deceive people, and he was very good at his job. But having been on the receiving end of Gemma's recent accusatory outburst all the old insecurities rushed to the surface, and Lisa's self-confidence plummeted.

'I'll take that out to him.' Gemma spoke softly as she leaned around Lisa to retrieve the toasted sandwich, and added it to the tray on which she had already placed a freshly made mug of tea. Now that the fire of frustration at her sister's self-deception had been exhausted, Gemma was feeling guilty. Lisa had always been happy to follow someone else's lead, and although over the years her lack of desire to take responsibility for anything had annoyed Gemma, she accepted that was the way Lisa was. But things had changed recently, and Gemma knew that Lisa could no longer rely on her to smooth everything over when life got rough. It was time for Lisa to take charge of her own life by making her own decisions and sticking to them.

Gemma walked over to Robin's table and placed the mug and the plate in front of him. With a pleasant smile on her face she asked 'Are you working in the area at the moment?'

'No, no I am not.' Robin said quietly, as he looked down at his lunch. After a pause he lifted his head, and shifted his gaze towards the serving window, searching for any sign of Lisa. Realising she was keeping out of sight, he turned his attention back to Gemma who had been studying him. In her experience every time Robin Morton came into the tearooms it meant trouble was brewing. 'Thank you for this,' he said, nodding towards the food and drink.

The next twenty minutes were spent in a chilly but well-organised exhibition of teamwork, as Gemma and Lisa took orders, prepared and served drinks and food, and cleared tables. When they next had a chance to stop for a few moments, Paul and Jennifer had gone, as had Robin Morton.

Lisa looked at her watch 'Well, I think that was the worst of the lunchtime rush. Will you be alright on your own if I go now?'

'Yes, I'll be fine. You go. Good luck at the hairdressers!' Gemma's attempt at injecting a friendly note into their discourse fell flat, as Lisa simply nodded, unhooked her bag from the back of the door, and left without another word.

Lisa walked the short distance up the Woodford High Street to one of the five hairdressing salons in the town. She had kept the same hairstyle of long blonde curls for the past twenty years, and although when she booked the appointment six weeks earlier she had no intention of changing it, she noted the large canvases depicting a variety of beautiful women modelling carefully created hair colours and styles, and decided it was time for a change.

Chapter 12

Tuesday 2nd August 2016, 3.00pm

'I just don't think these are right.' Cliff Williamson and his two employees, Nicola Stacey and Barry Johnson, were studying a pair of silver candlesticks which one of the stall holders in Cliff's antiques centre had placed for sale that morning in their cabinet. He passed one of them back to Nicola, 'See? The way the hallmark is blurry where it shouldn't be if it was through normal wear and tear.' As he handed the second to Barry he said 'And they are purporting to be by the eighteenth century silver maker Ebenezer Coker.'

Nicola peered at the marks. 'Oh! I see what you mean now. Yes, the marks are worn in places where there is no good reason for something to regularly be rubbing them down like that. So do you think these have been faked?'

Barry asked 'Why is the name Ebenezer Coker a red flag to you?'

Cliff shrugged. 'Only because there are so many fakes around carrying his name. Although it doesn't mean these are not silver; it could just be that the maker they are being attributed to did not make these candlesticks.'

Nicola carefully placed the candlestick she had been studying back on the glass shelf. 'It's a minefield isn't it? All this fake stuff flooding the market? First brass disguised as bronze, and now silver disguised as silver.'

Barry laughed as he put its mate alongside it, before he closed and locked the cabinet doors. 'I don't think this is a new phenomenon, Nicola. People have been faking antiques for hundreds of years.'

Cliff explained 'If you think about it, that is why antiques dealers specialise in one area of the trade, so they can be an expert in their chosen field. Although, Barry, when does a fake become an antique in its own right? Those candlesticks were probably made over one hundred and twenty years ago, which legitimately makes them antiques, but they are still fakes.'

Barry smoothed down his short grey beard to give himself some thinking time. He had worked for Cliff at Williamson Antiques since it first opened nineteen years earlier, and preferred to use his muscles to lift the antiques, rather than his brain to think about them. 'I suppose, because they are being marketed as one thing, when in fact they are something else.'

'Exactly. Those hallmarks, if as we suspect they are forged, are designed to give the impression that these candlesticks were made by a certain silver maker, when they are more than likely to have been made by somebody entirely different.'

'Antique fakes! So what happens next?' asked Nicola.

'I'll have to contact the dealer and tell him I am not happy about them, and explain my concerns. Unless he can convince me they are authentic, I'll have to remove them from sale. He should then send them up to the assay office in London to be checked for their authenticity. Depending on what they find, the chaps at the assay office will either destroy the candlesticks, or blank the hallmark and re-mark them with a modern hallmark.'

'Sounds expensive for someone!' commented Barry.

Cliff nodded 'Could be, for the dealer. Silver hallmarks are a legal requirement, so if anyone has been messing around with them then it is serious. The trouble is if we sell them through here, then I will probably be the one in trouble for selling illegal silver. Actually, now that I have thought about it, quick, unlock that cabinet again and we'll pop them in the safe until I can have a word with the owner.'

Their attempts to remove the candlesticks were interrupted by someone coming into the antiques centre.

'Robin, hello. You are like a bad penny. What undercover scheming are you up to this time?' Cliff moved away from the cabinet to draw the policeman's attention somewhere safer. The man's timing was scary.

Robin Morton shook his head. 'I can't blame you for feeling like that about me, Cliff, but my time as an undercover police officer has come to an end, and I am in here purely as a civilian customer.'

'Ah, but how can we believe you? You, the man who pretended to be an antiques dealer, and even went to the lengths of fooling me by taking on one of my stalls in here?'

Barry and Nicola looked at each other, and silently agreed to both find something important to do in another part of the antiques centre. Neither of them had much time for Robin Morton, and they were confident that Cliff could sort out whatever issue Robin had brought in with him.

Robin spread his hands out in surrender. 'All I can do is apologise for that deceit. Over the past few months I have been forced to realise how many people I have upset and hurt in this town, but it really wasn't my intention.'

'So why are you here? Are you sure your presence doesn't have anything to do with Hugh Jones' tragic death? You don't live here, you don't have any family or friends here, you have no reason to be here.'

'What can I say? I love this town! And for what it is worth, I am genuinely fascinated by the antiques world. All I ever wanted to do was protect the Trade. Look, if you are free this evening can I buy you a pint at The Ship Inn? No strings, I promise. I feel we have got off on the wrong foot, and I would like to attempt to start to put things right between us.'

Cliff didn't believe Robin's explanation for turning up in Williamson Antiques, or for that matter in the town of Woodford, but he was curious enough to accept Robin's invitation.

'Alright, I'll have a pint off you. I think that is the least you can do, after all the stunts you have pulled on me. Shall we meet at about six o'clock?'

Robin smiled with relief. 'Six o'clock, in The Ship Inn, and the first round is on me.'

'Ah, sorry mate, I can only stay for one. I have to be up for a training session in the morning.' And with that parting shot, Cliff called over to Nicola 'While it's quiet in here I'm going to pop up to Bridger's for some groceries. If you could do that thing when the time is right, I would appreciate it.'

'Right you are Boss. I'll do that thing as soon as possible. I expect I will have left by the time you get back here; I am going to Zumba with Sarah tonight.'

'Oh yes, I'll have to join you and Sarah Handley one evening, and find out what it is all about.'

'Any time, Cliff, any time! Men are always welcome.'

Cliff had no intention of joining Nicola and Sarah at one of their regular Zumba dance classes until he had practised first. He and Paul had watched them through the window once, to see what was so great about it. They had both been taken aback by how strenuous it looked, and how physically fit the instructors were. They agreed that it looked far too hard for them, and they preferred running where you only had to make sure you put one foot in front of the other, and your arms just joined in naturally. All that tricky footwork and intricate arm waggling put them off.

He walked the short distance up the High Street to the fruit and veg shop, barely noticing his journey. He hated to admit it but he liked Robin Morton, even though he did not trust his motives. Cliff was curious about the man's desire to get him on-side, and wondered what was occurring in the local antiques trade to make the policeman want to befriend him. He did not believe for a moment that Robin had left the police force. Grudgingly, he acknowledged that Robin's behaviour so far had only helped the antiques trade, by removing some of the bad elements from it. Even so, everyone was uncomfortable when he was around. Policemen tend to have that effect on innocent and guilty people alike.

Cliff stopped just before the shop's entrance when a new thought occurred to him, but it was lost when an elderly lady, taken by surprise by his sudden halt, bumped into him. After all of the kerfuffle which inevitably happens when two English people collide, where both want to take responsibility and apologise to each other while desperately trying to continue on their way as though nothing has happened, Cliff eventually made it through the doorway.

'Afternoon, Cliff.' Tristram, the shop's owner, came up from the back of the shop where he had been replenishing the basket of beetroot. 'You look a bit flustered, are you OK? Is it because you are contemplating a tricky recipe involving pak choi?'

Cliff laughed 'Yes, Tristram, you are spot on. But nothing so exotic. No, I was trying to work something out when I managed to trip up an old lady, and now I can't remember what it was I was thinking about. Tell me again, how do you boil an egg?' He appreciated Tristram Bridger's gentle teasing. When Rebecca first threw him out of the family home, Cliff moved into the flat above Williamson Antiques, and was suddenly in charge of making his own meals for the first time in almost twenty years. After a few days of admittedly very good pub dinners, and equally tasty takeaways from the local Indian and Italian restaurants, he knuckled down to taking responsibility for his own food. His first visit to Bridger's, the family-owned grocery shop on Woodford High Street, had been a major step on the road to self-sufficiency. Tristram had been a great source of easy-to-prepare and cook recipes for one, and enjoyed advising Cliff on which ingredients he could buy, and then use for three or four different meals so that nothing was wasted.

Cliff and Tristram were roughly the same height, both topping over six foot tall, but there their physical similarities ended. Tristram was slender and dark-haired with blue eyes, while Cliff was well-muscled and auburn haired with brown eyes. Although they had lived in the same town, and worked within feet of each other, since Cliff moved to Woodford over twenty years before, until the previous summer they had

94

barely spoken more than half a dozen words to each other. Even now they only ever conversed about food and recipes, but Cliff was tempted to share his concerns about Robin Morton's presence in the town with Tristram.

'Actually, I have just seen someone whose presence always seems to mean there is imminent trouble.'

'Ah' Tristram nodded. 'I wondered if you had seen him too. I don't think he wants anyone to notice he is back, but he has been around for a few days now.'

'Really? He seemed to be quite open about being here, and has even offered to buy me a drink in the pub this evening.'

'Has he? Well that does surprise me. If you say you have accepted his invitation I will be even more shocked.'

Cliff frowned before replying. 'Tristram, I am talking about Robin Morton. Who are you talking about?'

'Oh, oh I see! I'm talking about Simon Maxwell-Lewis. I suppose you do know he has been released from prison?'

'Oh him, yes I did know. He briefly came into the tearooms while I was in there yesterday, but thought better of it and left immediately. Where on earth is he living?'

'I don't know. Presumably he has moved to wherever his poor old mum has gone, now that their farm has been sold? Robin Morton, eh? Yes, he does seem to follow trouble around. The nature of his job, I suppose. Be careful.'

Cliff left Tristram's shop with a bag full of vegetables, and began to walk the short distance back to his antiques centre. Deep in thought, it took a few moments before Cliff became aware of a person deliberately keeping pace alongside him. He took a quick glance at the woman, wondering why she didn't either overtake him or speak to him if that was her intention. A second look made him stop in his tracks.

'Oh, oh that was so funny!' Lisa Bartlett was almost doubled over with hysterics.

'Lisa! I didn't recognise you! What on earth have you done to your hair?'

Cliff's words had the same effect on Lisa as if he had slapped her face. The laughter stopped in an instant, and she stared up at him, her mouth shaped in an 'O'.

'Er, I mean, wow, what a difference!' Cliff's feeble attempt to extricate himself from the enormous hole he had just dug in record time was too weak to be effective. He tried again. 'I didn't recognise you, Lisa, you look completely different.'

'Yes, I got that message' Lisa snapped.

'Right. In a good way I mean.' Cliff could see from Lisa's face that this was also not the right thing to say. He tried a different tack. 'Do you like it?'

'Well I did before I bumped into you,' Lisa muttered, and she walked quickly away from him.

Cliff stood helplessly watching her go, unable to think of a single thing to call after her to rectify the situation. It wasn't that Lisa's new hairstyle looked bad; it was such a shock to see her looking so different that nothing sensible or complimentary came to mind. He shook his head at his own ineptitude, and managed to at least get his feet to do what he wanted even if his tongue wouldn't, and continued his journey back to the antiques centre.

Barry looked up from the computer as Cliff walked in.

'What's happened to you?' he asked, as Cliff sighed his way over and dumped the shopping bag onto the counter.

'Oh, I am such an idiot. I have just seen Lisa Bartlett with her new hairdo, and I managed to make her feel terrible about it,' he groaned. 'She has had all her hair chopped off and dyed red. It is all spiky and pointy.'

'Has she? I wonder what prompted her to do that. My wife had all of her hair cut off when she was made redundant. Apparently it had something to do with empowerment. I thought she looked bloody awful, and so did she after she had it done. Fortunately it grew back, but it took a couple of years. It will be strange seeing Lisa with short red hair, after all these years of only knowing her with long blonde curls.'

'Yes, it was a shock. It does suit her though, I thought she looked fantastic.'

Barry thought for a moment, 'I'll have to pop next door to the tearooms tomorrow and have a gander. I am sure she looks great; after all Rebecca took the plunge to have her long dark curls cut shorter last year, and she looks gorgeous.'

Cliff declined to comment.

Chapter 13

Tuesday 2nd August 2016, 5.00pm

After her excruciating encounter with Cliff, Lisa decided she didn't want anyone else to let her know what a terrible mistake she had made, and walked quickly past the big Edwardian windows of the tearooms with her head slightly turned away. She continued down the High Street until she could take a left turn through one of the alleyways which provided a link from the road to The Green which ran the length of the back of the shops and offices. She turned left again and made her way up the narrow track to the small yard at the back of the tearooms where her car was parked. Lisa briefly considered ducking down so she would be less visible to anybody, namely Gemma, looking through the windows of the kitchen, but managed to stop herself and walked with a ramrod straight back to her car. She unlocked the driver's door and slid into the seat, before closing it as quietly as possible.

She checked nobody was looking in horror at her hair out of the kitchen window, and started the engine. The beeping of the car's inbuilt warning system to put on her seatbelt made her jump, and again she scanned the yard and back door to the tearooms, but no one came rushing over to see what all the noise was about.

Swearing furiously, she shoved her foot down on the clutch, pulled the gear stick into reverse, and attempted to leave the yard without releasing the handbrake. More noise as she hurriedly corrected her mistake, and then she was out onto the track, and with relief she was safely hidden behind the wall.

Lisa pulled impatiently at the seatbelt, but of course it kept locking, until eventually she managed to release her grip and try again. Safely belted in, and with the incessant noise of the alarm finally silenced, she let out a breath and looked ahead to the freedom of the road. Lisa put her foot down firmly on the accelerator. The car shot backwards in its original trajectory and hit the wall.

For a moment Lisa considered giving up, and going inside to seek Gemma's help. But then the memory of how hurtful her sister's words and attitude had been earlier that day made her recoil, and she put her head on the steering wheel and sobbed, all of the time wondering what it was her sister was trying to tell her. When tears began to drip onto her jeans she sat up, intending to search her handbag for a tissue, but caught sight of her reflection in the rear-view mirror and froze. The image staring back at her was frightful. Bloodshot eyes bled into black rivers of mascara, which in turn mixed with mucus. Her new haircut was styled off her face, so she no longer had her long curls to hide behind. The sight of her image was the shock Lisa needed to find some inner strength, and sort out her current problem. The urgency to find the packet of tissues forced her to look away from the horror story in the mirror, and reach over to retrieve her handbag from the foot well of the passenger side where it had been thrown with the force of the impact. But something else in the mirror made her look back into it again.

Somebody was watching her; she could see the head of a man peering around the wall which formed the entrance to the yard at the back of Williamson Antiques.

Embarrassed that she had been spotted after all, Lisa reached down for her bag, and scrabbled around inside it, relieved that the little plastic bag of tissues were easily located. Pulling several out, she blew her nose and wiped her face, before checking the rear-view, and then the side mirror, to see how close the man was to being able to see the mess she was in. She looked over her shoulder, and then checked in front of the car, but no one was to be seen.

Lisa was now worried he had gone to fetch help, and as she didn't want to see Cliff again that day she re-started the stalled engine, put the car into first gear, and carefully pulled away from the wall. Once she was clear of the entrance to the tearooms' yard, she jumped out to check the damage to her car, and to the wall. The wall looked unscathed, but she could see the marks on her car where it had collided with the stones. Fortunately it didn't look as though the lights had been damaged, and nothing was obviously hanging off the side or underneath, so she climbed back in and sped away before anyone could come and interfere.

Chapter 14

Tuesday 2nd August 2016, 5.55pm

Cliff locked the back door to Williamson Antiques, and turned to walk through the small yard which formed the car park for the antiques centre; the twin of the one at the back of The Woodford Tearooms. As he did so he caught a flash of someone walking past the entrance, but by the time he reached the track outside there was no one around. Assuming he was seeing things, he continued his journey up to the beer garden of The Ship Inn, where he saw Peter and Gemma Isaac sharing a jug of Pimm's together.

'Hello, you two; you look as though you should be sitting next to a swimming pool somewhere hot and exotic.'

Gemma grinned 'Blissful isn't it. I do like this weather.'

Peter wasn't looking quite so comfortable. 'To be honest I'd rather have a lager and be sitting indoors. I have been outside all day, working as the vet on call at one of the local equestrian one-day events, and have seen enough exhausted and dehydrated horses and riders to last me a lifetime.'

'Oh, he's just being grumpy because I said he couldn't have anything alcoholic until I have seen him drink at least a pint of this mocktail,' Gemma patted his arm.

'Alcohol is not the best form of rehydration, is it Cliff?'

Cliff laughed 'I thought you were drinking Pimm's! Mmmh, that does look refreshing, and your wife is correct Peter, that mocktail will be far better for you. Maybe I should have some of that, instead of the bitter I was planning to drink. I'm running with your niece, Caroline, in the morning Gemma, and I struggle to keep up with her as it is. Is that a 'thing' then? Horses can get dehydrated?'

'Yes, of course. Horses are much better at warming themselves up, then cooling down, and so when you combine it with a baking hot day like today, and a series of athletic exercises which test your stamina, then it can happen. Fortunately none of them will have any long-term effects, but there are now a few riders who have gained some essential knowledge about how to manage their horse's electrolyte consumption prior to, and during, exercise.'

Gemma groaned 'For goodness' sake, don't ask him any more questions. He'll only answer them, and I have already heard all of this twice this evening.'

Cliff laughed, and began to move away before a thought struck him. 'Gemma, is your sister joining you here this evening?'

'Lisa? No. Or at least, we haven't arranged to meet. She could be meeting someone else, I suppose, but she didn't mention it when I saw her this morning. Why?'

Cliff looked shifty. 'Um, I think I upset her this afternoon, and now I am meeting Robin Morton for a quick drink which I can't imagine will please her, either. I don't think I am her favourite person at the moment.'

'Oh, join the club,' scoffed Gemma. 'I overstepped the mark this morning by giving her a few home truths

102

about the state of her love-life and the part she has played in it. I think you are right; I imagine if she does turn up here then the sight of me enjoying myself with Peter, and seeing you having a drink with Robin, will not help her bad temper. Why are you meeting Robin, anyway? And what have you done to upset Lisa?'

'To answer your second question first: I think I was less than complimentary about her new hairstyle.'

Gemma sat up 'Her what? What's she had done to her hair?'

'She has had it all cut off, and dyed red. It looks very good, it really suits her, but I wasn't expecting it and I think I upset her quite a bit with the way I reacted.'

Gemma was quiet for a few moments, before she said 'Oh dear, I think this is my fault. I was quite sharp with her this morning, and more or less told her that if she wanted to be in a loving relationship then she needed to change.'

'That sounds a bit harsh, and not at all like you.' Peter carefully ventured an opinion, making sure he softened the criticism of his wife's actions with a compliment. After several years of living with his two daughters and his now ex-wife, Peter was aware of the minefield of criticising anything, and familiar with the close link between physical appearance and self-confidence. 'But you say this complete change suits her?' He looked over at his wife, hoping that she wouldn't follow in her younger sister's footsteps and have her long blonde curls chopped off.

'Oh it really does suit her! She looks great. Anyway, I had better go and see what Robin wants. In answer to your first question: I have no idea. But I'm about to find out. Enjoy the rest of your evening.' He waved as he walked towards the open doors of the conservatory at the back of the pub.

Chapter 15

Tuesday 2nd August 2016, 6.00pm

'Oh no, look who's here' groaned Tom Higston to The Ship Inn's chef, Amanda, as he spotted someone lurking outside the window.

'We are already busy, and it is early in the evening. I think it would be a good idea to ask Sarah to stay and help out, because things never go smoothly when that woman is around' she observed.

Tom sighed. 'I really don't want to ask, but I think you are right.'

'Ask who what?' Sarah appeared from upstairs where she had changed out of her everyday jeans into a pair of red and black leggings and a neon yellow top.

'I'm out of here' Amanda disappeared to the safety of the kitchen as the customer she and Tom had been discussing began to walk in through the door.

Tom inclined his head in the customer's direction. 'I hate to say this, but I could do with your help after all this evening, please. You know I wouldn't normally ask, but I am out of my depth with this woman.'

Sarah Handley was trying to get into the habit of having every Tuesday as a pub-free day. It started as just the evenings off, when she and Nicola would go to a local Zumba class, and then she began to take the afternoons off to concentrate on her antiques hobby.

Now she had a new venture in the planning stages, and was testing the waters to see if it was possible to have a whole day away from the pub. She wanted to fulfil her dream of owning and running a small antiques shop, and the opportunity had arisen in a new development on the other side of The Green. If the business took off then she expected to be away from the pub a lot more than for one day a week.

In the seven months since her husband's unexpected death, Sarah had become increasingly reliant on both Tom and Amanda to help her run the pub. She was retraining herself to take a back seat during opening hours, but was still in control of the administration. While Mike was alive they enjoyed running their businesses together, taking on all the responsibilities and only employing a minimum number of permanent and casual staff when they were needed. This meant they rarely had quality time away from their business together, but that was how they liked to live.

Now that Sarah was on her own she was tentatively exploring the deliciously decadent world of delegation. And so far it seemed to be working. Tom Higston was a personable young man in his early twenties, who had been expected to take his place somewhere within the large family farming business a few miles away in Brackendon. But after several years trying his hand at the various aspects of the business, including sheep farming and the farm's shop, he still hadn't found his niche. He started to look around at other options, and Mike and Sarah Handley gave Tom a few hours behind the bar during their busy times in the summer and again over Christmas. After Mike's death, Tom moved into position as Bar Manager and was happy to be a full-time member of staff. He was inexperienced in the intricacies of the pub trade, but had excellent people skills and was very capable at working both independently and as part of the team.

Amanda had worked in pub kitchens for years, and loved working for Sarah, but had no desire to take on any more responsibilities. She was married, with four children, and Sarah knew she could not expect Amanda to take over any of her own duties.

Between them, Tom and Amanda were managing the various part-time employees, and so far the team were working together very well. The atmosphere in the pub was welcoming and relaxed, with occasional high-jinxes between staff and customers.

But this particular customer was unique.

Sarah looked over and smiled a professional welcome to the woman and her companion, while her heart sank. The woman was a local resident of Woodford, who rarely came into the pub. She had long unnaturally black hair which always seemed to need to be re-dyed, and the sort of pale wrinkly skin which is developed from smoking several packets of cigarettes a day. Her facial expressions ranged from hard to angry, and her voice echoed her face. Her five foot eight inch frame was thin, and today she was wearing a short black leather-type mini-skirt which showed off her bony white legs, and a black vest top which revealed far more of her skinny chest and lack of bra than Sarah would have personally been comfortable to reveal. She was with an elderly lady, who was very well-turned out, and put Sarah in mind of Agatha Christie's lady sleuth, Miss Jane Marple. They had paused just inside the door, and were now making a show of deciding whether or not to stay. Sarah hoped they would choose to go elsewhere. They didn't.

'Ah, yes, Veronica Bank. I see what you mean, Tom. Don't worry; I'll stay here this evening.' Sarah fished out a clean polo shirt emblazoned with the pub's logo from underneath the bar, and put it on over the top of her exercise wear. They all kept spare clothes ready to change into at a moment's notice when inevitably drink or food sullied their work clothes, and everyone's uniforms went into a basket at the end of each shift, ready for Sarah to wash and iron when she had time.

Smoothly Sarah began to work alongside Tom, taking drinks orders and handing over menus, mentally adjusting to spending the evening waiting tables instead of whooping and jumping around for an hour with her Zumba friends. She sent Nicola a short text apologising for not being able to join her, and then turned her full attention to the matter in hand.

Veronica Bank, the woman they were concerned about, considered herself to be a Very Important Person in the town of Woodford, and once upon a time she and her husband had been integral to the town's social and business life. Mr Bank had been an antiques dealer who specialised in postcards. He was respected for his knowledge by members of the local antiques trade, and he was well liked within Woodford. He had raised tens of thousands of pounds for local charities by organising and participating in a variety of events, and his wife was never far away whenever there was a photo opportunity.

Since he died it became clear that Veronica Bank's involvement within the community was more to do with flashing her power and money around than altruism, and without her husband's positive influence she was fast gaining a reputation as an oppressor rather than a benefactor. Sarah was beginning to personally understand how grief could affect a person's character, but the woman's husband had died more than three years earlier, and the tolerance the townspeople used to have for her had run out long ago.

'Right, how is everyone today?' Veronica Bank said, as she claimed a larger area of the bar top than was fair from the two people who were already waiting for their drinks orders. 'Hot isn't it? Too hot for me.'

Sarah noted that she was using the cover of general conversation for rudeness, as usual.

Without waiting for an answer she continued 'Any tables free for dinner tonight? We want to be in the dining room, where it is quiet. We don't want to have to listen to screaming kids while we eat.'

Neither Sarah nor Tom were paying her any attention while they continued to serve the customers who were ahead of her in the queue, although both had one ear tuned to her requests.

'What are the Chef's Specials today?' Tom put a couple of menus on the bar in front of the two women, with a smile, and continued past to fetch a bottle of ginger beer from the fridge.

Sarah finished helping the young couple and turned to the woman and her companion. 'Hello Mrs Bank, did I hear you say you would like a table in the dining room? If you would like to follow me, I can take your order once you have had a chance to sit down and read through the choices.'

'Oh, no need, Mum and I can order now. It will be much quicker.' Veronica Bank gave one of those fake smiles, managing to imply that Sarah and her staff were slow and incompetent, without actually stating it. Sarah waited patiently, while she read out the entire menu to her mother even though the old lady had her own copy of the menu and was clearly reading it.

This was a game Sarah and Tom were familiar with: Veronica Bank would demand attention, and then once she had it would make the person wait an inordinately long time before she deigned to share whatever it was she wanted them to do for her.

Sarah could see that a table of three had finished their main courses, so with a polite 'I won't be long, I'll give you a minute or two to choose' she dashed off to clear their plates, with Veronica Bank's words 'Oh, we are ready to order now!' following her. She winked at Tom as she passed him, indicating it was his turn to take over. They played this game of tag with the, thankfully few, customers who enjoyed trying to monopolise one person's time when the pub was busy.

Once she had cleared a few more tables, and left dessert menus with the occupants, Sarah returned to check on Tom's progress with Veronica Bank and her mother. She was relieved to see Tom had been able to find a suitable table in the dining room, and had also been able to take their food order. For the next forty five minutes all was quiet from that table, other than a comment when their second course arrived about preferring thin-cut chips to the chunky ones which were listed in the menu. Tom apologised and reminded Veronica Bank that she could request thin-cut chips, as she had done on many previous occasions.

'Oh well, I would have thought you would know that I only like thin-cut chips' came back the smart reply. Again, Tom apologised, and left the couple to eat their dinner, kicking himself for falling into the carefully laid trap.

Sarah was finishing taking the payment from a satisfied couple who were raving about their choice of Portuguese seafood cataplana, and were requesting she pass on their compliments to the chef, when she became aware that Tom was hovering by her shoulder.

He said 'Sorry, Sarah, but I think you need to deal with this.'

'Mrs Bank?' she asked.

'Mrs Bank' he confirmed.

Together they walked through to the dining room, where Veronica Bank was waiting expectantly, while her mother looked as though she would like the floor to open up and let her fall through it and escape. Sarah and Tom were used to Veronica Bank's complaints before, during and after a meal, and Sarah was thankful that the woman had chosen to wait until both she and her mother had finished eating their meal before demanding attention from the pub's staff.

'Ah, Mrs Handley' Veronica Bank never used Sarah's first name. 'I asked this young man to fetch the Chef. I want to make a complaint. Please be so good as to fetch him immediately.'

Sarah had only once made the mistake of doing as she asked, and brought Amanda out of the kitchen at her request. It rarely happened in the pub, but sometimes a customer had a concern about their food, and Amanda was happy to hear feedback about the texture or seasoning of the dishes she created. If the person's point was deemed valid then she and Sarah would alter the menu to ensure there could be no more misunderstandings. But after that single encounter during which Veronica Bank made a huge fuss about her Thai red curry being too spicy, even though it was marked as Very Hot on the menu, and she had warned the woman when she ordered it, and given her the choice of a milder green curry, she decided to deal with Veronica Bank herself in future. Fortunately she rarely came to The Ship Inn; Sarah calculated she made an appearance only a handful of times a year, and every time she found something to complain about.

'I am sorry but Chef is extremely busy. Can I help you?'

After a bit of harrumphing and pushing her used cutlery and empty plate around in front of her, Veronica Bank said 'Well, I am very sorry to say that I am dissatisfied with this meal.'

She looked at Sarah expectantly. 'I am very sorry to hear that Mrs Bank. What is it that has caused you dissatisfaction?'

For a second Sarah thought she could see the woman waver, but it didn't last.

'Please tell Chef that the chips were far too potatoey.'

Sarah could feel her jaw drop. She took a quick peek at Veronica Bank's mother, who was attempting to shrink as far back into her chair as possible.

'Pardon? I don't think I heard you correctly Mrs Bank.' Sarah spoke clearly, ensuring that all of the other diners could hear. 'Did you just say that you are unhappy with your meal, which you have eaten in its entirety, because the chips were too *potatoey*?'

Tom was aware that everybody in the various rooms in the pub were trying to listen to Veronica Bank's latest outburst. Her behaviour in the town was legendary. This woman had developed a habit of driving around the narrow country lanes in a top of the range sports car which apparently was not equipped with a reverse gear, nor could its tyres come into contact with mud at the edge of the road. She would drive at high speed past passing spaces towards oncoming vehicles, and flap her hands and arms at the astonished driver insisting they reverse, regardless of how far that needed to be to enable her to continue on her journey. She would then drive at approximately forty miles an hour on the main 'A' road up to Swanwick or down to the coast, holding up all the other traffic on the single carriageway sections.

Another behaviour for which Veronica Bank had become notorious was to go to one of the local shops, arrive at the counter with a full shopping basket, wait until the contents had been rung through the till, and then complain about the price in a loud voice. She would then leave the goods on the counter and the bill unpaid, and walk out of the shop declaring she would be shopping at Tesco in future. Fed up with her behaviour, one by one the shopkeepers banned her from their premises. She was also infamous for being the only person Gemma and Lisa had ever refused to serve in The Woodford Tearooms.

In a world where mental illness and dementia are often ignored, the local people of Woodford tended to stand out as a considerate and compassionate community, and it was generally assumed Mrs Bank was ailing into old age, even though she was probably only in her fifties. None of the local business owners had acted in haste; indeed many had given her discounts or free goods over several months or even years, before making the decision to prevent her from affecting their profits permanently. Sarah and Mike had ended up giving Mrs Bank several free meals because of her complaints over the three years since her husband died, but today Sarah decided that enough was enough.

'Ah,' she said. 'Potatoey chips. That will be because of all the potatoes Chef puts into them. Do you have an alternative recipe she could use?'

She could see a flicker of something in Veronica Bank's face. Their eyes locked and an understanding flew between them. Gotcha, she thought to herself. This was no mentally ill or grieving widow, this was someone who needed to be the centre of attention, someone with more time on her hands than she was used to, someone who needed to exert power over others, and someone who could eat elsewhere in future. 'No?' Sarah persisted. Veronica Bank had looked away from her; Sarah had a strong suspicion she was struggling to prevent her features from breaking out into a smile. 'Well in that case I suggest you go and pay for the meals you have both eaten, and don't return to my pub, because I am afraid that our chips will always be potatoey. Goodbye Mrs Bank.'

To the resounding sound of applause, with a few wolf whistles and cat calls, Veronica Bank held up her hands in defeat. She gracefully assisted her mother over to the bar, where her mother paid their bill in full, leaving a very large tip.

The remainder of the evening session continued smoothly, with several more people than usual commenting about how much they enjoyed the food and service. Sarah and Tom both worked hard to ensure they didn't allow the comments to degenerate into a bitching session about the woman, after all if the chips were too potatoey for her taste buds then she was entitled to express her opinion, and no harm had been done. Whatever the reasons for Veronica Bank's behaviour, Sarah was pleased she had finally been able to call the woman's bluff.

Chapter 16

Wednesday 3rd August 2016, 11.30am

Nicola finished her phone conversation. 'Well, that sounds like a good call. The lady has inherited a pile of silver cutlery and wondered if we want to sell it for her. She is going to bring it all in later today for you to have a look at.'

Cliff rubbed his hands together 'That does sound good. I hope the tines and blades are not too worn, otherwise I'll have to tell her to scrap it all. I heard the candlesticks had been collected.'

'Yes, I pointed out the wear on the hallmarks to him, and he thinks the same about it as you do, although he is not happy about it. I bet they are going to be scrapped.' She sighed 'I do hate how many quality silver items go to be scrapped. All of those beautiful pieces of jewellery, and the figures that sculptors have put so much time and energy into creating. It makes me sad to think of it all being destroyed.'

'I agree with you about most of the jewellery. It breaks my heart to think about the history of design all being lobbed into the melting pot. I think you might be right about where those candlesticks we removed from the cabinet yesterday will be heading. When I spoke to the owner he was furious because he bought them as part of a Lot from one of the London auction houses, and now he has checked the rest of the silver he has his doubts about most of that too. He is sending the whole Lot back and is demanding a refund, and has promised to let me know what they say about it. The auctioneers won't tell him who consigned the items, obviously, but he knows one of the porters who thinks it was a woman, and is going to look up the information for him.'

'Mmmh, sounds dodgy to me. I didn't think auction houses were meant to reveal the name of the vendor without their permission?'

'They are not. It is illegal. But, well, you know how these things work. With a tenner here, fifty quid there, you can find out anything you want.'

Nicola shook her head. 'What a mess. And all because you noticed something didn't look right with the hallmarks. If you hadn't said anything, none of this would be happening now. So, how was your evening?'

Cliff looked up at Nicola's sudden change of subject. She had been working alongside Cliff for more than two hours, trying to work out a way of casually dropping the meeting with Robin Morton into their conversation. So far he had failed to mention anything about it, and there had been no obvious opportunities for her to introduce the subject. When she arrived for work Nicola had been expecting Cliff to be full of the latest gossip from the undercover policeman, but as he didn't seem to be in the mood to share she decided to force the issue.

'What? Oh, good thank you. I had a pint with Robin, and then came back here. That recipe Tristram gave me for the pomegranate salad worked out well. It was superb with the tuna.'

Nicola peered at Cliff to check he wasn't being facetious, and concluded he genuinely thought she would be interested in his culinary skills.

'Oh, well that's good then.'

Cliff looked up at her tone. 'Eh? Are you being sarcastic?'

'Of course I am! I want to know what Robin Morton needed to see you about. You know, your date with him at The Ship Inn last night?'

He laughed. 'I'm only teasing you. I wondered how long you could last before giving in and asking me. In fact, I thought you might have already been on the phone to Sarah Handley to find out what she knew.'

'I did think about it.'

'Not that she would have been able to tell you anything. Veronica Bank was in there, creating a fuss over nothing as usual. Something about the chips tasting too much like potatoes.'

Nicola groaned. 'There had better be more to your meeting with Robin than cooking your tuna steak and preparing your pomegranate salad and what Veronica Bank had to complain about this time.'

'Does there?'

'Oh come on, there must be more to it. Spill the beans!'

'You should have rung me and asked if you were that desperate to know! Or better yet, come and joined us.'

'Oh I couldn't do that. I didn't want to appear too nosey, and anyway he was very specific about asking *you* out for a drink. Are you sure he didn't want to talk to you about anything in particular? What did you discuss? What was he asking you?'

'Not half as many questions as you are. Did it occur to you that maybe he really did just want to spend some

116

time in my company? People do, you know.' He winked at her.

'Cliff ...' Nicola said, in a warning tone.

'Alright, alright,' he said as he settled down in his chair behind the counter. 'Go and make us a coffee, and I will tell you all about my evening.'

Much to Nicola's frustration, the antiques centre was suddenly busy with an influx of customers for the next forty minutes, most of whom had heard about Veronica Bank's latest episode and were eager to voice their opinions. Everyone felt that Sarah had handled Mrs Bank's behaviour competently, and there were plenty of comments about how well Sarah was coping since the death of her husband. There was also a lot of discussion about where Veronica Bank would try to eat out in Woodford in the future. She had already been barred from the next pub down the road, The Royal Oak, and everyone knew the landlord of The Boot - technically in the village of Brackendon, but the locals considered it to be a Woodford pub - wasn't likely to put up with her nonsense.

By the time everyone had left, and the place was quiet, the coffees had gone cold, and Cliff insisted she make them some fresh ones before he would tell her about his evening.

Infuriatingly, Cliff waited until he had made a big deal about sniffing the aroma, and then tasting the coffee as though he was sampling from a newly opened bottle of wine.

'CLIFF!'

Chuckling he gave in. 'OK, here goes. In a nutshell, Robin Morton is desperately in love with Lisa Bartlett, and wants me to pave the way for him to get back into her good books.'

Nicola folded her arms. 'Well I don't think that is a good idea, do you? For one thing, you are not in the school playground. For another, other people's relationships are none of your business, particularly given your poor track record in that department. And for a third, he is so dishonest he must have the word DECEITFUL written through him like a stick of rock!'

'You are not keen on the idea then?'

'No!'

'I thought you wouldn't be, which was why I didn't want to discuss it with you. You are giving away some subtle signs there, Nicola! Don't worry, I agree with you, and I told Robin I couldn't get involved between him and Lisa. For one thing I wouldn't feel comfortable interfering in Lisa's love life; especially after the mess I made of things yesterday with her.'

'Good. The sooner that man leaves Woodford, the better.'

'Ah, I said I couldn't be involved between him and Lisa, but I didn't say I wouldn't spend time with him. I actually quite like the chap; and not just because he liked my tuna and pomegranate salad.'

'You're not telling me you invited him back here for supper are you? Are you mad?'

'Not at all. When you think about it, he has never done us or our businesses any harm. He really has been looking out for us. Yes, he has lied about his purpose for being here, and his real name, which isn't Robin Morton by the way. But he had to, didn't he? He could hardly have done his job as an undercover policeman if he told everybody what he was doing.'

'Are you being serious? You are really going to take his side in all of this?'

'I don't think it is about taking sides, is it? He had a job to do, which he seemed to do very well. Yes, it was unfortunate …'

'Unfortunate!'

'Well, alright, cruel, that Lisa Bartlett got caught up in it all. But he is genuinely in love with her. You should have seen him last night, Nicola. He is desperate to make it up to her.'

'I don't see how he can? How can Lisa, or any woman for that matter, ever trust someone again who deceives them in the way he did? She could take him to court, you know for what he did to her. There are plenty of cases now where women have successfully prosecuted policemen for tricking them into romantic relationships.'

'But that's the point, Nicola. He didn't do that to Lisa, did he? He didn't use her in his investigations, or need any information from her. He genuinely liked her. He freely admits that in the beginning he was just looking for a casual relationship while he was based here in Woodford, and you can't blame a guy for that, can you? It isn't as though he promised her ever-lasting love, or anything. But once things got serious between them, he was stuck. He didn't want to break it off, because he wanted to be with her. When it was all over, he did go and explain everything to her.'

'So what has changed?'

'He says that meeting Lisa changed everything for him. Up until then, he was committed to his job. He believed he was not cut out for any long term relationships. He was married in his twenties when he was a bobby on the beat, but one month later his wife was killed in a car accident with a drugged up driver. Robin was devastated, and decided he would never let himself be open to the pain of that time again. The thought of being in a relationship with someone else was incomprehensible to him, and so he didn't try. After a short period of mourning, he headed over to join the undercover police, and specialised in the antiques trade. His parents were antiques dealers, well, they still are apparently although I don't think I have come across them before, and he felt comfortable in that environment. He enjoyed his work, and put all his energies into creating and immersing himself into the characters necessary to do the job. Some of them would only last a week, others he lived as that person for anything up to five years. It suited both his profession and his emotional state not to try to replace his wife with anyone new, and he was happy to have a handful of relationships with women who were not the marrying kind.'

Nicola sniffed. 'I thought that was all men.'

'Now, now, don't be like that. Anyway, he said that when he met Lisa, he thought she was another one of them; someone who didn't want a life partner, but just someone to fool around with and push away the loneliness. But he told me that after a short time he realised he wanted more than a few nights here and there with her. I won't go into all the details; suffice to say we were both blubbing like babies while he was talking. I don't know how therapists can keep it together when someone starts pouring their heart out to them.'

'You really believe him, Cliff? He is an expert at manipulating people to believe in the persona he exhibits, you know.'

Cliff sighed. 'I knew you were going to say something like that. Look Nicola, I honestly think he is telling the truth. If you could have seen him you would too. Anyway, Lisa seemed to feel the same way about him,

120

so he said that he tried to combine his career with a fulfilling, loving relationship with Lisa.'

'Humph, when you say he *tried* there seems to have been one thing he didn't put any effort into. A truly healthy relationship has honesty at the heart of it, as you well know.'

Cliff looked a little bit annoyed at Nicola's reference to the affair he had enjoyed during his marriage to Rebecca. He and Rebecca had moved on with their own lives, and he wished that people like Nicola would do the same. He knew how badly he behaved, and every minute of every day he was paying for it by being separated from his family, no longer able to live with them in the family home. He also realised how lucky he was that neither Rebecca nor his children held his past behaviour against him, and that his relationship with his children had surprisingly grown stronger since he and Rebecca had parted.

'From Robin's point of view he thought he was making the best decision by keeping the true details of his work from Lisa, partly because his employers dictated that he did not reveal anything to anybody outside of the chain of command. He now realises that combining a career as an undercover officer and having a loving relationship with Lisa Bartlett is not possible, so he has made the decision to leave the police force.'

Nicola looked sceptical. 'Are you serious? You fell for that story? You really believe he gave up an extremely well-paid job, doing something from the sound of it he was very good at, for a woman who won't even give him the time of day? Come off it Cliff, you are not so naïve, and neither am I.'

Cliff ran his hand through his hair. Eventually he said 'I really did believe him. And I still do. That is why we came back here for something to eat. The pub wasn't the right place to have a heart-to-heart, and so we continued our conversation up in my flat, and he spent the entire evening talking about Lisa Bartlett. The man is besotted! I mean, she is nice enough, and easy on the eye, which reminds me of another piece of gossip I must share with you, but John is absolutely head-over-heels in love with her.'

'What did you call him?'

Cliff looked shifty. 'Ah. That's another thing. His real name. It is John Thomas.'

Nicola looked at him for a few moments, and didn't know whether to laugh or cry. 'Idiot,' she muttered, as she gathered up their coffee mugs, and began to walk up the stairs towards the kitchen.

'No, wait, Nicola, it really is! He showed me his passport, and driver's licence.'

Nicola ignored him, and carried on climbing.

'Nicola!' Cliff called after her. 'It's true! Oh, and the other thing I meant to tell you: Lisa Bartlett has had all of her blonde curls chopped off, and is now a short-haired red-head!'

Nicola kicked the door shut with her foot.

Chapter 17

Wednesday 3rd August 2016, 12 noon.

Lisa was thoroughly fed up with all the comments about her hair. 'Why do people feel the need to make a judgement?' she grumbled to her daughter, Caroline.

'Because they are all in shock, mum, as am I. I can't believe you have done it.'

'Yes, alright, you have made your point. Several times. But it is done now, and I'll just have to wait for it to grow out.'

'You won't keep it like that? It really suits you, you know. I think it looks much better than before. When it was long it dragged your features down; now it shows off your cheekbones. And the colour accentuates your blue eyes. If you want my opinion, which I know you don't, I think you should enjoy it. At least now people will be able to tell you and Aunty Gem apart.'

'Well, there is that I suppose. Although I quite liked the fact we used to look so similar.' She peered in the mirror which was fixed to the back of the large walk-in larder door. 'Do you really think it suits my eyes?'

Caroline rolled hers, and left the kitchen to take an order of crab, fennel and watercress salad to a lunchtime customer. The cowbell on the front door rang to alert her to someone new coming in.

'Hi Nicola,' she greeted the newcomer, before gathering up the empty bowls and plates from a table where a family of three were studying the list of desserts. 'Do you think you have room for a pudding after all that cheese toastie?' she asked a young boy, guessing he was about six years old.

He grinned and pointed at the strawberry ice cream. Caroline checked with his parents, who agreed with their son's choice and also ordered one each for themselves, and she returned to the kitchen balancing the dirty dishes and with the order for three ice creams in her head.

'I'll be with you in a minute, Nicola. Are you looking for something to take out?'

Nicola was leaning on the wide shelf which formed the window which separated the kitchen from the customers. 'Yes please, Caroline. But there is no hurry; I haven't chosen yet. What are you doing here? I thought you didn't work here anymore now you have your own tea wagon.'

Caroline groaned. 'Oh, believe me, I would rather be over there than here, but Aunty Gem isn't feeling very well so I have popped over to help Mum out for an hour or two.'

'And she is grabbing the opportunity to use our oven to make some more of her delicious ginger cake!' Lisa appeared behind her daughter and gave her a bear hug. 'The smell is driving me mad. You will let me be the taste tester for you, won't you darling?'

'I am always willing to help either of you in that department' offered Nicola. 'Oh Lisa, I love your new hair!'

'Thank you Nicola,' she beamed, and then faltered. 'Although, I guess Cliff warned you before you came in so you were prepared?'

'Oh Mother! You are so exasperating. Why can't you just take the compliment?' Caroline put an extra scoop of ice cream into the glass bowls, to make up for briefly losing her temper.

'Yes he did tell me he saw you in the High Street on Monday, but it doesn't change what I said. Both the colour and the style really suit you.' Nicola was pleased Cliff had warned her, because the change was so dramatic that she suspected she would have been lost for words. At least this way she was prepared, and could genuinely express her approval.

'Well, thank you Nicola. I will try to do as my daughter tells me to, and accept your compliment as it is meant. I am still not sure if I like this new look, though.'

'Oh, I expect it will take you a while to get used to it. When I change mine from afro to relaxed, or vice-versa, it takes me a few days to be comfortable with it. Catching glimpses of myself in the mirror can be a shock!'

Lisa laughed 'Yes! I know what you mean. And when I went to wash it in the shower this morning there was nothing there; all I had to do was run my fingers through it with a minimal amount of shampoo and conditioner, and it was clean. It was so much quicker than having to deal with long hair, and all the washing, rinsing, conditioning, waiting, rinsing, combing, arghh!'

'Yes, I noticed how quick you were,' chipped in Caroline, as she returned from delivering the ice creams to the family with the little boy. 'Usually you are in that shower for fifteen minutes or more while I am waiting outside after my run!'

Lisa laughed again, pleased that her daughter's earlier outburst was behind them. 'Well, darling daughter, it is *my* ensuite shower. I think I should be allowed to take as long as I want.'

'Yes, but your shower is so much nicer than the one in the family bathroom,' grinned Caroline, aware that now her brother had moved out of the house she couldn't use the excuse that he was hogging the bathroom as a reason to use her mother's any more. 'I wonder if that colour would suit me?'

'I am sure it would,' Lisa studied her daughter's dark brown straight bob. 'You have the same skin tone and eye colour as I do. But your hair is such a lovely deep and rich colour, I think it would be a shame to disguise it.'

Nicola nodded 'I agree with your mum. Save the hair colouring for when you start to go grey. With the amount of exercise you do, every time you have it re-dyed you will be forever having to deal with colour running down your face and neck when you get hot and sweaty!'

'No chance of that happening to me' smiled Lisa. 'The closest I get to exercise is walking thousands of steps while I serve customers in here. And no, before you start Nicola, I am not joining you and Sarah Handley for any of your various exercise classes!'

'Ah, you'll change your mind. Eventually.'

Lisa ignored her. 'Another reason why I like this style is that it was dry in minutes. Before, if I didn't use a hair dryer it used to take hours for my hair to dry. Oooh the freedom! I will be able to go to bed with damp hair, it will only take me a minute or so in the morning to repair the damage. When it was long I had to brush it all out and then plait it or something, to hide how horrendous it looked. Anyway, enough about my appearance; what can I get for you?'

When Nicola left a few minutes later, with a brown paper bag full of brie and grape sandwiches and a couple of slices of apricot flapjack, she passed Robin Morton as he was entering the tearooms. She was tempted to stay to see what happened, but knew she would be no better than a voyeur, and so continued on her way back to work next door.

'Oh God, more drama,' Caroline breathed when she saw him. 'Mum, don't look now, but your ex has just walked in again. Would you like me to serve him? I said don't look!'

'Ah, Robin. Don't be silly, of course I am going to look if you tell me not to! No, don't worry, love, I'll do it. I might as well get all of the reactions to my new hairstyle over with as quickly as possible.'

Taking a deep breath, Lisa pulled her shoulders back and walked out of the kitchen with her head held high. She saw that he had sat at his favourite table, over in the corner of the room.

'Hello, Robin' she greeted him with a fixed smile, determined to see this meeting as an opportunity to demonstrate her professional attitude. Robin had been an infrequent customer to The Woodford Tearooms since their break-up the previous year, after a short but intense romance lasting a matter of weeks, but just recently he had been turning up every day. Usually either her sister or daughter served him, and Lisa only occasionally had to deal with him when she was running the tearooms on her own. 'Would you like a few minutes to choose, or do you know what you would like to order?'

His face was a picture. Lisa could not prevent a broad grin stretching her mouth from one side of her face to the other, as she watched him do a triple take before his mouth dropped open. 'Lisa? Wow. You look fantastic! Cliff said you were trying something different with your hair. What a difference. I love it.'

Lisa's grin swiftly turned into a blush. 'Oh, oh thank you Robin. You are very kind to say so.'

'No, no I mean it. That colour really suits you. I loved your hair the way it was, but this is even better. You can see your whole face now that it isn't hidden behind masses of hair.'

Thoroughly embarrassed by his attention, and feeling disturbed by how much his approval meant to her, Lisa pointed to the menu on the table in front of him. 'So, what would you like to eat?'

'Oh, um, a cheese salad and a glass of ginger beer, please. Thank you, Lisa.' A few seconds went by while they did nothing but stare at each other with big smiles on their faces, until Lisa forced her feet to move, and she hurried back to the relative safety of the kitchen.

She was greeted by her daughter, who was standing in the middle of the room with her arms folded across her chest, and a stern stare on her face.

'What was that?' she hissed. 'And don't pretend you don't know what I am referring to.'

Lisa could feel the blush on her cheeks turn into burning heat under Caroline's disapproval. 'I don't know what you mean. Robin was simply complimenting me on my hair, and then placing his lunchtime order.' She broke her gaze away from Caroline's steely blue eyes, and moved to one of the work surfaces to prepare his food, aware that Caroline was still watching her. 'Anyway, I don't know why you are having a go at me. You are always going on about what a nice man he is, and how I should make an effort to be friendlier with him.'

'Not like that! You two were practically having sex out there in the café!'

'No we weren't! Don't be so silly. That's enough. I don't want to hear any more about it. That man is part of my past; not my future. You are just being difficult. All I was doing was accepting a compliment from a customer, and taking his order. Now drop it. I don't want to discuss this subject any more.' She turned to the spring onion she had been slicing, and finished the task before starting on a red pepper.

Thinking silent thoughts about people who protest more than the accusation warrants, Caroline left her mother in peace for a few minutes, and switched the dishwasher on. A movement in the yard outside caught her eye, but by the time she had raised her head and looked properly, whoever had been there was gone.

Chapter 18

Thursday 4th August 2016, 8.00am

Natasha Holmes sat down at her wide mahogany partners desk, with her hands splayed on its red leather top, the whirlwind of energy she had brought with her temporarily lulled while she prepared herself for the day ahead.

Natasha wondered if she had been too hasty in accepting the latest suitor's invitation. Dafydd Jenkins was a successful silver dealer, whom Natasha had known to speak to for a number of years. The previous Friday, the accountants for Kemp and Holmes had invited all of their clients to a black tie evening (obviously the clients had to pay for the privilege): a champagne-fuelled opening night for a blockbuster film, at the cinema in Swanwick. Bertram tried to avoid social occasions like this one, but Natasha always went to such networking events to represent their business, and because she could write them off as expenses; she was happy to go on her own, or in company, and that evening she went by herself, confident in the knowledge she would know many of the people attending.

Dafydd Jenkins homed in on her as soon as she arrived, ensuring she had a glass in her hand at all times, and remaining by her side for the entire evening.

She allowed him to drive her back to her apartment at the end of the night, and invited him inside for a nightcap, which they both knew was a euphemism for sex. It had been almost three months since her last sexual encounter, and Natasha was more than ready. Dafydd proved to be an eager lover, and she thoroughly enjoyed herself, but when she made it clear he was not expected to stay the night he began to sulk, which swiftly cancelled out any appeal she had found in him. He had not made contact since he left her apartment in the early hours of Saturday morning, but five minutes ago Dafydd had phoned to ask her out to dinner. Natasha realised she was pleased to receive the invite, and accepted immediately. They agreed that he would collect her from her flat at half past seven that evening.

But now as she sat at her desk Natasha was wondering what had prompted him to break the ice. She felt a little uneasy about the situation. Her thoughts were interrupted by a knock on the door.

'Come!' she called, sharply.

The blond tousled head of Crispin Keogh appeared around the door. 'Hi Natasha, I hope we are not interrupting anything important?'

'No, no, come on in. What can I do for you, Crispin?'

The rest of his body appeared, his clothes looking just as crumpled as his hair, and he was closely followed by the more smartly turned out Jason Chapillon.

'Thanks Natasha. I'd like your advice on one of these silver items we have been processing, and thought I'd also bring the new boy, Jason Chapillon, to meet you again. I know you haven't seen him since his interview.' Crispin ushered Jason in front of him, towards the desk.

131

'Hello Jason, welcome to Kemp and Holmes. You boys are in early this morning.' Natasha stood up and leaned over the desk to shake his hand. Jason wished he had wiped his hands dry on his trousers before entering her office, but it was too late now. He was so nervous all he could do was smile, showing more teeth than he intended, but his facial muscles were not working as he wanted them too.

Natasha surreptitiously smoothed her hand down the side of her black skirt, giving Jason even more reason to lose focus as his eyes followed the feminine outline of her hip. Natasha was firmly against any workplace romances, but she allowed herself a secret smile at the knowledge she could still be sexually attractive to a young man in his early twenties. Maybe her instincts about Dafydd - who must be at least fifty years old - were right after all. She had always preferred much older men, but as her years on the planet were clocking up she wondered if it was time to drop her age limit on a prospective life partner.

Crispin's voice interrupted her thoughts, and brought her abruptly back to the present. 'We have spent the last three days checking and cataloguing the silver which came in from those two house calls last week, and putting everything we were concerned about to one side, as you asked us to. We didn't find anything suspicious in that collection, but here is one which was brought in on Monday. We thought we had better bring it in here for your expert opinion, and check we are on the right track.'

'Thank you. What is the problem with it?' Natasha picked up the silver bowl and began to inspect it.

'We're not happy with the hallmark.' Natasha noted that Crispin was including Jason in his assessment, even though the young man had shown no knowledge

132

of the pitfalls which could arise when appraising silver for its authenticity during his interview. She liked that about Crispin, and hoped that some of his professionalism would rub off on Jason. 'See? The whole thing has been stamped vertically, and yet it appears in a horizontal line along the side of the bowl.'

Natasha nodded. 'Yes, this does look suspicious. Put it with the other items you are concerned about, and I'll come and have a look later to see if I can verify whether it is genuine.' She looked at her watch. 'Keep putting everything you have already listed on one side in your workroom, together with a print out of the catalogue so far before you leave, and I'll check it all before I go home tonight as usual. Anything else you are concerned about put on the other side of the room with a note outlining what it is that bothers you; there was a candelabra yesterday which took me a while to work out why you had set it aside. I guess it was because one of the sconces was a bit bashed about, so you were worried about its condition rather than any concerns you had about its authenticity?'

Crispin nodded 'That's right, sorry I should have said. Yes, we didn't think the quality was good enough for the silver sale, but that it would be fine for one of the general sales.'

Natasha smiled to show they were not in any trouble. 'You made a good call. I put it with the items for the next sale, but was going to check you hadn't spotted anything I didn't. Thanks for bringing this bowl to me. I had planned to come down and check everything before we go to print anyway, just in case, but please do bring anything like this to my attention if you spot it.'

'I guessed you would want to double-check our work at the very end. Thanks Natasha. Come on Jason.'

Crispin beckoned to his colleague, who seemed to be stuck in a trance.

'Oh, oh yes, right, thank you, bye Miss Holmes.' As soon as they were out of her office, Jason whispered 'God, she is gorgeous! Pure sex on legs. She can search my workspace any time she wants.'

Crispin groaned. 'For goodness' sake don't let her hear you! She can't bear innuendo.'

Jason had been horrified when Crispin told him that Natasha regularly patrolled the workrooms, both during and after office hours. 'But that stinks of Big Brother! Does she not trust us? We are adults, after all.'

'Well, I am, I don't know about you' Crispin had laughed. 'Look,' he explained 'don't take it personally; it is just the way she works. She saw how much stock went into Slippery's private collection while she worked for him at Swanwick Auctions. She is determined that Kemp and Holmes will never treat their customers with the same dishonesty. Natasha takes great pride in this company's reputation, and will sack anyone who has sticky fingers. If you don't like it, you will have to find somewhere else to work, and quickly. Natasha has a habit of appearing just when you don't want her to, and she will know if you are not being honest. But so long as you are straight with her, and work hard, then she is brilliant to work for.'

Crispin's words were making Jason think he would like to see as much of Natasha as possible.

'She is single, right?' he checked.

Crispin laughed 'You have no chance, mate. Give up now. Natasha Holmes is so far out of your league. She'd eat you for breakfast.'

Jason reflected that he quite liked the sound of that.

Chapter 19

Thursday 4th August 2016, 10.00am

Bertram Kemp was not an early riser, and liked to be able to arrive at his office long after all of his employees had begun the business of the day. He also liked to leave early, usually by three o'clock in the afternoon. He projected a relaxed approach, which belied an efficient and productive system. He employed good workers, treated them well, and enjoyed reaping the rewards.

But every now and then something would occur which meant he had to step out of his comfortable routine. The antiques trade relies on honesty and trust, but also runs smoothly on gossip and scandal. The recent mysterious death of one of their own, Hugh Jones, a well-liked and respected silversmith, had sent choppy waves through the industry, and the rumours were out of control.

Normally Bertram stayed one step removed from the scandals which frequented the business. He could spot a warning sign and take a large step away from any trouble which was brewing. Someone would suddenly start paying their suppliers with cheques, which then bounced, instead of the usual cash or card; a marriage breakup could take years due to a prolonged and expensive divorce settlement, resulting in a successful business disappearing from the landscape and taking a number of other businesses down with it; a dealer would finally succumb to a life of heavy drinking and smoking, and die, leaving a string of unpaid bills and missing stock. All of these events occurred if not weekly, then monthly, and each one would leave a huge hole. Sometimes those holes swallowed up other businesses which could never recover; others barely caused a ripple, and would be forgotten by the few who were even aware of their demise. Bertram's ear to the ground was acute, and he was canny in his way of preventing the downfalls of other people from dragging him with them.

But he had been taken by surprise by recent events, and he had a feeling that the truth about the death of Hugh Jones was still a long way from being revealed. Bertram had only ever had legitimate dealings with Hugh, and never had an inkling that Hugh was anything other than an honest member of the antiques trade.

Grand Tour bronze figures in the form of Roman ones are very collectible, and are legitimate. Modern reproduction furniture also has a legitimate place in the market, although many antiques dealers would like to heat their houses with it. The crime takes place when the maker tries to conceal the provenance of the item, or the seller describes the nineteenth century vase as made in the sixteen hundreds.

The two issues which concerned Bertram were: he had liked and more importantly trusted Hugh Jones as a genuine member of the antiques trade, and he was not ready to believe he had been deceived; the fake silver pieces which were turning up were very good, and the quality of the craftsmanship was indicative of Hugh Jones' work. After forty years in the business, Bertram was disturbed to think he may have been so thoroughly hoodwinked by the silversmith. He was also perturbed that no rumours of Hugh's dodgy dealing had reached his ears until Hugh's untimely death. He wondered if the luxury of managing his own business in the relatively hands-off way he had chosen for the past few years was preventing him from having his ear to the ground after all.

Bertram had been at his desk for over three hours by the time the clock in Swanwick's town square chimed to mark ten o'clock in the morning. In the beginning Bertram had not been a fan of the way the antiques trade had moved so easily onto selling via the internet, and he had taken a very long time to accept that it was a major part of the way auction houses interacted with their customers. Natasha had gently but persistently ensured that Kemp and Holmes had a good online presence for their auctions, and now Bertram was grateful for her foresight. He had been checking the sales catalogues for other auction houses, and had made a list of seventeen silver items which raised his suspicions. Without seeing the bowls, candlesticks, and trays in real life so he could get a feel for them, he could not be sure that they had been faked in some way, but he thought he could detect a pattern emerging, and he did not like its implications.

Armed with his notebook, tucked into the inside breast pocket of his suit jacket, which he wore despite the heat of the day, Bertram began to stroll along the corridors in the direction of Crispin and Jason's workroom.

He paused outside for a few moments, and observed the two men working; one blond head, one brown, bent over their desks. Bertram had not been keen on Jason's appointment to their payroll, but Natasha had persuaded him that her decision had nothing to do with any desire on her part to upset Slippery Stan, and everything to do with the need for their auction house to expand their staffing numbers. Bertram was aware of Natasha's motives in trying to do as much damage to Slippery Stan's auction business as she could, but he also trusted that she would pull out all the stops to ensure her actions benefited their joint enterprise in the long term. He just wished Natasha could find peace, and no longer feel the need to control and dominate people she felt had wronged her in the past. Admittedly Slippery had been a complete nightmare for her to work for, with his fondness for groping certain female staff, and Natasha had suffered at his hands, literally, until she managed to leave Swanwick Auctioneers.

He frowned as he thought about another of her recent appointments: Lydia Black, who was due to start with the company on the following Monday. Her father's reputation had reached Bertram's ears, but until Natasha's insistence on appointing the school leaver over four more qualified and experienced candidates, Bertram had not heard of any recent relationship between Natasha and Paul Black. He wondered what the story was there; he knew there had to be one.

He knocked on the glass door as a courtesy, and pushed it open without waiting for a response.

'Good morning chaps. Hello Jason, how are you settling in?'

Jason hurriedly stood up to shake hands with his new boss. 'Good morning sir. I am very well, thank you.'

Bertram smiled 'Bertram is fine; no need to call me sir.'

'Thank you,' Jason sat back down at his desk.

'Ah, I see you are processing the silver items for our sale in October. Have you encountered any problems?'

Crispin spoke up. 'We have had a few queries, like this bowl where the hallmark has been stamped horizontally with marks which are vertical.'

He walked over to the table and cupboard where they were storing the items once they had catalogued them, and picked up a small silver bowl with ornate handles to either side.

Handing it to Bertram, he said 'Natasha is keeping an eye on everything, and anything we are concerned about we have been putting on this shelf here so she knows we have spotted something. We took it over to her this morning, so she is aware of it already.'

Bertram could see immediately the issue Crispin had raised. The hallmark looked as though someone has melted a spoon into the side of the bowl, hallmarked side outwards. He nodded, and gave the bowl back to Crispin.

'Good. Well spotted. We can't afford for our auction house to gain a reputation as somewhere which passes faked items as genuine.' Bertram picked up a set of six teaspoons and inspected them closely, frowning as he did so. 'Do you know who brought these in?'

Crispin checked his list. 'Ah, yes, they came in as part of that whole canteen of cutlery,' he indicated the large box next to where Bertram was standing. 'A lady called Mrs Edwards brought it in. Her husband died recently, and she is moving into one of those warden-controlled apartments, and there won't be room for wedding presents like that. Poor old lady, she was so upset to be parting with them all. She and her husband had been married for over fifty years, and every year they took out all the silver from where they stored it in a big old sideboard in their dining room and hosted an anniversary meal for their best man and bridesmaids from their wedding day. She was very sad, because none of them were still alive; she is the only one left. You were in the process of checking them weren't you Jason?'

'Oh yes, I checked all of them. They looked fine to me.'

Bertram opened up the box. 'You checked every single piece in here did you?'

'Yes, I did.'

'So why did you leave these teaspoons out?'

Jason shrugged his shoulders. 'Sorry, they were the last things I checked, and I must have forgotten to put them back in.'

'That is not the way we do things at Kemp and Holmes. Here we respect other people's property, and until this entire canteen of cutlery is sold every single item belongs to that lady. The situation only changes once the auction has taken place, and a buyer has paid for the items, at which point they change ownership. These are not ours to misplace, lose, or separate from their companions.'

'Unlike my last place,' muttered Jason.

'Quite,' said Bertram sternly. He fixed Jason with a surprisingly hard stare. 'We have high standards here, and have earned a solid reputation in a relatively short space of time, but as we all know a reputation can be ruined in a day. If you are going to remain as an employee of Kemp and Holmes Antiques Auctioneers and Valuers, then you need to make sure that you immediately discard any illegal or even vaguely dodgy practices you picked up whilst working elsewhere.'

Jason shifted uncomfortably, suddenly feeling as though he was on trial. Nobody had warned him that Bertram Kemp could be so fierce; he had always believed he was a teddy bear, who was being led by the balls by Natasha Holmes. Realisation that he had underestimated both partners in this business washed over Jason like a cold sweat.

Bertram paused, allowing Jason to speak. 'Of course, you are quite right. I am so sorry. I have allowed myself to get into sloppy habits. I assure you I meant no harm, but thank you for reminding me that these are not just items to go into an auction, they are someone's belongings. I am keen to improve my attitude towards our customers. I am afraid I have become conditioned to treating our customers, and therefore the antiques they bring to us, as commodities. I have only been here for three days, but already the professional approach of Kemp and Holmes is rubbing off on me. I promise I won't be so lax with my duties again. I love it here, and want to stay.'

Jason's words had the positive effect he was aiming for, and Bertram's normal calm demeanour reappeared, much to both Jason and Crispin's relief. He beamed at Jason. 'Good, that is good to hear. I am pleased to see you are settling in to working here at Kemp and Holmes, and I do hope you will be here for many years to come.'

After he left, Jason suddenly shivered. 'Ugh, that was unpleasant. I had no idea Mr Kemp could be so hard!'

Crispin had worked for Bertram and Natasha ever since the auction house opened six years earlier, and it took him a moment or two to reply.

'Nor me, Jason. Nor me,' he said, quietly.

The two colleagues returned to their work with renewed concentration; both trying to leave the unsettling experience behind them. But a chill remained in the room for several minutes afterwards, despite the heat of the day.

Chapter 20

Thursday 4th August 2016, 1.00pm

Paul Black frowned as he peered through his loop and studied the hallmark on the silver tankard, and then compared it to the one on the silver serving spoon on his desk. Running his hand through his longish brown hair he wondered if he had time to pop down to the men's Barber Shop on the High Street, before a knock on the door interrupted him.

'Come in' he called out. His frown turned to a smile and he stood up, his bad mood evaporating as he walked around his desk to give his visitor a hug and a kiss, which turned into a smooch.

'Mmmmh, maybe we should change our lunchtime plans?' suggested Jennifer Isaac, in between kisses.

Briefly Paul contemplated whisking her off for the short walk around to his cottage, before remembering that he had two appointments with clients that afternoon, the first of whom would arrive in less than an hour. Reluctantly he pulled away, and checked his trouser pockets for his wallet and keys.

'Sorry darling, as tempting as you are the only quickie I can offer you at my desk today is half a sandwich from The Woodford Tearooms.'

Jennifer sighed with mock despair 'Oh, alright then. Comes to something when my dad is having more sex than I am! The walls in Gemma's cottage are paper thin.'

'What do you mean? Last night we were both tired and had an early start this morning.'

'Alright, don't stress, I am only teasing you.'

'Anyway, now that you don't sleep there anymore, their love life shouldn't be a problem for you.'

'I am not talking about good old regular night time sex in their bedroom, Paul. Only two weeks ago I walked in on them in a compromising position in the kitchen. Eugh! That is an image no daughter should ever see. Anyway, I'll raise your half a sandwich with a whole fruit and nut flapjack, also from The Woodford Tearooms.' She waved a paperback in front of him, before sitting down on the other side of his desk. 'To be honest I haven't got time for more than this either; my next appointment is over in Stormy Vale. A horse with intermittent lameness, and the owner is going out of her mind with worry.'

Paul wasn't listening. 'On the kitchen table, eh?'

'Stop! I want to erase that image from my mind. Let's talk about something else.'

'Well, let's go and have our picnic on The Green, rather than sitting in here. It is such a beautiful day, come on.'

They left his office together, giggling, and Paul turned back to lock the door, causing Rebecca to raise her eyebrows. She had been working for Paul at Black's Auction House for almost a year, and she could only think of one other occasion when he had locked that door: and the event which followed ended in violence.

Paul saw her expression and shrugged his shoulders, the frown returning as he said 'Just something not right with those hallmarks, Rebecca. They all look suspiciously as though they have been made from the same silicon mould. I think in the present climate it is better to be safe than sorry.'

'What do you mean?'

'Well, each part of the hallmark should be stamped individually. Hang on a minute, I'll show you.' Jennifer sighed as he beckoned to Rebecca to follow him, as he unlocked the door to his office.

Handing Rebecca the loop, he said 'First, look at the hallmark on this silver specimen vase. Now look at the hallmarks on this tankard, and then the ones on the serving spoon.'

Rebecca had never used a small magnifying eye-glass, known in the antiques trade as a loop, so Paul had to show her the best technique of putting the loop to her eye, and then moving the object until the hallmarks were brought into focus. She carefully studied each one as Paul watched.

After a while she looked up. 'Sorry Paul, I don't think I know what I am looking for.'

'OK, let me show you. On the vase, look at the Birmingham mark, see? The anchor. Now look at the same mark on the tankard, and on the spoon.'

'Let me see?' Paul passed the loop over to Jennifer, who copied Rebecca's technique, and studied each piece in turn.

'I agree with Rebecca, I am not sure what it is I am meant to be seeing. Do you want to look again Rebecca?'

'Yes please,' Rebecca took the loop, picked up the spoon, and concentrated again. 'Why on earth does Birmingham have an anchor as its symbol? Surely it is located about as far away from the sea as you can get!'

'Ah, legend has it that when the authorities decided that each city should have its own identifying mark, the officials from Birmingham and Sheffield met in a public house to discuss it. The pub was called the Crown and Anchor, so Sheffield's mark is a crown and Birmingham's is an anchor.'

'Mmmh, I believe you, thousands wouldn't,' she muttered.

'Right, look at the mark on the spoon. Do you see that miniscule aberration to the top right of the impressed mark?'

Rebecca squinted, moved the spoon backwards and forwards a bit, before finally exclaiming 'Yes!'

'Good. Now look at the mark on the vase.'

'Nope, sorry Paul, I can't see it on here.'

'That's OK. Now look on the tankard.'

'Ah, yes, I can see it on this one.'

She went to pick up the vase again, but Paul stopped her. 'That's it. You have seen what I wanted you to see. The same flaw is on the Birmingham hallmark for both the spoon and the tankard. Cliff spotted the same thing on a pair of candlesticks one of his stallholders was selling in the antiques centre, although on those it looked as though somebody had tried to rub out the flaw, but all they did was emphasise the error.'

'So what does that mean?' Jennifer asked. 'That the stamp used to make these marks two hundred years ago has a flaw in it?'

'No, not exactly.' He handed the loop and the spoon back to Jennifer. 'If you now study the lion passant mark, and the date letter on each of those three items, you will see that they are all positioned in exactly the same way on the tankard and the spoon, but on the vase there is a slight variation between the date letter and the lion passant. Now, these are only four examples, if we include Cliff's two candlesticks, but for all four of these items to turn up here in Woodford at around the same time, with the same flaws in the same places, is beyond coincidence in my view.'

'So what happens now?' asked Rebecca.

'I have to contact the vendor and tell them I cannot accept these two items in my auction. The vendor should then send them up to the assay office for verification, but if they do that and the tankard and the spoon turn out to have been faked, then the vendor will probably not get a penny back in recompense and the items will be melted down by the assay office.'

'That doesn't sound very fair!' Jennifer looked upset at the thought of the two inanimate objects being destroyed.

Paul shrugged. 'That's the way it is love. Come on, we have wasted enough time on all of this. Let's go and eat our lunch on The Green.'

Chapter 21

Thursday 4th August 2016, 1.15pm

After the happy couple had left the coolness of the building to walk in the bright summer sunshine over to The Green, Rebecca turned her attention back to proofreading the catalogue for Black's next auction. It wasn't long before she was interrupted by the telephone on her desk. Her heart sank when she recognised the whining tones of one of Black's regular customers, Mrs Wheeler.

'Oh Rebecca, I am so glad I caught you. I thought you would be having your lunch.'

'Hello Mrs Wheeler.'

'Oh, I was expecting to leave a message on the answerphone. I know how you young people insist on taking breaks every few minutes throughout the day.'

'No, no, I am here, hard at work. How can I help you?'

I have missed my calling; I should have taken up a career as an actress, what I really want to do is slam the phone back down, Rebecca thought to herself.

'Well it isn't you I want to speak to. I want to speak to Mr Black.' Rebecca could hear the indignation building strength in the lady's voice.

'I am sorry but he is out of the office at the moment, and won't be able to return your call until much later this afternoon because he has a number of appointments in the diary. Is it something I can help you with Mrs Wheeler?'

'Well, you will have to do, I suppose. I want to talk to Mr Black about that Vienna bronze of a dog which I bought in your sale on Friday. I took it all of the way up to Swanwick Auctioneers for their free valuation day this morning, and Mr Simmons informs me it is made from brass. Needless to say I am very upset to discover that I have been deceived in this way and I expect Mr Black to recompense me immediately!'

Rebecca pulled a face, and then realised she was being watched through the glass front door of the office. Feeling the colour burn its way onto her cheeks she turned away slightly so the voyeur could only see the back of her head, and attempted to soothe Mrs Wheeler's ruffled feathers.

'Can you give me the item number please?' Rebecca called Mrs Wheeler's account up on the computer, and could see the item the angry lady was referring to. 'Ah, yes, I see Mrs Wheeler. It is listed in our catalogue as a painted figure of a dog. I cannot see any mention of the style it was manufactured in, or the material it was made from.'

'Oh don't you try and wriggle out of it like that!' Rebecca could almost feel the angry vibrations coming out of the handset she was holding. 'Everybody in the room believed it to be a Vienna bronze, and well you know it. I would never have paid such a high price for a simple brass ornament! I was so humiliated when Mr Simmons dismissed it in front of everyone, *everyone*, as a brass trinket.'

Rebecca rolled her eyes. So that was what the telephone call was all about. Mrs Wheeler had got carried away by the excitement of the auction room, and bid high above the true value of the figure. Now she had egg on her face and was desperately trying to pass the blame for her own lack of self-control onto somebody else. Rebecca guessed that the lady, believing she had won a bargain, had hotfooted it up to Swanwick with her prize. Knowing Mrs Wheeler, she would have made sure everyone was watching when she produced the item for Slippery to value, intending to feign surprise when he revealed it had an even higher value than the one she paid. Her embarrassment when she was bluntly forced, because Slippery was blunt when he was faced with low priced items, to face the reality that she had paid far too much money for it must have been acute.

Rebecca knew that there was no way that Black's Auction House was liable for Mrs Wheeler's error, but she was also kind enough to allow the lady to save a bit of face by suggesting she bring it in, and put it into the next general sale if she no longer wanted to own it. Mrs Wheeler tried to bluster her way into receiving lower commission charges, but Rebecca held firm. There was no reason to reduce the auction house's earnings; the mistake was not theirs, they had listed the item accurately. In addition, Mrs Wheeler was not such a good customer that they needed to keep her sweet to retain her business.

Finally, Mrs Wheeler agreed to Rebecca's suggestions and she hung up, still grumbling, but Rebecca knew the lady understood the status quo. Leaning back in her chair and stretching her arms up over her head, Rebecca revelled in the cracking noises, stretching first her left side and then her right. Slowly lowering her arms back down, the noise of the front door opening made her start, and she suddenly remembered the man who had been watching her. Relief flooded her face as she saw who was walking in.

'Hello Cliff! I am very glad to see you.'

Rebecca's ex-husband looked surprised at her welcome. Rebecca was rarely effusive in her greeting.

'Really? Is everything alright?' he asked, gesturing towards the telephone.

'Oh yes,' she flapped her hand at it. 'That was just somebody who had made a mistake and wasn't ready to admit it. No, I am relieved it was you lurking outside, and not someone else. I keep seeing Simon Maxwell-Lewis around the place. Or at least I think it is him. I have yet to actually see the person properly.'

Cliff jumped to defend himself 'What do you mean lurking? I have only just arrived!'

'You mean you weren't watching me while I was on the telephone?'

Cliff looked worried. 'No, I promise you Rebecca, I have just walked up the path and come straight in through the door. But now you mention it, I keep catching someone out of the corner of my eye too. I hadn't given it much thought until now. Surely Simon wouldn't bother stalking us?'

Rebecca shrugged. 'Why not? He resented you enough to try to ruin your business, and break up our marriage. What makes you think all of that would be forgotten once he was sent to prison for his actions? I would have thought a prison term would have made everything ten times worse. Anyway, if you don't think it is Simon, who do you think it is?'

'Well, as I said until now I haven't given it much thought. But as you have brought up the subject, I suppose there isn't really anyone else it is likely to be is there? Maybe we should let the local police know? I'll send Ian McClure a text now.'

'Is it worth it? What would you write? "Sorry to bother you PC McClure, but I keep seeing someone who isn't there"? I don't think Ian would appreciate a request for help couched in those terms.'

Cliff laughed 'Well, when you put it like that, it does sound a bit flimsy. I'll cobble something together; I still think it is worth doing.'

'But what can Ian do? We don't even know that it is Simon. Or anybody for that matter. We both might be imagining it.'

'True. Unlikely, but possible. At least if Ian is aware of our concerns he can put the wind up Simon, and warn him to keep away from us.'

'I have a better idea; why don't you just mention it to your new best friend,' Rebecca said, slyly.

For a few seconds Cliff looked confused, before understanding relaxed his face and made him laugh. 'Oh, the Woodford grapevine is impressive! My evening out has reached you already has it? I suppose you are talking about Robin Morton? Or John Thomas, as he assures me he was named by his parents.'

Rebecca fell about laughing. 'You are not serious? John Thomas! Surely no mother and father would look down at their new-born and hate him so much they would make him carry that name around for the rest of his life. No wonder the poor man chose undercover police work as a career. It gave him the opportunity to live with a different name.'

Cliff shrugged 'That is what he told me on Tuesday night.'

Rebecca looked sceptical. 'And you believe him? Come off it, Cliff.'

Cliff spread his arms out 'Why would he lie? No, I mean' as Rebecca roared with laughter 'he is practised enough at lying, so why would he make up such an unlikely name? Oh, stop laughing.'

He looked so grumpy that Rebecca tried to do as he asked.

'OK, OK, just suppose he is telling you the truth, then why now? I mean, why would he tell you his real name?'

'Ah, well, that is where it gets interesting.' Cliff walked over to the kitchenette, and sat down on one of the chairs. 'This is why I have come to see you. To ask for your advice on the matter. Robin, or John …'

Rebecca shook her head 'call him Robin. I am not convinced about this John Thomas business.'

Cliff nodded in agreement. 'I can understand that. But anyway, Robin says that he has resigned from the police force, and is trying to return to civilian life. He says that he knows that while he was working as an undercover policeman there was no way he could have a deep and loving relationship with another person, and for a long time he was happy with that. But since he met Lisa Bartlett everything has changed for him, and he now realises what he has been missing. He wants me to help to smooth the way forward with Lisa. What do you think I should do? I don't want to get in the middle of anything, and I certainly don't want to assist him if all he is going to do is break Lisa's heart all over again. But, Rebecca, if you had seen him on Tuesday night like I did, you would have believed him too. What shall I do?'

Rebecca looked disbelieving. 'Are you seriously telling me that whatever-his-name, and let's face it, we still don't know for sure what is on his birth certificate whatever you believe, wants to give up the lifestyle he has been immersed in for goodness knows how long, so he can skip off into the sunset with a good woman? I thought he was hanging around so much because of the murder, or suicide or whatever, of Hugh Jones. If you want my opinion, I think you should grow up, and stop believing in fairy tales.'

Chapter 22

Thursday 4th August 2016, 5.30pm

'Oh hello, this is Paul Black from Black's Auction House calling. Just to say that I am very sorry, but we won't be able to enter the tankard you brought in into our next sale. I have some concerns about it, and will be happy to discuss them with you when you come to collect your goods. Thank you.'

Paul ticked the phone call off his To-Do list, relieved that he had got through to the answerphone and not a 'real' person. It was never pleasant to make calls like that one, and he hoped the failed vendor, an elderly lady who occasionally put items into Black's to sell, would not be too disappointed.

Paul shut down the computer, closed the blinds at his office window, and locked the office door behind him. Rebecca had already left, so the reception area was deserted and quiet. As always she had tidied up before she went home, so there were no stray coffee cups, teaspoons or food wrappers lying around, and all Paul needed to do was set the security alarms.

He strolled through to the section which formed the auction house's warehouse and sales room, and checked there were no lingering members of staff or customers. He loved being the only one in this space. He sat down on a chair, part of an Edwardian dining set of eight which were consigned in the next furniture sale, and listened to the silence. The sounds of several different working timepieces filled the air, and he followed the dust motes as they darted and fell in the rays of the late afternoon sunshine which streamed high up through the stained glass window of the former chapel.

Paul allowed his thoughts to drift over all of the ups and downs of the week so far: the thrill of early morning sex with Jennifer on Monday; the fury at discovering his daughter's betrayal a few hours afterwards; the peace brought about by Sarah's sensible advice in the pub; feeling pumped up and excited at achieving his running target first thing on Tuesday morning; the joy at being able to take time out and share a cheeky lunch with Jennifer later that day; the huge volume of work he had achieved both yesterday and today. Tomorrow was going to be another busy day at the auction house, and Paul was looking forward to it. And then it would be the weekend.

For as long as Paul could remember he had chosen work over leisure. By choosing to make a living in the antiques trade he could easily work for seven days a week, and certainly while he was married, and he and Christine were growing their family, he had chosen to spend more time at work than was strictly required. When he was bored of work he would 'entertain' himself by playing around in relationships with other people, rather than concentrate on his own family life. Once the marriage broke down Paul jumped into and out of another marriage, and throughout it all he pursued, and caught, a large number of women. The amount of affairs he had was greatly exaggerated, mainly by Paul himself, but they were still too many to be healthy. Paul never took holidays, and besides running and weight lifting, he didn't have any other hobbies. What free time he did have was spent in the pub.

His liaison with Natasha Holmes had been one of many which followed the pattern of: catch the eye of pretty girl; pursue her for a few days, if she gave in easily run away immediately after sex, if she played hard-to-get hang onto her for a few weeks; either way move on to the next one. But Natasha had not played by the rules. She had been a curious mix of easy to catch but hard to complete the game with. When he did finally persuade her to let him into her bed, he followed his normal pattern of failing to return her phone calls. Usually after a few days, the woman would get the message and leave him alone, deciding that he was not worth her attention, but Natasha was different. She came from a large family who were spread over most of the south-west, and had relatives in the midlands, the south-east, as well as a large number in London and surrounding areas. Once Natasha realised she had been played, it only took a couple of telephone calls before the wrath of the family came down on Paul, and his father's business.

For months he would discover that his car tyres were slashed, the liveried Black's Auction House's van would have its paintwork scratched and windows smashed, when he or his staff turned up for appointments someone else would have been there two hours earlier and bought all of the good stuff. The auctions themselves were constantly disrupted by noisy conversations drowning out the legitimate vocals from the rostrum or the buyers in the room. Items would be sold for vastly inflated sums of money, but then the buyer would fail to pay, and the ornament or painting would have to be re-entered into another sale weeks or even moths later, where it would fetch much less than originally expected because it was no longer termed fresh-to-the-market. Both vendors and buyers would have to run a gauntlet of intimidation on their way into and out of the building.

Eventually it came to light that one of Natasha's relatives was an employee of Black's, which was how the people behind the disruption seemed to always be one step ahead of the auction staff. Paul's father made the decision to pay a large sum of money as settlement, both for the former employee and to Natasha as compensation for her broken heart. Paul was given a stern telling-off about his treatment of women, in particular his wife, and a final warning.

Being threatened with the sack by his own father was probably the biggest shock of Paul's life. He could not believe that his dad would turn against him in that way. For a few days he sulked, and looked for other auction houses to move to in an effort to teach his dad a lesson. It wasn't long before he realised that with his track record and the trouble which seemed to follow him around, no one of any standing would take him on. He also worked out that if he stayed with the family firm, he would inevitably end up taking over from his father, and be running and owning the place, something which was almost impossible to do without family money and influence.

From that time on, Paul began to take his role at Black's Auction House more seriously than he had before. His passion was for the auctioneering business, and he had a vague interest in antiques, but until he was faced with the prospect of it all being snatched away from him, he had never really appreciated how important the antiques trade was in his life. He stopped taking his position there for granted, and began to try to be an integral part of the team with his father and colleagues, to build on the hard work which had gone before him. Once he changed his attitude he found that chasing women was less important, and concentrating on developing the business into the successful company it was today was far more fulfilling.

Unfortunately although he spent less time messing around with other people's lives, his attitude towards women did not undergo such a positive transformation. He continued to treat them as pieces in an exciting game, like the way a cat teases its prey until it has had enough and either bites the head off or discards it for other predators to devour. All that had changed was the numbers were lower.

Now he reflected on how life had changed for him in the past year. The day Jennifer Isaac walked into his life, or rather straight past him in The Ship Inn, 'Paul Black, Ladies' Man' was finished. He tried all his usual techniques on her, but she wasn't interested, and let him know she thought he was creepy. Normally Paul would count this as the unlucky woman's loss, but something about Jennifer bothered him, and he couldn't leave her alone. He tried to take his mind off her by playing around elsewhere, but was frustrated to discover that he didn't have the desire. Eventually Jennifer saw in him something worth engaging with, when he wasn't even trying to draw her in. Paul was left defenceless in a vicious attack by someone he had counted on as a friend, and as he lay in the hospital bed he abandoned all attempts at seduction and instead allowed himself to accept natural friendship from a highly desirable woman. Over the next few months he and Jennifer navigated the troughs and peaks of a relationship between two people who had very different outlooks on love, but as he sat alone, in the peace of his auction house, he was content that the future could only be smooth sailing for the pair of them.

Paul sighed. He felt happy, and fulfilled. Jennifer had agreed to wear his engagement ring, although she was not ready for marriage. Yet. And he was happy to go along with her wishes. He reflected that once upon a time he would have seen her reticence as another level in the game, and taken up the challenge of convincing her to change her mind. Now he was comfortable with living with her choice, and when the time was right for both of them, they would make their vows and keep them, for the rest of their lives.

Paul felt an overwhelming sense of well-being and peace.

But then he could feel the tension in his jaw as he thought about his daughter's decision to leave school, and go to take up an apprenticeship with somebody she knew he despised. Why could life never be simple?

Chapter 23

Thursday 4th August 2016, 8.30pm

One hour into the date, and Natasha was seriously regretting her decision to go against her instincts and see Dafydd again. Whereas he had seemed sweet and charming the week before, tonight he was pompous and boring. He was clearly determined to show her what she would be missing out on if she chose to reject him again, but all he was doing was convincing Natasha that she would never put herself through another evening like this one. She could feel her whole body tense with embarrassment at his behaviour.

Dafydd had booked a table for them at a fabulous fish restaurant which was one of Natasha's favourite haunts, half an hour from Swanwick. She regularly ate there on her own, and the staff knew her well. Dafydd did not have a clue that Natasha was familiar with the restaurant, and Natasha thought it interesting that he assumed the place was out of her league. He made a big show of keeping their destination a secret, until with a flourish he parked in the market square outside the building. She would have found this behaviour sweet, if he hadn't been behaving in such an imperious manner.

He flamboyantly opened the door to the restaurant, and ushered her inside before him, something she would have hated if this was her first visit there. Natasha could never understand why sending the woman into a strange pub or restaurant first was considered to be a gentlemanly thing to do. All that happened was the woman came to an awkward halt while she tried to get her bearings, and work out where to head for, all the time trying not to draw attention to herself from the people who were already safely ensconced inside. She supposed that was the point: to put the woman out of her depth so she could be rescued by the man. Fortunately on this occasion Natasha knew exactly where to go, and she was greeted by the maître d' like the old friend she had become. All of this passed by Dafydd, who was busy making a fuss about ensuring they had the exact table he had requested when he telephoned earlier that day.

When they had been shown to their table, Dafydd pushed the maître d' out of the way, pulled Natasha's chair out for her himself, and then pushed it in under her. This was another convention Natasha hated, because unless the man took out the woman's legs when he pushed it back in, there was no way the chair would be in the optimal position for comfortable eating and drinking. Once she had hoiked it to her own satisfaction, she buried her attention in the large menu. It slowly dawned on her that Dafydd was planning to choose and then order for both of them. He had already sent the waiter to fetch them both a cocktail, which Natasha was not very happy about because she only wanted to drink wine that evening. When she attempted to demur, Dafydd talked over her, but the waiter picked up on her discomfort, and when the drinks arrived he quietly let her know that hers was non-alcoholic.

Natasha was in a quandary. Should she continue with the evening, or call a halt to it now? It felt a bit like that sinking moment when she had once gone to view a flat with the expectation of buying it, but knew before the owner opened the front door that it didn't matter how well presented the interior would be, she could not stand to live in an apartment which was located opposite the lifts. It was rare that Natasha found herself in a situation where she was not in control, and usually she was perfectly capable of taking care of herself. On that occasion she had politely explained her feelings, and apologised. The owner accepted her apologies, and in less than thirty seconds the awkwardness had been replaced by a request from the owner to come in and view the flat, and provide feedback on any other details the estate agents should have included in the sales blurb. This situation was very different. Natasha was aware she had hurt Dafydd's feelings on their first date, and was prepared to put a lot of effort in to make amends.

But then he ordered oysters for them both.

Natasha loved oysters, and the ones served by the restaurant were always superb. But Dafydd ordered them with a startling degree of sexual innuendo, making sure that everybody on the surrounding tables knew what his plans for Natasha's body were once they had returned to her flat.

With her cheeks burning in a red which was a close match to her Christian Louboutin lipstick, Natasha excused herself and walked briskly to the Ladies, where she gave herself a few minutes to make a decision and formulate a plan about what to do next.

Once her pulse rate had returned as close to normal as she thought it could go, she headed back out and found the maître d'. Briefly explaining that she was on a date which was not working, she gave him enough money to cover the cost of the food and drink they had so far ordered and consumed, plus a substantial tip, and asked him to book a taxi for her. Fortunately there were a few idling outside in the market square, and so with her escape plan locked into place, Natasha made her way back to the table to her unsuspecting date.

'Dafydd?'

He looked up with a smug look on his face. While she was away he had been busy posting on his Facebook profile about their date, and had been receiving suitably encouraging replies from his male friends.

'Dafydd, I am terribly sorry, but this evening is not working for me.'

His face was a picture of shock, and for a brief moment Natasha could feel her resolve wavering. But then he spoke.

'What?' He stood up so fast he knocked his chair over. Jabbing his finger at her he began to rant. 'What do you mean "this evening is not working for you"? I collected you from your door, and chauffeured you all of the way out here for an expensive meal, with all of the alcohol you could want, and you say "this is not working for you"! Is this place too upmarket for you or something? Would you rather I had taken you to Burger King or Kentucky Fried Chicken? For God's sake Natasha, grow up and at least try to appreciate it when a cultured man shows you a good time. Now be a good girl and sit back down, and eat those oysters I paid for.'

Natasha had stayed silent throughout his diatribe, and waited until she was sure he had finished. Quietly, she said 'I think you have perfectly demonstrated why I do not wish to spend another minute in your company.

Goodbye Dafydd. Oh, and by the way, I have paid for those oysters. Good night.'

Leaving him standing open mouthed, Natasha walked out of the building and into her waiting taxi. Dafydd's display had been so loud that everyone in the restaurant was watching him, and so he had a large audience when he went to sit down on his fallen chair, only to land in a heap on the floor on top of it.

Chapter 24

Friday 5th August 2016, 8.30am

Lisa Bartlett looked up as the cow bell tinkled to signify someone was entering through the front door of the tearooms. Her spirits plummeted as she saw who it was. Taking a moment to compose herself, she checked the rashers of bacon under the grill were going to need another couple of minutes, before taking a deep breath, forcing the corners of her mouth to lift, and walked out of the kitchen.

'Robin. Again. I think we are going to need to get you a loyalty card if you don't complete your police investigation very soon. You never did say what you were working on?'

Robin Morton had been standing looking around the room for somewhere to sit, but as far as he could tell all of the tables were occupied, although many with only one person. He was taken aback by Lisa's tone, which was uncharacteristically sharp, and floundered as he realised he had lost the use of his voice. He wanted to explain that his reasons for coming into the tearooms on a daily basis had nothing to do with his former career. He would have liked to have told Lisa that he was no longer a serving police officer, and that he loved her, and wanted to spend the rest of his life with her.

'No? You are not going to explain? All Top Secret is it? Well here is a question I am sure you can answer. What would you like to order to eat?'

Robin stared at her, willing his mouth to work but he was incapable of simply asking for a cup of tea.

Lisa was livid. She had been stewing over Gemma's words to her at the beginning of the week, and had come to the conclusion that her sister was accusing her of being a 'victim' rather than having any say in her own destiny. She decided it was because of people like Robin who preyed on her vulnerability that made Lisa so miserable, and she was not going to allow anybody to treat her like that again. This man had been using the tearooms, *her* tearooms, for some underhand purpose, and she was not happy about it. Lisa wished he would have the decency and respect for her feelings to stay away, but as he clearly did not it was time for her to stand up for herself. Unlike Samson, Lisa felt as though having her long hair cut short had given her strength, and she was embracing the powerful feeling.

By contrast Robin was feeling overwhelmed, and briefly considered slinking back through the door and away up the High Street. He was sure that during their encounter two days earlier there had been a spark of their former attraction, but today Lisa seemed to be furious with him again. Gratefully he noticed somebody he recognised, and asked her if he could join her.

Madeleine Powell's father had been a colleague of Robin's, and in recent months Robin had been part of an investigation into his murder. In the course of the investigation Madeleine discovered that she had relatives in Woodford, and as Robin sat down at the table opposite her he was struck by the familial similarities she shared with her new-found half-sister,

Rebecca Martin. Today Madeleine had her long black curly hair tamed in a plait which hung down her back. It was stylish while at the same time practical for her job as the manager of the Woodford Riding Club.

Lisa was impatiently tapping her foot, and standing over him with her pen and order pad at the ready.

'Hang on a minute, please Lisa. I'll just check the menu.'

'Will you? I'd have thought you knew it off by heart by now.' She turned on her heel and marched back to the kitchen.

Robin, wishing the ground would swallow him up, hurriedly reached across the table for the menu, but managed to knock over the small posy vase containing a single yellow rose bud and an awful lot of water. Madeleine was eating a cooked breakfast, her first food of the day since starting work at five o'clock that morning so she could exercise three horses before the summer heat made it unpleasant for both horse and human. She had her hands full with a knife and fork, and so both of them watched in horror as the glass smashed to the floor, followed by the water which poured off the edge of the table and formed a small pool. Frozen, with the menu in one hand and the other, for some reason he could not explain, clutching the edge of his chair, Robin stared helplessly at the mess.

'OH MARVELLOUS' shouted Lisa from the kitchen, where she was in the process of plating up three full English breakfasts but could see where the sound was coming from.

'So sorry, I am so sorry!' Robin was jolted out of his static state by the rare sound of Lisa shouting, and he came running into the kitchen. 'Just tell me where the mop and bucket is, and a dustpan and brush, and I'll clear it up. I am really sorry.'

'Yes, so you have already said,' snapped Lisa. 'Everything you need is in there.' She pointed to a cupboard behind the door, and marched out with the laden breakfast plates.

A couple of other customers left their tables to help Madeleine and Robin clear away the mess, and in less than five minutes all traces of the smashed glass, petals, and water had vanished. As had Robin. His purpose in regularly coming into the tearooms had been to ask Lisa out on a date, or at the very least engage her in conversation, but his nerve kept failing him. Today she was clearly not in a good mood, so he cut his losses.

The rest of the morning continued in a more orderly way, and at half-past eleven Gemma came in to work the lunchtime shift with Lisa. Lisa's mood was not improved by her sister's half-hearted attempts to work, and she was getting annoyed that every time she turned around Gemma was standing on the steps outside the back door, gazing at the happy holidaymakers on The Green. While she stomped around the kitchen, huffing and muttering under her breath, Lisa began to consider for the first time if running the tearooms with her sister was how she wanted to spend the next few years. Taking over The Woodford Tearooms had been Lisa's idea, but she knew she wouldn't be able to do it on her own. She had persuaded Gemma to become her business partner, mainly because Gemma was the one with catering experience. In fact, Lisa had agreed to give up her job when she married her husband, because he wanted her to stay at home. Once their first child was born, Lisa was relieved not to have to juggle work, home, and a baby, and until she made the difficult decision to leave her domineering husband she had never felt the need to go against his wishes. The discovery that he had been growing a second family a few miles away was the catalyst she needed to cut him out of her life.

Lisa and Gemma quickly formed a successful working partnership, and Lisa had been happy working alongside her sister for the past five years. She had never been in any doubt that this was what she wanted to do, until now. Gemma's words to her at the beginning of the week had a profound effect, and as the days went past Lisa became more resentful about their meaning. As she ran around doing the lion's share of the work, Lisa began to wonder if the time had come for her to follow in her daughter's footsteps and set up her own business, away from her sister's influence. In between serving customers and clearing tables, Lisa started to think about what she could do if she decided to ask Gemma to buy her share of the business.

By two o'clock the tearooms contained only two customers, so Lisa decided she would take the rest of the afternoon off, and let her sister take the strain instead. She felt bad that she was being so unsympathetic to Gemma, who was clearly not feeling one hundred percent after her recent bug, but overwork and a sensitive ego prevented her from gaining any perspective on the situation. Still in a foul mood she drove home, and was only slightly mollified by the sight of a bunch of flowers on her doorstep. Assuming they were from Robin, she snatched them up, and ignoring the attached card she stomped through into the utility room and debated whether to throw them straight into the bin. Undecided, both about what to do with the flowers and whether to rock the boat and break up the partnership with her sister, Lisa left the flowers in the sink, while she went upstairs to shower and change.

Chapter 25

Friday 5th August 2016, 2.45pm

'Sorry! Sorry I'm late!' Jennifer apologised to Madeleine Powell, as she drove through the gates of the Woodford Riding Club.

'Don't worry about it; you have given me a chance to give Baby a proper brush, including her mane and tail. There she is, all ready for you.' Madeleine pressed the button to close the electric gates behind Jennifer's car, and then walked over to join her as Jennifer retrieved a bag from the foot well of the passenger side.

Jennifer glanced across to the gleaming bay mare standing quietly at the wooden rails next to a grey Welsh cob, both of them dozing in the shade of the stables and gently swishing their tails in half-hearted attempts to keep the relentless flies away.

'Thank you Madeleine, she looks great. My first client of the day couldn't catch his horse, so instead of just popping in, spending a few minutes discussing the pros and cons of 'flu vaccinations and general health of his horse, followed by a quick injection, I spent twenty minutes watching him chasing the naughty thing around the field, and another twenty joining in.'

'Forty minutes? That seems like a long time. Couldn't you leave, and come back later?'

'Well, I did think about it, but my visits this morning were arranged in a sort of semi-circular route, so I wouldn't have been going back past his yard. The horse's vaccination was due today, so if we had left it until tomorrow he would have had to start the whole programme from the beginning. I thought it was better for both the horse's well-being and the owner's wallet that we persisted until he was properly vaccinated today.'

Madeleine followed Jennifer as she walked over to the wooden shed which served as the yard's administration, refreshment, and place in which to shelter from the bad weather base. Also, for busy people like Jennifer, it could be used as a changing room. Jennifer walked inside with her bag, and as Madeleine went to close the door for her, Jennifer said 'Oh don't bother with that, I'm only changing into my jods. Come on in, I want to hear all about this TREC competition you are holding next month. Hearing about people who are actively doing something with their horses will take my mind off the owner this morning, who seems to think that treating his horse like a human is the right thing to do. If I had known then what I know now I would have just driven off after the first few minutes, but as they say, General Hindsight never lost a battle!'

'Oooh I like that. Go on then; tell me what happened?'

'Well, I was a bit annoyed when I pulled up and saw the horse was still out in the field. The owner knew I was coming at half past eight, and because I got caught behind a herd of sheep the Higstons were moving from one field to another along the Farnham Road going out of Brackendon, I was a few minutes late, so it wasn't as though I caught him unawares. He is one of those

171

people who think they have a special bond with their horse, when really the horse runs rings around him.'

Madeleine rolled her eyes. 'Yep, I know the sort. He is so desperate not to upset the horse he doesn't ask anything of him, and because the only thing he ever does is feed him, the horse always comes running when he turns up?'

Jennifer nodded 'You have got it in one. His farrier was working at the yard where I travelled to for my next appointment, and he laughed when I explained why I was late. He is thinking about dropping the owner as a client, because he won't take any advice, or allow the farrier to handle the horse as he would like to. He finds the horse heavy and unresponsive, but the owner is insistent that all he should do is click his fingers and the horse will hold his own leg up. Of course, the horse doesn't, and I doubt very much he could, do this for the length of time the farrier needs to take the shoes off and apply new ones, and so every time he and the owner have to have this discussion, with the owner implying the farrier is a lesser horseman than he is.'

'Is this horse ever asked to do any form of work?'

'Nope. The owner loves him very much, and takes great care in making sure he is rugged, groomed, petted, he is fed this latest commercial horse feed which is all Natural, whatever that means, his stable is immaculate and the field is poo-picked and properly maintained. But from what I can gather the horse never does anything more than move around at liberty from the yard, through the gate to the field, and back again. The farrier was also saying that he doesn't understand why the owner wants the horse to be shod, because he never leaves the yard or field.'

Madeleine shook her head. 'Mind you, from what you are saying the horse would probably be in a lot of pain from his feet if he didn't have shoes on. You know the mantra "A healthy foot needs a good diet and plenty of exercise".'

Jennifer nodded. 'True. I hadn't thought of it like that. This barefoot stuff is making me look at everything in a different way. Of course none of this is the horse's fault, it never is, which makes it harder to walk away. Anyway, when I arrived the owner was mucking out the horse's stable. He saw me, picked up a head collar and lead rope, and went out to the field. The horse promptly turned and walked away. For the next twenty minutes the horse stayed about six inches out of reach, varying his speed depending on how fast the owner was moving. It would have been funny to watch if I wasn't on a time limit.'

Madeleine laughed 'I can just imagine! What a very clever pony. So he wasn't worried about being caught then?'

'Not in my opinion, but the owner claimed the horse was scared of vets, and that was why he couldn't catch him.'

'What a load of nonsense.'

'Mmmh, that's what I think. Far more likely he was behaving like that because he had been cooped up in a stable all night, and was turned out onto a lovely field of grass one hour earlier!'

Madeleine nodded. 'I think you are probably right there. But also, why didn't the owner have the horse ready and waiting for you on the yard if he expected there would be a problem?'

'Exactly.'

'So how did you catch him in the end?'

'I went and got a bucket and put some of the fashionable horse food in it. He soon got over his fear of vets then!'

'I bet he did.' Madeleine chuckled. 'What did the owner say?'

Jennifer sighed 'Oh, I got an earful about how he and his horse have a connection which doesn't require bribery. And then the horse was a complete nightmare to inject. He wouldn't stand still, for a start. It must have taken us about another fifteen minutes to complete giving him the vaccination. I honestly think the horse would have been happier if the owner hadn't been there; the man was making such a fuss and kept going on about how sorry he was that the horse was having to go through such a traumatic ordeal. It is fair to say that is one owner who will not be sending me a Christmas card this year.'

'It is amazing how intuitive horses are to our attitudes and emotions. It would be interesting to remove that particular owner from the vicinity and see if the horse still posed such a big challenge.'

'I think the horse would have been absolutely fine if he was managed differently. Fortunately the rest of my clients were a lot more clued up about horse behaviour than that one; even the lady with the horse who had been sent to a so-called trainer to be "broken", and the trainer had done exactly that.'

'I do hate that word. And that approach to starting a young horse. I once worked for a woman who started all of the youngsters in her yard unshod, so that, and I quote "they will be so busy thinking about how much their feet hurt on the road, they won't have time to mess around". She had no understanding of how to produce barefoot performance horses, and didn't want to know. She deliberately worked them with sore feet,

174

and of course all that happened was she produced a string of three- and four-year olds who learned to brace against the rider when ridden, and who associated work with pain. After a few weeks they would be shod as a rite of passage, and then the horses' behavioural problems transferred from pain-related issues to ones based in mistrust because those early chances to build positive communication between horse and rider had been abused.'

'I bet none of those poor horses lasted beyond the age of about seven years old before they broke down with tendon and ligament injuries. My old practice up in Shropshire made a lot of money out of the owners of horses who were started in that way. But enough about all that; come on, I want to hear all about this competition you are holding here next month. Tell me what TREC is?'

'Let's talk as we ride.' Madeleine picked up a blue marker pen. 'Where shall we go? The Trailway? It should be fairly quiet at this time of day. Most of the tourists will either be enjoying themselves down at the beach, or will have already walked or cycled this section by now. There should only be locals using it, and most of them will sensibly be staying indoors, or even still be at work.'

'Good idea, let's go along there. It will be a lot cooler on the sections which are lined with trees.'

Madeleine wrote their proposed route and rough timings up on the whiteboard, along with their mobile phone numbers, as a safety measure so that any staff members or livery owners would have an idea of where they were if something should go wrong while they were out on their ride.

The two women left the comparative cool shade of the shed, and walked out into the bright sunshine, which was compounded by the dusty dry whiteness of the concrete yard and hardcore tracks. Silently they greeted and then tacked up their respective horses, before each mounted from the large wooden purpose-built block. Madeleine was up in the saddle first, and she and her horse, Sonny, stood patiently waiting as Jennifer and Baby finished getting ready.

Together they rode out of the yard, and walked the short distance to one of the many access points which ran the length of the Trailway.

'And breathe.' Jennifer could feel her shoulders dropping several millimetres further away from her ears as she consciously scanned for tension in her body, and allowed herself to relax into the rhythm of the horse's movement. 'Isn't this bliss? We are so lucky to be able to ride out at this time of day, when everywhere is so quiet.'

Madeleine laughed. 'Well, if you don't count the sound of the cockerel over there, or the lawn mower in that garden, or the motorbike which I can hear but not see.'

'Ha ha yes, if you don't count all of them.'

'So, you want to know about TREC?'

'Yes please, what does it stand for?'

'Oh, I am not sure. The sport originated in France, so it is called *Le Trec* over there, and the three sections all have French initials too, but that isn't important. Basically you have three tests: Orienteering, which ranges from about twelve kilometres to over forty kilometres depending which Level you are in; a phase where you are tested on how slowly you can canter your horse along a marked section, and then walk back as quickly as possible, without breaking gait or deviating from the route; and sixteen obstacles which you have to negotiate in various ways, such as reversing between two poles, or jumping a log, or

176

standing still without holding the reins for ten seconds. The local group have booked our yard for a full competition on the second weekend in September.'

'Are you doing it?'

'Oh yes! This is too good an opportunity to miss! I used to compete in the arena TREC events where you do everything but the orienteering when I lived in Hampshire, but I never had the opportunity to try a full competition like this one because I was always working when they were on. Why, do you fancy having a go?'

'I do now, I haven't ever heard of it before. That motorbike is getting closer isn't he?' Jennifer turned around and looked behind them. 'Oh, it's OK, he has stopped. He is on his mobile phone.'

Madeleine suggested 'We can enter as a Pair if you like? That way we do the orienteering section together, and our individual scores for the control of paces and the obstacles course are combined. I am sure Baby's owners would let you borrow her for the weekend.'

Jennifer laughed 'OK, let's do it. But, on the subject of Baby, I have decided that I am ready to have my own horse again.'

'Aha! I thought so. I suspected you were thinking along those lines for a while, and I have been keeping an eye out for a suitable horse for you, just in case.'

'Really, Madeleine? That is kind of you. My sister Alison and I always had ponies when we were children, because Mum ran a riding school and Dad was a vet, so they had easy access to the little devils nobody else wanted. That was how my sister and I learned to ride. We never had good, well-mannered ponies, and were forever being bitten, kicked, and dumped on the ground. It taught us both to have respect for the animals, and made us learn how to gain their trust so they would let us do everything we wanted to. I do not want to go back to those lessons again; I am too old and want a nice, easy horse now! In fact, this time around I want a unicorn.'

'Don't we all!' laughed Madeleine. 'Sonny here was my unicorn. How long is it since you had a pony of your own?'

'Oh, it must be over twelve years I think? Whereas Alison loved competing in the Pony Club games, and moved up to horses and eventing competitions when we were teenagers, and is still going out most weekends during the season, I was always more interested in studying to be a veterinary surgeon. I don't know when, exactly, but at some point I just stopped riding. It has only been in the last few months since you have been working here, that I have rediscovered my love for horses.'

'I think that is a useful attribute for an equine vet,' Madeleine dryly observed.

'It is quite shocking how many of my mentors and the professionals I have looked up to over the years don't like horses any more. I am sure nobody chooses this profession, and spends all those years training for their qualifications, if they don't like horses in the beginning. But somewhere along the line many of them develop a dislike for them.'

'I know. I have met a few. That is why I was so pleased to discover how perfect both you and your father are for this job. So, tell me more about your plans for horse ownership.'

'After all this time observing and handling other people's horses, I can see what type of horse I want. I don't suppose Baby's owners would ever sell her to me, would they?'

'I am sorry, but they would never let her go. Although you could maybe talk to them about having her permanently on loan? Bloody hell!'

Both horses took off as the motorbike, which had been following them for the last few minutes at a distance, suddenly roared up behind them. Jennifer was caught by surprise and shot sideways out of the saddle, hitting the ground hard. Luckily Madeleine stayed on her horse, although they travelled several metres before she was able bring him back to a walk. She managed to turn him around, and looked back to see what had happened to Jennifer. Horrified, Madeleine could see that the motorcyclist was off his bike, and appeared to be molesting her. Sonny was still trembling with fear, and his entire body felt braced and ready to flee at any moment, but Madeleine asked him to walk forwards towards the scene of the accident. She was trying to keep her nerves under control so she could help Sonny to calm down, but at the sight of the motorcyclist assaulting Jennifer she knew she had to do something. She shouted 'LEAVE HER ALONE!' and immediately lowered her voice and stroked Sonny's neck 'It's OK, we're OK.'

The motorbike engine was still running, and the rider looked over his shoulder at the sound of Madeleine's voice, to see Madeleine and Sonny approaching, so he finished whatever he was doing to Jennifer, jumped back on the bike, and roared away in the other direction. With the motorbike disappearing into the distance, Sonny was able to gain enough confidence to trot along the last section of the track towards Jennifer, who was still lying, immobile, on the ground.

Madeleine jumped off her horse, and called to Jennifer as she looked around for somewhere to securely tie Sonny. Hearing the sound of hooves on the hardcore, she saw that Baby had come back to join them. As there wasn't anywhere sensible to use as a tying up post, she first secured Sonny's reins to his saddle and then carefully approached Baby, who was shaking from the top of her ears all of the way down the length of her body to her tail. Talking in a calm voice, Madeleine was still trying to coax a response out of Jennifer, while attempting to rescue Baby's reins which were dangling dangerously in front of her trembling front legs. Fishing in her pocket, Madeleine found an open packet of Polos, and cautiously held one out in the palm of her hand. Baby was far too scared to lower her head and investigate the treat, but didn't appear to be ready to turn and run again either, so Madeleine left her where she was and went back to Jennifer, who was beginning to stir. The last thing she wanted was for either horse to panic and run over the top of Jennifer as she lay injured.

'Jennifer? Jennifer? No, don't move. Stay still for a second or two.' Madeleine pulled her phone out of the holder attached to her belt, and began to press the numbers 999. 'Hello, we need an ambulance and the police here immediately. We are on the Trailway near the Brackendon Road entrance, and we have just been attacked by a man on a motorbike. My friend fell from her horse and is unconscious.'

The next few minutes were taken up with trying to establish how badly injured Jennifer was, and helping the emergency services to find their exact location. Fortunately another couple of horse riders and three dog walkers appeared, so the two horses were safely removed from the scene and led back to the yard, and Madeleine gave the dog walkers her hi-viz tabard to use to signal access from the road to their location for the emergency services to see. In what seemed like half an hour, but in real time was only four minutes, the sound of the air ambulance could be heard, and shortly afterwards the sirens of the police cars. The helicopter was able to land in one of the fields which ran alongside the Trailway, and it was only a short clamber up the bank from there to the track where Madeleine and Jennifer were waiting.

By this time Jennifer was trying to sit up, clearly dazed and sore, but otherwise wanting to convince herself and anybody who would listen that she was unhurt. Madeleine moved back to allow the paramedics, doctor, and police to ascertain Jennifer's condition, and was comforted by the dog walkers and one of the PCSOs. She was unable to tell them anything about the motorbike or its rider, other than it was black and noisy, and the rider was dressed head-to-toe in black leathers and a motorbike helmet. Watching the health professionals check Jennifer, she suddenly remembered the assault.

'Oh, Jennifer, he was touching you!'

Jennifer carefully shook her head. 'Was he? I don't remember.'

'What's that?' Eagle-eyed PCSO Jean Driver had spotted a white envelope on the ground near to where Jennifer had been lying. She hunkered down next to it, and then fished out an evidence bag from one of the numerous pockets of her uniform. Carefully retrieving it, she held it up so everyone could see the writing on the front of it. The envelope was addressed PAUL BLACK, URGENT.

Jean could see there was something inside. 'Is this yours?' she asked Jennifer.

'I ... I don't think so. Is it?' Jennifer looked up at Madeleine, who shrugged.

'I don't think you had it on you when you got changed into your riding clothes earlier.'

'Let me see that,' PC Ian McClure took the envelope from Jean. Both he and Jean knew Jennifer and Paul were a couple, so they didn't need to ask who Paul Black was.

The ambulance crew were ready to move Jennifer, and the police stepped out of the way as they lifted her on to the stretcher and carried her the short distance to the waiting helicopter. As she watched her friend go, Madeleine felt an overwhelming urge to cry. Jean saw this, and put an arm around her, which set Madeleine off properly. Delving deep into another of her pockets, Jean produced some tissues. Within seconds the flood was over, and, in between sniffs, Madeleine said 'Right, if you don't need me any more I had better go back and see to those horses!'

'We will walk back with you,' Ian said, and after thanking the kind members of the public who had all rallied around and given practical help where they could, the trio walked briskly back to the yard.

The two horse riders had alerted a couple of the livery owners who were at the yard, and they let them in through the electronic gates. Once inside the livery owners took charge of Sonny and Baby, while the two horse riders tied their own horses up at the rails. They were encouraged to make themselves a drink in the refreshment shed, and were waiting to hear that Jennifer and Madeleine were safe. By the time Madeleine appeared, accompanied by her police minders, Sonny and Baby had been untacked, checked for injuries, lightly hosed down with cold water, and turned out onto the hardcore track which was their home during the daytime. Both horses had taken advantage of the sandy area to get down and roll, and were now standing blissfully munching on hay, looking filthy but otherwise unscathed.

Once inside the shade of the shed, Ian explored the contents of the envelope. All that it contained was a single sheet of white paper, on which were printed the words THINK AGAIN.

Ian held it up 'Do you know anything about this, Madeleine?'

She shook her head. 'No, I am sorry, it means nothing to me.'

They had already discussed whether or not the motorcyclist intended to spook the horses, and Madeleine had not been sure at the time, but the presence of the envelope in such close proximity to Jennifer's fallen body, and its contents, added a sinister aspect to the event.

Ian frowned. 'Try to think back. What exactly did you see?'

Madeleine closed her eyes and pictured the scene. 'I'll be honest with you Ian, it is all a bit of a blur. Everything happened so fast. One minute we were riding along, side-by-side, chatting about horses, and the next all hell broke loose and my horse was bolting along the Trailway, close behind Jennifer's riderless horse! OK, let me think. We could hear the motorbike for a few minutes before it all happened. He was behind us for a while, and then he stopped and was using his phone.'

'To do what? Take photos? Speak to someone? Text?'

Madeleine closed her eyes again. 'Ummh. I'm not sure. He was looking at it when I looked back at him, so he could have been doing any of those things.'

'And then?'

'Well, Jennifer and I carried on chatting, and then he was right behind us.'

'So did he deliberately drive his bike directly at your horse? Or at Jennifer's?'

Madeleine shook her head. 'I really don't know. I am sorry. One minute we were riding along, enjoying the peaceful countryside, and the next I was galloping off, while Jennifer was lying unconscious. When I eventually managed to stop Sonny and look back to see where Jennifer was, the motorcyclist was crouching over her, sort of like this.' Madeleine then did a pantomime of showing Ian and Jean what she thought she saw, using a folded up rug in place of Jennifer, and using her own body to shape the actions of the motorcyclist.

'See? Jennifer was lying on her left side like this, and he was leaning over her, with one knee on the floor and the other next to her back, while he … he …' Madeleine took a deep breath 'Oh, I see!'

'What?' asked Ian and Jean in unison.

'Well, I thought he was fiddling around in her shirt, you know, touching her breasts, but he could have been trying to put that envelope inside there. When I shouted at him, he leapt up and immediately rode off on his bike. Before you and the air ambulance reached us, Jennifer had regained consciousness and was rolling around trying to sit up, so the envelope could have got dislodged and fallen out. I was distracted, trying to secure the horses so they didn't run off again, or worse, trample all over Jennifer, so I wasn't really paying attention. Then all the people, dogs and more horses were around us, so the envelope could have got trampled and moved.' A thought suddenly struck her. 'Has anyone told Paul what has happened?'

Chapter 26

Friday 5th August 2016, 6.00pm

'What is all this then? Are you copying me?' Paul leant over and gently kissed Jennifer's forehead, as she lay on the bed in the Accident and Emergency ward of Swanwick Hospital, where Paul had been treated several months earlier.

Jennifer laughed 'I was thinking that too! No, I am fine, not even close to being as badly damaged as you were. They only brought me in to check I didn't have a serious head wound. Madeleine said I was unconscious for a short time, and the health professionals take injuries caused by falls from horses very seriously. Other than a whopping great bruise on my left shoulder where I landed on the track, and another random one on the inside of my right thigh which I have no idea how it got there, I am just a little tired. It has been a very long day, and I really want to go home now.'

They were interrupted by a team of hospital staff.

'You are that auctioneer, Paul Black, aren't you? I have seen you on television!' one of them said.

'That's right. I have never been recognised before,' Paul pretended to straighten his non-existent tie. 'Are you a fan of the show?'

'Oh yes, I watch it every week. Antiques For All is one of my favourite shows.'

'Really? Do you collect anything in particular?'

'Yes, …'

The sound of someone loudly clearing his throat interrupted Paul's conversation with one of the nurses, and the doctor stepped forward to talk to Jennifer.

'How are you feeling now?' he asked.

'Absolutely fine, no problems, just a bit tired.' Jennifer was doing her best to look bright and alert.

'That's good. We think you were saved from serious damage by your riding hat, but you have still had a concussion, and although no bones are broken, that knock to your shoulder is going to be sore for a few days. I'll leave you in the capable hands of this star struck nurse to talk to you about the warning signs to look out for, in case things are not as stable as you think they are, and then you can go home.'

Jennifer smiled with relief, and then listened to the instructions the nurse was giving her. Within minutes she and Paul, armed with a handful of advisory leaflets, were walking down the corridor and heading towards the exit. It took a few minutes to find Paul's car, because he had been in such a hurry to see Jennifer he had not paid attention to where he parked it. Eventually they found it by walking up and down the rows of vehicles and pressing the key fob repeatedly until the flashing lights indicated the end of the frustrating game of hide-and-seek. Jennifer gingerly lowered herself into the passenger seat, and even more gently pulled the seatbelt across her body.

'I am going to have to hold it out here' she said, as she used her right hand to pull the belt away from her left shoulder.

'I will drive as carefully as I can' promised Paul, as he navigated out of the car park at a snail's pace.

Jennifer groaned.

'What? What's the matter? Are you OK?' Paul stopped the car abruptly, causing Jennifer to squeak in alarm, before she began to giggle.

'Oh, that was so funny! I was about to suggest you drove less carefully, and a bit quicker, so we could get home before midnight, but then you did exactly what I didn't want you to do and performed an emergency stop!'

'Well I don't think it is funny,' grumbled Paul as he put the car back into gear, and pulled away.

'Aw, my famous boyfriend,' teased Jennifer. 'I thought that nurse was going to ask for your autograph!'

'I am amazed she recognised me. I am probably only in two programmes every series, and then only for a total of about two minutes, if that.'

'When are the television crew next back at the auction house?'

'I think in a few weeks' time, in September. Look, enough about my fifteen minutes of fame. What exactly happened this afternoon? With all of the fuss going on in A&E I haven't had a chance to ask you. When Ian phoned he said that a motorcyclist deliberately tried to run you over on the Trailway?'

Jennifer shook her head. 'I'm sorry, but I really don't know what happened. Madeleine may know more. One minute we were plodding along having a chat, the next I woke up on the floor with a banging headache and fighting the urge to throw up everywhere. I can't think of any of my clients who would be so vindictive as to do that to me. There have been a few difficult horse owners this week, but I haven't killed anyone's horse, or lost someone a potentially lucrative sale by failing a prize stallion at a vetting, or anything like that. I even had one slightly annoying client this morning, but he was nothing unusual, and it seems a bit of an overreaction to try to run me off my horse.'

'Ian wondered if Madeleine was involved, you know, something to do with her dad, but the presence of the envelope addressed to me makes it look as though you were the one being targeted, and she just got mixed up in the attack.'

'What envelope?'

Paul carefully slowed down to stop at the red light at a set of traffic lights. 'There was an envelope on the ground near you. It was addressed to me, and inside it said THINK AGAIN.'

Jennifer, who hadn't been looking particularly well before, paled significantly. 'What on earth does that mean? That this was deliberate after all? The motorcyclist frightened our horses on purpose?'

'It does look like it, doesn't it?'

Jennifer asked 'You don't know where the envelope came from?'

Paul shook his head. 'I have no idea. You weren't carrying it with you when you went riding?'

'Not that I can remember. Why would I? But why try to get to you through me? It must be something to do with you, or your work, Paul. What has been going on in your world that would make somebody behave so dangerously?'

Paul shook his head. 'I am so sorry if this does have something to do with me or my work, but I cannot think of a thing which could result in an attack on you.'

For the rest of the journey back home to Woodford, Jennifer was kept occupied with concerned friends contacting her by text or phone calls. Paul continued to drive with a lot more care and attention than he normally did, desperate to avoid causing any more pain to Jennifer's injured shoulder. Quietly, he kept track of the dark coloured sports car which, either coincidentally or deliberately, was following the same route as they were.

Chapter 27

Saturday 6th August 2016, 8.00am

'You are sure you are feeling OK? No headache, dizziness, sickness?'

Jennifer was getting a little tetchy with her father, who had turned up on the doorstep of Paul's cottage an hour earlier. 'Yes, Dad, I have told you about a million times I am absolutely fine. Please, stop going on about it!'

Peter said 'I have to admit, you do look very well. Are you going to be alright on your own, here? Why don't you come back with me, and you and Gemma can spend the day resting together. I would be much happier if I knew you were both keeping an eye on each other.'

'Why? What is wrong with Gemma?'

Peter shrugged. 'She doesn't know. She has been feeling a bit under the weather for a few days now. She was meant to be working at the tearooms today, but Lisa and Caroline are going to swap their shifts around so they can cover for her.'

Jennifer stretched her body along the length of the sofa, resting her head on the cushions Paul had placed there for her before he left for work half an hour earlier, and yawned. 'She has probably been working too hard. Those tearooms are always busy whenever

Paul and I go in there, and now that Caroline is spending more time with her own project I do think that Gem and Lisa need to take on more staff. I'll pop round later and check on her if you want, Dad?'

Peter frowned. 'It is not ideal. You were knocked out yesterday, Jennifer, I do wish you would appreciate how serious that could be. If only your sister lived closer.'

Jennifer snorted 'You are making a bit of an assumption there Dad. How do you know Alison wouldn't be too busy to play nursemaid to me today, even if she was close enough to pop over? Please, please stop making such a fuss. I feel absolutely fine, I have not had any problems since I left hospital yesterday. I will go and check on Gemma later this morning; she is only a few doors down the road, so I won't be over-taxing myself by walking round there. Now, go to work. The sooner you get moving, the quicker you can be back to check that neither Gemma nor I have expired.'

Peter wasn't sure whether to laugh or cry at Jennifer's last comment, but he did as she suggested, after first gently patting her head and giving her a kiss on the cheek.

Breathing a sigh of relief at the sound of the front door closing behind him, Jennifer settled down to watch the first in a series of videos Madeleine had recommended. It was rare that she had the time to spend even half an hour in front of an educational DVD that wasn't work related; she was looking forward to the luxury, and had decided to make the most of being on the receiving end of a terrifying incident.

A knock on the door broke her concentration. She had already left her prone position and was sitting up with amazement and watching, slightly open mouthed, as the American former dressage rider performed beautiful rhythmic canter pirouettes on a white horse who wasn't wearing a bit in his mouth. Leaving the DVD running, Jennifer went to open the front door.

'Sarah! Good morning!'

'Oh Jennifer, I am so pleased to see you up and about. The pub was full of your accident last night, so I wanted to come and see for myself how you are, before this morning's grapevine begins to spring into life.'

Jennifer laughed 'Come on in. I was about to put the kettle on for a cuppa. Would you like one?' Without waiting for an answer, Jennifer turned and walked back through the hallway, through the living room and into the small open kitchen area just beyond.

Sarah followed her, stopping in the living room and continued their conversation 'If it's not too much trouble? From what I was hearing last night, I would be the one making you a cup of tea! That is, if you could manage it through the straw you would have to use because of your broken teeth and jaw.'

'Oh, honestly, the gossips around here are ridiculous! I am absolutely fine, other than a few bruises and feeling generally a bit sore. The doctor said that my riding hat saved my head from serious damage, although I was unconscious for a short time so I have an excuse to go shopping to replace it with a new one. My left shoulder, hip, and for some obscure reason the inside of my right thigh are looking rather colourful this morning. Dad has already been round with a collection of arnica products, so within a few days there won't be any marks on me.'

'Good grief, who is that?' Sarah was looking at the television screen, and the horse and rider were executing perfect canter circles, but now the rider was riding bareback, and with nothing but a piece of string around the horse's neck.

'Amazing isn't she? This is someone Madeleine recommended. In fact Madeleine has given me a whole list of people who run these online courses, including an amazing Dutch horse trainer who also has a whole network of instructors over here, which means there are clinics I can go to, and she has told me about an American equine vet who shares masses of knowledge about nutrition.'

'Thank you,' Sarah accepted the mug of coffee Jennifer had brought through from the kitchen for her. 'So yesterday's accident hasn't put you off riding horses then?'

'No, of course not! Although, we don't think it was an accident.'

Sarah looked at her in horror. 'You don't mean the trail bikers rode at you both on purpose do you?'

'Oh, no, it wasn't a trail biker, or even more than one person. This was a motorcyclist who was following us for a little while, before he drove straight at my horse! Or at least that is what Madeleine thinks happened. I can't remember anything once we were on the Trailway.'

Sarah was silent for a few moments. 'That is absolutely terrible to think about. Why would anybody want to do that? Anything could have happened to you! For one thing, even if the motorcyclist wasn't concerned for yours or the horse's safety, he put himself in a very vulnerable position by coming so close to your horse's hind legs. And Madeleine's horse. It sounds as though she had a lucky escape. Has anyone else reported something similar happening to them?'

Jennifer shook her head. 'No, Ian says this is the first he has heard of it. I have ridden on that track loads of times in the past few months, and other than the occasional idiot cyclist or badly behaved dog owner, I have never had any problem before. Especially not from the motorcyclists. I meet the trail bikers regularly, and they are always brilliant; they pull right over to the side, turn their engines off, and have a banter with me as I ride past. I bet they will be furious to hear about what happened yesterday.'

Sarah shrugged. 'Maybe it was someone with a grudge against horse riders, and it was unfortunate that you and Madeleine were riding along that stretch of the track at the time?'

'Maybe, but this seems to have been a deliberately targeted attack at me, because of my relationship with Paul. Whoever did it left a warning note for him.'

'You do realise that means somebody tried to murder you?'

'Oh don't be ridiculous!'

'No, I am serious. You always hear about people who break their necks, or suffer such severe trauma to their skulls that they die from their injuries. If that motorcyclist deliberately drove at you and your horse, then he was trying to kill one or both of you.'

They both sat quietly for a few minutes and watched the screen, as the American, now on the ground, played at Liberty with her horse.

'On a lighter note, I have decided to buy myself a horse.'

'Have you? When will you find the time to ride it?'

Sarah had been toying with the idea of owning her own horse, and was keen to hear how Jennifer planned to manage.

'Now that could be a challenge, especially as Dad and I have some major plans for the practice we need to put into place over the next two years. But I think that it

194

must be like having a baby, don't you? There is never a "right" time to have a baby, and if you keep putting it off until you have, oh I don't know, reached a good point in your career, you are earning a decent income, you own your own home, you have found the right man, whatever is on your list, then you would probably never reach that stage.'

'True. But it is a big responsibility to have, financially too. Nicola and I have been talking about sharing a horse, but then we would never be able to ride with each other if we did that! Also, if I owned my own horse I wouldn't get to ride all the lovely horses over at Brackendon Western stables, or Madeleine's horses at the Woodford Riding Club. I do like having the variety.'

'Yes, I understand what you mean. But don't you want that?' Jennifer gestured towards the screen. 'See the connection they have? I would love to have that kind of relationship with a horse. I have talked to Madeleine and I could keep it at livery with her, so once the practice is based at Wellwood Farm, and now I am living at Paul's cottage, I would be less than seven minutes away. In the winter I would make good use of the floodlit arena, and the indoor school. My horse would be living out with other horses, and Madeleine and her staff would take care of all the poo-picking, feeding, and maintenance of the tracks and fields. I am sure I can do it.'

'Mmmh, you do make it sound tempting. Although I think we should all be putting our energies into finding out who this bastard motorcyclist is before he tries again.'

'I don't think it has totally sunk in yet, probably because I can't really remember anything. Paul is very concerned, and has been contacting everyone he can think of to try to find out who was behind this. You know what the antiques trade is like; it won't be long before somebody speaks out I am sure. I don't think there is much either you or I can do about it, other than be more aware of our surroundings.'

'You are probably right, but I think when I go back to the pub I will get the Regulars onto it as well. At the very least I can get the correct story of what happened circulated so that no innocent trail biker is unfairly accused. I'll make us another cuppa, and you can tell me how your search for your new equine partner is going.'

Chapter 28

Saturday 6th August 2016, 10.00am

Natasha stretched luxuriously in the hot tub, revelling in the pleasure of having the open-air space to herself, and wriggled her toes, smiling at how good the red nail polish made her feet look. It was a shame she did not have a man waiting at home to compliment them too, but for the time being Natasha was happy to fulfil her own need for love. She was beginning to despair of ever finding the right life partner.

Diva's Spa, located in Swanwick Sports Centre, was one of Natasha's favourite places to be when she needed to properly relax, and it was also probably the only time Natasha could be seen in public without make-up and with her hair messy. For this reason on the rare occasion someone from the local antiques trade or a member of the public who attended the auctions made use of the saunas and steam rooms, they never recognised her, which suited Natasha perfectly. After her disastrous date a couple of days earlier with Dafydd, she felt the need to pamper herself, and a day at the spa always hit the spot. She was a Gold Member, and one quick online visit to their website the evening before had booked her place for the day.

Natasha lay back and closed her eyes, enjoying the warmth of the sun on her face. She was not a sun-

197

worshipper, and rarely had enough time away from work to sit or lie under the sun's rays, but for a few minutes half-lying/ half-floating in the large open air hot tub, this felt very good.

The door from the indoor section of the spa opened, and a couple of women walked out onto the wooden decking surrounding the hot tub. The peace and isolation Natasha had been revelling in was broken, and she inspected them through barely open eyes. She could see that they had similar facial features to each other, although one was clearly older, and although Natasha hadn't seen the younger woman for a long time she guessed they were mother and daughter. She wondered if the older woman recognised her this time, because they both acknowledged her with a knowing smile, and then continued their murmured conversation in which Natasha was clearly not included, and settled down on the sun loungers behind Natasha's head. In her opinion it was a waste of time spending all that money to come to a spa and then just sit out in the sunshine instead of making use of the facilities, but Natasha noticed the younger woman was limping and appeared to have a newly created tattoo on her leg which had not yet healed and was very raw in places. Presumably it was not safe to enter the water with a wound like that.

Now that her peaceful spell was broken, Natasha opened her eyes fully, and slowly eased herself upright and lazily inspected her environment. The wooden decking into which the hot tub was positioned was surrounded by white painted railings, entwined with a perfumed pink flower. Natasha had no idea about gardening or plants, but she appreciated the management's attempt to disguise the location. Whatever the climber was, it hid the ugly view of the street below, although the noise of the people and traffic could not be disguised.

Another person emerged from the connecting door, and she padded her way along the decking, before discarding a cream and gold coloured dressing gown and towel, which all guests were given to use, onto one of the brightly coloured sun loungers. Natasha shuffled along the underwater bench to make room for the newcomer, and deliberately closed her eyes again.

'Hello Natasha. Fancy seeing you here. How are you?'

Natasha was not fond of making small talk, and rarely engaged in it. But here she was trapped, so she opened her eyes to see who was talking to her.

'Tanya, hello. I am very well, thank you. And you?'

'I am great, thank you for asking. This is a treat, isn't it? I have never been here before. Daft isn't it, when it is right here on my doorstep. Oooh, I have just indulged in one of those hot stone massage treatments, and my whole body feels loose and light. Amazing! Have you had one?'

'No, no I haven't. Oh, is that the time? Sorry, I have been in here for far too long. Enjoy the rest of your day.'

Natasha had planned to spend the whole day at the spa, but she decided that after only one session in the lavender scented steam room, and one cedar based sauna, followed by the mineral-filled hot tub, she was feeling revived, and didn't want it ruined by having her former colleague forcing her to make polite conversation. She made the decision to cut short her time there, and instead head back home and spend the remainder of the day catching up with book number three in the Logan McRae series, *Broken Skin* by Stuart MacBride. She had stumbled across the series via another of her favourite authors on Twitter, and was now hooked. Natasha enjoyed her own company, and if it wasn't for the fact that she had chosen the antiques trade as her profession, and specifically owning and running an auction house, she could have happily stayed in deliberate solitary confinement for days on end. Several hours alone at home with a good book was an appealing prospect.

Ignoring the other women in the changing rooms, she showered and dressed, reapplied the mask that was her make-up, tamed and subdued her dark hair back into its formal straight bob with perfect fringe, and gathered up the rest of her belongings from the locker. Pushing the spa's complimentary towels and dressing gown down the laundry chute, she walked quickly through the reception area, and out to the car park, eager to get home and snuggled up on her huge cream-coloured sofa with her book.

Natasha rummaged in her Marc Jacobs bag for the car keys, found them, and stopped dead. Her beautiful silver blue Jaguar XK8 had been trashed. The tyres were slashed; the soft top had been ripped open; every panel had been scraped with a knife; the lights were all smashed; and the words: THINK AGAIN were scratched into the paintwork.

Chapter 29

Saturday 6th August 2016, 11.00am

It was one of those warm sunny summer days in Woodford when all the holiday-makers were out and about visiting local tourist attractions, and the locals had all decamped to the beach. Lisa and Caroline were alone in the tearooms, having served a total of five customers so far that day.

'You might as well go, Caroline. I am sure I can manage here today. There is no point both of us hanging around twiddling our thumbs.'

Caroline jumped up from the chair she had been sitting on 'Great, thanks. I have some more plans for the new café I want to put into place. Oh, Mum, I forgot to ask earlier. Why have you got flowers for Cliff Williamson in the sink in the utility room?'

Lisa looked at her daughter in confusion. 'What are you talking about?'

'Those white lilies? Were you meant to bring them in for him today? Has someone died?'

'White …? Oh! Those flowers. Robin Morton dropped them off at the house yesterday. I expect he was apologising for smashing one of the glass vases. As if his presence in here wasn't toxic enough, he is now destroying the place. You know, I told you about it.'

Caroline pulled a face. 'So why is the card addressed to Cliff?'

Now it was Lisa's turn to look puzzled. 'Is it? To be honest I didn't even look for a card. In fact, I was going to chuck them away, I was so furious with him. What an idiot. Fancy thinking he could buy me a crappy bunch of flowers and all would be forgiven.'

'Actually they are a very expensive bunch of flowers, so if they had been from Robin to you then maybe it would have been worth your while to give him another chance.'

'Oh don't be so ridiculous, why on earth would I do that? I am surprised that you of all people, who lived through the awful way your father behaved towards us, should think it would be a good idea for me to go back to a relationship where I was treated with that level of disrespect.'

'Oh come on Mum, Robin is nothing like Dad. For one thing, Robin actually likes you, and I think he has a huge amount of respect for you. It was the nature of his job which made him lie to you about where he was and what he was doing. It isn't as though he was like that about anything else.'

'Well that just proves my point' Lisa pointed her finger at Caroline triumphantly. 'Robin chose a career in which lying and deceiving people is integral to its success, and from all accounts he is very good at it. Anyway, you hardly saw him. How would you know anything about the way he behaved the rest of the time?'

'Oh, I give up. If I was in your shoes I would give him a second chance. But I am not, and it is your choice. But it still doesn't explain how the flowers turned up at our house.'

'Yes, that is strange; why would he be leaving flowers for Cliff at my front door?'

'I think the bigger question is why would Robin be buying flowers for Cliff! Mum, do you know for sure that Robin left them there? If they aren't for you, I can't imagine why he would drive all of the way over to our house, when he could just go next door to Williamson Antiques?'

'Well, now you ask, no I don't know that it was him. I just assumed it was, because of all the fuss in here.'

'Tell you what, I'll go home and change, and pick up some paperwork, and then I can drop the flowers off on my way past.'

'Thanks, love.' Lisa was annoyed with herself to discover how disappointed she felt that the flowers hadn't been from Robin to her after all. She had spent the past twenty-four hours feeling indignant that Robin should think he had the right to go to her house for any reason, let alone something as pathetic as bringing an apology bunch of flowers for her without the guts to speak to her face-to-face. Now she felt deflated. And, for a few minutes, very lonely.

Not long after Caroline left, there was a sudden rush of a dozen people all wanting something to eat and drink. Lisa was kept busy for the next two hours, taking orders, preparing meals, serving customers, and clearing away afterwards. But once the place was empty again, the sense of loneliness came flooding back.

By four o'clock she decided to close early. Since the lunchtime rush there had only been two people in who had shared a pot of tea between them, and Lisa decided enough was enough. She tidied, swept and washed down the kitchen, and the tables and floors in the tearooms, and made sure everything was in order for

Gemma to open up the next day, if she was feeling well enough. Otherwise Lisa knew she would be the one opening up, and probably on her own.

After she had set the alarms and locked the doors, Lisa decided to pop next door and find out what the story about the flowers was all about. Rather than walking around the back of the buildings to the alleyway which led to the High Street, and then walking up to the front of Williamson Antiques, Lisa decided to set herself a challenge. She had to unlock the back door and switch off the alarms, before re-locking the back door from the inside, re-setting the alarms, and running through to the front door, and quickly unlocking, opening and then shutting it again behind her, before the alarms could be triggered. Giving herself a mental 'High Five' for achieving the challenge, Lisa congratulated herself on taking another risk. Gemma's words at the start of the week still stung, but Lisa was slowly beginning to understand that if she wanted more out of her life then she needed to put more into it.

She walked the few steps to the front door of Williamson Antiques, and pushed her way inside. The building was lovely and cool, and Lisa realised it had been several weeks since she had last been in. After a quick glance around the corner at the empty counter area to see if Cliff or Nicola were there, she began to look at the items for sale on some of the stands and cabinets. After a few minutes she heard voices, and the sound of footsteps on the white wooden stairs which led from Cliff's flat down to the sale room.

'I'll give you a ring if I hear anything else.'

Lisa could feel her heart rate rise at the sound of Robin Morton's voice. She tried to hide, but too late realised she was standing the other side of a glass cabinet.

Robin saw her and raised a tentative smile, before hurrying through the front door.

'Lisa!' Cliff was nervous after their last meeting, and determined not to upset her again. 'How are you?'

'I am fine thank you Cliff. What did he want?' she asked, gesturing to the door Robin had just dashed through.

Cliff quickly decided that telling Lisa all about Robin's plan to win back her affections probably wasn't the best timing, and so he tried to change the subject. 'Robin? Oh, nothing much. Just some scary stuff that has been happening around here recently. I was hoping he could shed some light on it, but he hasn't had any contact with his former colleagues for a few weeks now.'

Lisa gave him a disbelieving look.

'Hey, your daughter was in earlier with a bunch of flowers for me. She said they had been delivered to your house? Do you have any idea who from?'

'Nope, no idea at all. I assumed they were for me, and so I didn't even notice the card with your name on it. Doesn't it say who they are from on the card?'

'No it doesn't. It just has this really strange message. THINK AGAIN.'

Chapter 30

Saturday 6th August 2016, 12 noon

Natasha was furious. The Jaguar had been a lavish present to herself five years ago, to celebrate Kemp and Holmes Antiques Auctioneers and Valuers being in profit after only their first year of trading. To Natasha it symbolised both her personal and professional success, and she loved it. For Dafydd to attack her car so thoroughly was a declaration of war, and she didn't waste any time in telephoning the police to report his actions.

Much to her surprise, the police turned up within minutes. She had expected them to fob her off with a crime number and a vague promise to speak to her 'sometime next week', but instead two officers had promptly started the investigation into who had committed the damage, and why. They explained that they took damage to property very seriously, and the use of a knife in this way could indicate that the person responsible was ready to use it on a human being.

All of a sudden Dafydd Jones wasn't a man she felt pity for; for the first time in her life Natasha was terrified of another human being. She gave the police his details, and hoped they would lock him up somewhere he couldn't reach her. She regretted inviting him back to her flat on that first night after the film, because now he knew where she lived. It was bad enough when rejected lovers tried to hassle her in her workplace, although at least there she had people who could block access to her. But even though her apartment building had a security door at the entrance, people were forever propping it open so that anyone could walk in off the street. Once inside, there was nothing to stop a person from gaining access to the front door to her flat. Resolving to keep her mobile easily accessible every time she went home, in case she needed to call the police again, and wondering where she could get hold of some pepper spray, Natasha tried to think of other precautions she could take against unwanted and possibly violent attention. Briefly, she wondered if Dafydd was one of the silver dealers involved in Hugh Jones' case.

She watched tearfully as her car was loaded onto the back of a breakdown truck. The staff at the spa were magnificent in their cooperation with the police, and in taking care of the shocked victim. They made one of the treatment rooms available, and Natasha was ushered inside with a complimentary cup of tea and a glass of water. Once she felt strong enough she joined the police in the security centre, where they were shown the spa's CCTV. Fortunately the car park was well covered with cameras, and the destruction of Natasha's Jaguar was recorded clearly. The video showed a black motorcycle coming into the car park, ridden by a black-clad motorcyclist, and parking up next to Natasha's Jaguar. In less than two minutes the motorcyclist had slashed the roof, run around the outside of the car with his knife pressed firmly into the paintwork, and had scratched the message in big capital letters along one side. He proceeded to further mark the paintwork with a series of symbols which the police could not decipher, but now that she could see them from a distance via the camera, Natasha recognised instantly. As a final act of destruction, he kicked every single one of the lights, both front and back, smashing the glass and covering the ground with it. The police guessed that his leather trousers must have protected his legs, but it looked as though at least one shard of glass had slipped inside one of his boots, because he could be seen bending down, unzipping and then removing it, before shaking it thoroughly, and pulling it back on. He must have left his bike running, because as soon as his boot was back on his foot, he jumped on and tore out of the car park.

Natasha could tell by the shape of him, and the way he moved, that the perpetrator was not Dafydd Jones. Dafydd was stocky and moved like a former rugby player, whereas this person was much taller and leaner. The knowledge frightened her even more, because it meant that he either had an accomplice, or he was in a position to pay someone to terrify her. Whatever the truth of the matter, there was absolutely no way she was going to give him a third chance. Who on earth believed that engaging in criminal damage was a good way to seduce a life partner?

She made the decision to do something she hadn't done for years, and thought she would never do again. She telephoned her parents for help.

Chapter 31

Monday 8th August 2016, 8.55am

Lydia Black took a deep breath and tried to steady her nerves before she walked underneath the midnight blue wooden sign with the name Kemp and Holmes Antiques Auctioneers and Valuers painted in gold. It crowned the archway through to the building where the business was based, and Lydia walked on through the car park, and into the large reception area. The last time she had been here was the day of her job interview, when she was so sure that Natasha Holmes would never choose to give the daughter of Paul Black an apprenticeship, she had not felt at all nervous. Curiosity had been her over-riding emotion on that day.

Her phone chirruped to let her know someone had sent her a text. A quick glance showed her it was from her father; she chose to ignore it. Lydia and her brother had no memories of their father living with them. He and Christine separated when their children were both very young, and in those early years he had very little time for them. Lydia grew up with a mother who suffering from depression, and a father who was flitting from one relationship to another. Throughout her childhood her ambition was to be rich and famous so that she could buy a big house for her mother to live in where she could be safe and happy. How she would achieve all of those things was not something Lydia was very clear about at that age, and from one week to the next she would change her plan. Sometimes she wanted to be a television presenter, and she idolised Cat Deeley, Fearne Cotton, Holly Willoughby and Katy Hill. Other weeks she was going to be the next Britney Spears or Christina Aguilera.

By the time Lydia was ten years old, Christine had successfully turned her own life around and was a much happier person than she had been for most of Lydia's early childhood. At last Lydia was free to be the child she had never really been able to be, instead of feeling the weight of adult responsibility for her own mother. For the next few years she was a handful at home, a fiend at school, and often terrorizing the neighbourhood by not being either at home or at school.

On her thirteenth birthday Lydia abruptly changed her ways. In a reverse transformation to most of her peers, Lydia became very serious about her present and her future, and began to put into place a series of achievable targets. Taking care of her mum was no longer her overriding desire; her mum was one of the most sorted people she knew. She had also grown out of the vague wish to be famous, without a clear idea of how she would achieve it. But she did still want to be rich.

Lydia was bright. She was far too bright for the rigid academic structures which rule the British school system, and consequently she was bored. Woodford School was the usual mix of superb teachers with a small percentage of people who should never have chosen working with children as their profession. Lydia's form tutor was one of those who clearly did not like children, and had no business working in a school. She intensely disliked Lydia, and it was unfortunate that the school operated a system within which the students kept the same form tutor throughout their time at the institution. For the first two years the woman put far more energy into trying to get Lydia excluded than she did putting effort into finding out what could engage the youngster. Fortunately she was the only adult Lydia regularly came into contact with who behaved in this way, and others on the payroll, both teaching and support staff, worked even harder to keep Lydia with them.

There was one teacher in particular, her mathematics teacher, who was able to see through the aggressive and uncooperative attitude she presented when she could be bothered to stay in her timetabled lessons, and who encouraged her love of learning. He would set her, and others in her class, practical tests such as working out each curriculum subject department's share of the whole school's electricity bill, or understanding why it would be cost effective for the tennis courts to be relaid with a more expensive surface than the one preferred by Brackenshire County Council.

As part of her decision to focus on the road to her future financial security, Lydia asked her father for a small role in the family business. Black's Auction House had never featured strongly in Lydia's life, mainly because her father had so little time for her. She knew where the building was, but had only been inside a handful of times. She knew nothing about antiques, and was not interested in learning about them, but she did love computers, and she knew that her father's business was becoming increasingly dependent on them. She also knew that this was causing her father a great deal of stress. Lydia took her proposal to her father in the belief that he would welcome her natural abilities, and he would appreciate the efforts she was putting in to mend their fractured relationship.

Paul knocked her aspirations back with a cruel 'Over my dead body'.

For two weeks Lydia reverted to her wild and rebellious behaviour. She successfully persuaded a tattoo artist to ink an image of the Greek goddess Selene onto her bicep, and added another three piercings to her right ear. She lost her virginity to one of the sixth formers.

After the fortnight was over, Lydia returned home, and went back to school, determined to continue her studies so she could leave with the highest qualifications she was capable of achieving.

Two years later, while scanning the careers section of the local paper online, and still smarting from another knock back when her father refused to fund a trip to Borneo where she wanted to work with a group who were attempting to save the orangutans from the devastation which humans were forcing on them in the rainforest, Lydia spotted the advertisement which was to change her destiny.

She quietly prepared for the interview by finding out as much about Kemp and Holmes Antiques Auctioneers and Valuers as she could online, and even snuck in to observe one of her father's auctions incognito, wearing a pretty summer dress she 'borrowed' from her mother's wardrobe and replacing her normal white pancake foundation plus heavy black eye make-up with a light bronzer, and minimal rose and greens powders accentuating the depth and colour of her eyes. Lydia diligently carried out her research, and her efforts were rewarded by achieving an apprenticeship with her father's sworn enemy, Natasha Holmes.

Lydia Black was ecstatic. As she walked towards the front door her heart was singing. This was the first day of the rest of her life.

Chapter 32

Monday 8th August 2016, 12 noon

Lunchtime in The Ship Inn had been a busy one, with plenty of holiday makers dropping in for sustenance. Woodford was a useful resting point for people who wanted to use the Trailway, which ran for more than fourteen kilometres from Woodford down to the coast. It provided a safe off-road route for walkers, cyclists, and horse riders, and was a popular amenity for tourists and locals alike.

A former local, Simon Maxwell-Lewis, had also made his first appearance in the pub since he was taken into custody and then sentenced to a term in prison. Simon had been one of the pub's Regulars for many years, and had never been the source of any problems in there, but Sarah wasn't sure about allowing him to resume his previous stool at the end of the bar, because he had caused a number of Woodford residents a lot of emotional and financial stress before he was imprisoned the previous year. She and Tom agreed to watch and see how his presence affected the usual smooth running of the pub, and at the first sign of trouble they would bar him for life. He sat quietly, with his pint, and when he finished it he left, without incident.

Once most of the customers had followed suit, Sarah checked that both Amanda and Tom were happy for her to take off for the afternoon. Mondays were usually a quiet day in the pub, and Sarah was hoping eventually to make it another of her days off, creating a useful two-day combination in which she could concentrate on her developing antiques business. She knew she needed to employ another full-time member of staff to support Tom and Amanda, but was still analysing the type of person and the duties which would need to be fulfilled.

After a quick change out of her basic uniform of polo shirt with the pub's logo, and jeans, she was surprised to find that she could comfortably fit into a summer dress which had been lurking in the back of her wardrobe for several years. She reflected that all the Zumba classes and swimming sessions she was enjoying this year were having a positive effect on her figure. She refused to believe that grief could have resulted in her recent weight loss.

She drove for an hour up to Brackenshire's county town of Swanwick, and after carefully negotiating the narrow entrance designed for horses and carriages rather than her dark blue Mercedes sports car, she found a parking space, and walked into the auction rooms. Immediately she could feel her shoulders relax, and realised just how stressful the interaction with Simon Maxwell-Lewis had been for her, even though his time in the pub had been incident-free. She took a moment to reflect that in the past she and Mike had always handled customers like him together, and although she had Tom by her side this time, it wasn't the same. It was another indication that her time as a publican was coming to an end.

Swanwick Auctioneers was established in the 1950s, by two brothers. It was successfully run as a family business for several years, but over time the children of the two brothers found other things they wanted to do instead, so the auction house's porter, Barney Simmons, ended up taking sole charge by default. The brothers maintained an interest for as long they could, but ill-health and eventually death caused them to relinquish all control of the business. Barney had a son, Stanley, who was keen to follow in his father's footsteps, and for the past twenty-five years the name Swanwick Auctioneers had become synonymous with 'Slippery' Stanley Simmons.

Sarah particularly wanted to view this month's sale in person, because she had seen in the online catalogue a portrait miniature she thought may have been painted of a member of one of the families she was currently researching. Sarah was a keen family historian, and although in recent months, since her husband's death, she had lost the passion she once had for it, in the last few days she could feel her interest being reignited.

As she walked in through the main entrance she could see Slippery Stanley Simmons in all his glory, monopolising a conversation between a group of men Sarah assumed were antiques dealers. She didn't recognise any of them, and continued past uninterrupted. While she was waiting for Slippery's assistant, Tanya Gordon, who appeared to be the only person doing any work, to unlock one of the cabinets so she could study the portrait miniature, she felt someone's hand on her arm. Since Mike had died, Sarah had very little bodily contact with anyone else, and her instinct was to snatch her arm away.

'Sorry Sarah, I didn't mean to startle you!' Linda Beecham was very apologetic, and this made Sarah feel guilty for her reaction.

'Oh, don't worry Linda, I was so focused on making sure I don't miss my turn I wasn't aware you were there.'

'I see good ol' Slippery is leaving Tanya to do all the work, as usual,' said Linda as she looked around in vain for someone else who could help them. 'Which item are you interested in?'

Sarah pointed towards the painting. 'That portrait miniature of the gentleman. Can you see it? The one in a silver frame.'

'I see it, on the second shelf down? Ah, here's Tanya now.' Linda Beecham was a local antiques dealer who had a stand in Williamson Antiques, and regularly stalled out at the local Drayton Flea Market, and more recently at Sarah and Cliff's new venture, the Woodford Flea Market. She and Sarah were a similar age, both in their late thirties, and their shared interest in antiques was forming the basis for a growing friendship.

'Tanya, I love your new look!' Sarah gazed admiringly at Tanya's hair, which had gained some subtle highlights and was styled in a swishy bob instead of the hanging strands which usually surrounded her face.

Blushing, Tanya self-consciously gave her head a little shake to emphasise the soft movement of her hair.

'Thank you, Sarah. I decided I needed a change.'

'It really suits you. Maybe I should try something different,' Sarah absent-mindedly gave her own straight mousey-brown hair a pat.

'Oh, I think you look great. You look as though you have been working out?'

217

Pleased, Sarah said 'Yes, I have. Nicola and I began going to Zumba a few months ago, and now we have also started something called Strong by Zumba. Have you heard of it?'

Tanya shook her head, but looked interested, so Sarah continued 'Oh, it is an amazing HIIT class, where you …'

'Tanya, Tanya!' Another customer was calling for help.

'Sorry Sarah, I had better go and help him. I would like to know more about these exercise classes though. I am sure I have seen an advert at the leisure centre.'

'Oh, yes, they do them there. Give it a go.'

Tanya smiled her thanks, and moved further down the line of cabinets to help another customer.

'She and Nicola went to the same school in Woodford,' Sarah said to Linda. 'Nicola says that Tanya was a real wild child in those days, although it is hard to believe now, she is always so quiet. Don't you think that something must have happened to make her blossom like that? She looks like a different person today; much happier than normal.'

'I should think that years of working with Slippery would drain the life out of anyone. Maybe she has decided to find herself another job and is going to escape his slimy clutches. Can you imagine it?'

'I dread to think what it must be like to work for him; he is pretty ghastly. Oh, that's a shame,' now that she had the chance to study the painting close up, Sarah could see almost immediately that the subject of the portrait was not the man she had hoped it would be. 'It isn't him after all. Never mind, it would have been a fluke if it had been.'

'If you ask me you have had a lucky escape there. This frame has been faked to make it look as though it is the original for this portrait.'

Sarah looked at Linda in astonishment. 'How on earth can you tell that?'

'See, here,' Linda pointed to the maker's mark on the back of the silver frame. 'This mark is far too crisp to match a three-hundred-year old frame.'

Sarah peered closely at the marks which had been stamped into the silver. 'Do you know, I have never paid much attention to the frames which surround my paintings. It is the quality and authenticity of the picture, who the artist was, and who is portrayed that have been my concerns.'

'I suppose that could be the difference between you as a collector, and me as an antiques dealer? You are going to have to learn to change your focus now,' Linda winked.

Sarah groaned. 'Oh, there is just too much to learn! I had no idea there were these pitfalls. I am going to have to have a rethink about trying to make a living out of antiques.'

'I may have a solution to your problem. Don't give up on your dream, but maybe think about it from a different angle. Have you considered going into partnership with someone else?'

Sarah's face brightened up. 'Do you mean with someone like you?'

'Well, I have been thinking about it, ever since you first mentioned your plans. You always said you were not planning on giving up the pub, and I couldn't see how you could possibly run the two businesses side-by-side, even with the marvellous Amanda and amazing Tom. We would need to sit down and properly go through the finances, our expectations from the project, and how much commitment we can both give to it, but other than all of those details, and more that I haven't even thought about yet, what do you think?'

Sarah laughed 'Even if you hadn't just demonstrated why I need someone with far more antiques knowledge than I have, the answer still would have been yes! I would love to work with you.'

'Fantastic news! Is it OK if I hug you now?' Linda teased.

Chapter 33

Monday 8th August 2016, 6.00pm

'Cheers!'

'Cheers!'

Sarah and Linda raised their glasses in a toast to their joint venture.

'What are you celebrating, ladies?' Paul Black appeared from the snug, where he and Jennifer Isaac were about to have a quick supper before heading back home.

'Paul, have a drink!' offered Sarah, as she waived the bottle of Prosecco in his direction.

Holding up his hands in defence, Paul backed away a couple of steps 'No, no, I have an early start in the morning. I am trying to get back on track with my running, and have an eight miler planned with Cliff.'

'Quite right,' said Sarah. 'Good for you. Although Linda probably has an even earlier start, don't you Linda?'

'I certainly do! I have to be on the road by half past four tomorrow morning, to make sure I am in time for my pitch at the antiques fair up in London. But I can have a small glass of bubbles now, you know, just to show that I am a team player.'

'Ha ha, I like your way of thinking. I am going to enjoy working with you. Of course, I am being very naughty because I missed out on my afternoon swim by going up to Swanwick and checking out the auction.'

Linda groaned. 'I really should do some form of exercise, but I can't find anything I enjoy doing.'

Sarah looked her up and down with obvious jealousy. 'Hmmh, don't tell me are one of those lucky people who stay slim and gorgeous whilst eating and drinking whatever they like? Our business partnership may be over before it starts if that is the case.'

'Business partnership? Are you going into the pub trade?' asked Paul, determinedly not eyeing up Linda's svelte figure clad in its usual attire of jeans and T-shirt.

'No,' laughed Linda. 'I will leave that to the professionals,' she said, gesturing to Sarah, and to Tom who was working on the other side of the bar.

Sarah explained 'You know I had plans to open a little antiques shop over in the new development on Wellwood Farm?'

'Yes,' said Paul, 'although I can't help thinking of it still as the Maxwell-Lewis farm.'

'I know what you mean,' nodded Sarah. 'That whole situation is so sad; poor old Mrs Maxwell-Lewis. Did you know her son, Simon, is back in town?'

'Yes I did,' Paul said carefully. Simon Maxwell-Lewis was high on his list of suspects for the motorbike attack on Jennifer the previous Friday, although as yet he could not find a reason why Simon would want him to 'think again'.

'He had a drink in here today. I was in two minds about serving him, but I suppose he has done his time, and so long as no one objects too strongly then I don't have reasonable grounds to bar him.'

Paul stayed silent. He had been to see PC Ian McClure that morning to find out how the investigation was going, but Ian did not have anything he could tell him. Paul hoped that if the police also believed Simon was a suspect, then Ian would have at the very least warned him about it.

Sarah was oblivious to Paul's concerns, and carried on. 'Anyway, back to our little celebratory drink. I have been struggling to find the time to source and purchase enough stock, and it is harder than I thought it would be to take more of a back seat in this place' she gestured vaguely around the bar. 'At the weekend I had a chance to think about it seriously, and I came to the conclusion that I don't have enough know-how of the antiques trade to run a retail business, and I was all for jacking it in, when this Guardian Angel appeared at my shoulder!'

'Sarah and I have been having a number of casual chats about her plans over the past few months, and this afternoon I asked if I could join her, and here we are!' Linda waved her glass in the air, skilfully failing to spill any of the bubbles. 'I have more than enough stock to fill the retail space in the planned shop, and if we can employ a third person then I am sure we will be able to staff it properly. We think the buildings over at the farm will be ready next month, and we plan to open in October.'

'Hang on a minute, let me get Jennifer over here. She will want to hear this too.' Paul disappeared into the snug, and emerged less than a minute later with a tired-looking Jennifer. She smiled at the two women, who in contrast were full of energy and clearly enjoying themselves.

'Jennifer! How are you feeling? You look a lot better than you did on Saturday morning,' Sarah gave her an enthusiastic hug, which made her wince.

223

'I am a lot better thank you. My shoulder is still too sore for me to get back to work properly, but Dad has set me up with a load of paperwork to do so I am relieved to be out of the house again. Hopefully I'll be fully fit before the end of the week.'

'Why? What happened? Were you kicked by one of your patients?' Linda asked.

'No I wasn't, fortunately. My horse was spooked when I was out riding on Friday, and I stupidly fell off.'

'There was nothing stupid about what you did; it was that bloody motorcyclist who was behaving stupidly,' growled Paul, who was determined not to allow Jennifer to put herself down over the accident.

'Anyway, enough about that; it is old news. Paul tells me you two are celebrating, and we will all soon be business neighbours!'

Linda look surprised 'You and your father are moving your equine practice over to Wellwood Farm?'

Jennifer laughed 'We are hoping to, Linda. We haven't signed the final papers yet because we have some serious financial questions to resolve before we do, but if everything goes to plan we will be making the move before the end of the year. The owners, the Barker family, are very keen for us to base ourselves at Wellwood Farm; as you know Mrs Barker used to run the Swanwick Irish Draught Stud, and she is eager to promote equine health. The lease on our surgery runs out soon, and the owners want to develop the buildings as flats rather than renew it with us, so we need to move somewhere. The thought of packing up the entire surgery and hospital and moving it, even if it is only a few miles down the road, is terrifying!'

'Oooh yes I can imagine, but exciting too? We are going to have a lovely little community over there. I was a bit concerned when Sarah first started talking about it, that the location was too tucked away, and nobody would visit it. I thought they would get as far as the High Street, and not bother to venture down the track to the farm'

'Oh, I think the real antiques nuts will find you,' said Paul. 'They will be attracted by my auction house and Cliff's antiques centre, and continue on to your shop. Now that Caroline's mobile café is a bit more established, and once the other shops get moved in and started, I can see the place thriving.'

'Yes, I agree with you, Paul. Antiques buyers will go anywhere for a bargain, and the other businesses will attract passing trade too. Here you two, join us and have a glass,' Sarah expertly poured from the bottle. 'Oh Jennifer, are you allowed to drink so soon after your head injury?'

'Yes, I have had no problems since Friday so a glass of bubbly would be lovely. Thank you, and Cheers!'

Chapter 34

Tuesday 9th August 2016, 6.35am

Linda Beecham sighed as the fifth person in as many minutes began to tell her about the latest scandal to hit the antiques trade.

'What an idiot. Apparently he stitched one of the big silver boys up for more than forty grand! How stupid can you get? No wonder they put out a contract on him. He deserved everything he got if you ask me. The police have seized all of his money, and his stock of course.'

Linda was trying to unpack the contents of her van onto tables so she could stall out at the big London antiques fair, along with over seven hundred other stall holders. She was setting up on an outdoor pitch, and it was one of those beautiful dry and sunny mornings which make everything a joy. But so far nobody had wanted to buy, or even look at, what little of her carefully selected stock she had managed to display, and she was rapidly losing patience. The dealer's face was a discomforting mixture of horror and excitement at someone else's misfortune. This had the effect of making Linda want to throw the dregs of her coffee at him. Instead, slowly and deliberately, she began to list the errors in the man's story, counting the points on her fingers as she did so.

'Firstly, Hugh Jones had a wife and three small children who deserve our compassion, and at the moment they have no access to joint bank accounts or any immediate way of making money, so maybe you could channel your judgemental energy into finding a way to help them. Secondly, I worked with Hugh, and think he was one of the good guys in the business, so I believe that he was an innocent who got mixed up in the sort of silly deal which any of us could have done, and he, and his family, have paid an extraordinarily high price for his mistake. Thirdly, and again this is only what I believe from the information I have received, Hugh did not steal anything; he paid for the silver salver at a price agreed with the seller, Adrian Edwards. And the fourth and final point I am going to make on this subject: the amount involved was nearer two thousand pounds than forty thousand.'

The man's expression slowly changed to one of shock as he listened to Linda. With his hands clutched to his cheeks he said 'Oh Linda, I had no idea! Of course, you are right. He did a lot of work for me, and I never had any complaints about him. Except that he was very slow in returning the silver once he had finished with it. I trusted him too; never had any doubts about giving him tens of thousands of pounds worth of stock to mend. Poor, poor Hugh. And yes, of course, his family. His wife is a lovely lady. I hadn't thought of it like that. I wonder if anyone has set up a collection for them? I'll go and find out, and if not I'll do it. How awful. I feel terrible now.'

'What is awful?' the low gravelly voice of John Robson, an antiques dealer in his late sixties who had been involved in the trade since he was a boy, interrupted the man, who took advantage of John's arrival to slink away, determined to try to make amends for his enjoyment at someone else's misfortune.

Linda sighed. 'Oh, you know, the news about Hugh Jones. I have heard several different versions this morning and it is only' she quickly checked her watch 'twenty-five minutes to seven. It all happened weeks ago, and yet for some reason it is STILL the main topic of conversation amongst antiques and general dealers. It is as though somebody keeps feeding a new rumour in every week or so to keep the story alive.'

John said nothing, simply raised his eyebrows and stared at her. Linda suspected he knew even more than she did about the death of Hugh Jones, and the circumstances leading up to it, but he clearly wasn't going to share any information with her. After a few moments she asked 'Any chance you have walked over here to buy something, rather than spread unpleasant gossip like everyone else?'

John chuckled and looked at the sparsely covered tables she had set up in front of her van. 'I would love to buy something from you Linda, but as you don't appear to have much to sell I will come back later, with coffee. White, no sugar?' He winked, and walked on to the next stall.

Linda gave a 'Humph' of frustration and proceeded to haul the boxes from the van and dump them on the tables.

'Hi Linda, you are looking particularly ravishing today! I love your dress; very summery.'

Linda looked around and immediately felt a lot happier at the sight of Sarah Handley. Laughing, Linda gave her a hug. 'Oh you are a sight for sore eyes, or should I say your voice is good for sore ears. This lot are full of distasteful gossip, and I am thoroughly fed up of hearing about it. I am just going to refuse to talk to the next person who tries to bring it up. And thank you very much. As you know I am more of a jeans and T-shirt kind of girl, but my sister gave me this dress and as the weather forecasters said it is going to be a boiling hot day today, I thought I'd give it a go. I wasn't sure if large flowers were really my thing,' she said as she glanced down at the long white maxi-dress printed with several big yellow sunflower heads.

'I think that dress compliments your figure, and I love the matching scarf you have tied around your head.'

Linda put a hand up to check it was still in place. 'Well, when you have long grey hair it is usually a good idea to tart it up in one way or another. Anyway, let's change the subject, you know I am never comfortable discussing my appearance. What do you think of this fair now that you have finally made it up here for your first visit?'

'Oh my goodness this place is amazing! You were absolutely right about it. I can't believe how big it is. It makes our little Woodford Flea Market look like a Scout's jumble sale. Before I go off and get lost for several hours, would you like a hand unpacking these boxes?'

'Oh Sarah, I would love some help, thank you. But I don't want to hold you up from finding some bargains?'

'Oh don't worry about that. Now that I know you are on board with the shop I can stop stressing about volume and start to concentrate on quality.'

'Yes but all of the bargains will be gone in the first hour.'

Sarah shrugged. 'Look, this is my first time up here and to be honest, I am feeling a bit overwhelmed. Please let me help you for a while, and then I'll walk around once the dealers have finished racing everywhere. Some of them would cut your throat to get to a good deal first, wouldn't they? I think they have been sharpening their elbows while waiting in the queue to get in.'

'Cutting of throats is a bit of a sore subject this morning' Linda said, grimly. 'Well, if you are sure you can spare the time, please can you start with that box over there? Just lay everything out and tuck the empty box underneath the table. Thank you.'

For the next few minutes Linda was pleased to have her time taken up by genuine buyers rather than gossip-mongers, as both the antiques and general dealers finally began to pile onto her stand. While Linda was taking money and giving change, and fielding questions about the quality and age of goods, Sarah Handley relished the chance to observe the behaviours of the people while she unwrapped and arranged Linda's stock on the four tables. Although she was a frequent visitor to the Drayton Flea Market which was fairly local to Woodford, and she and Cliff and recently set-up the Woodford Flea Market, Sarah had never worked behind an antiques stall before.

Sarah watched in awe as a dealer walked by pushing a heavy-looking but well-balanced trolley load of furniture, and then she grimaced and held her breath as another man tottered past carrying several items piled on top of each other in his arms. She hoped he would make it safely back to his car without dropping anything, but sure enough within a few steps he had dropped the lot. Glass smashed and objects rolled away, causing several people to leap into action to prevent the man's newly bought items from demolishing the stalls in the immediate vicinity of his accident. The fair's marshals and members of the general public appeared from nowhere to help, and within a couple of minutes the whole disaster area had been cleaned up, and two strangers assisted the man to carry the remains of his damaged belongings to his car. Sarah's attention was next caught by a customer who was browsing the table in front of her and appeared to be wearing a golfing costume from the Victorian era, including thick woolly socks and plus fours, in the heat of the London summer. She tried not to stare at the transvestite in his fluorescent pink tight shorts and swirly patterned frilly see-through blouse, or at the shocking state of another man's toes which curled over the end of his flip-flops. She tried to breathe as shallowly as possible as a woman waved her cigarette in Sarah's face while demonstrating what she thought was wrong with a delicate silk fan with an ivory frame, and waited for the burning tip or falling ash to cause even more damage to the one hundred and fifty-year-old fashion accessory.

After the woman had put the fan back in its box, surprisingly unscathed, and left the stand, Sarah turned to see Linda laughing at her.

'Your face! What a picture. I take it this fair is a bit of a culture shock after Brackenshire's Drayton Flea Market?'

'I'll say. Blimey. I think some of the images I have just seen are going to stay with me forever.'

'Ah,' Linda winked, 'there was more blue blood running through the veins of one or two of the people who have been to this stall in the last fifteen minutes than ever stands on the balcony of Buckingham Palace for a photo shoot.'

'No! You are kidding me? None of them look as though they have two pennies to rub together, let alone know which knife and fork to use at a three-course meal. I was watching one or two of them very closely to check they weren't going to pocket any of your stock.'

'Don't be fooled by appearances; I think every single one of those dealers who has passed by here is a millionaire, if not a multi-millionaire. Most of that lot have more high-end antiques stashed away in their houses than you will see in the whole of this fair. But I am glad you were being alert to the possibility of the small thieving element of the antiques trade. I hope one of the people you were suspicious of was the smartly dressed woman?'

Sarah looked puzzled as she tried to remember seeing a woman in amongst all of the male buyers. 'Not the one you were talking to? The lady with the elegant blonde bob, and wearing a simple string of pearls around her neck? I thought you two were best mates the way you called over to her.'

Linda smiled 'There is nothing a thief hates more than having attention drawn to them. Did you notice how all of the stallholders were calling out her name as she walked past? We were alerting everyone to her presence. She won't be back for a while now, thank goodness. It is hard enough to earn a living in this business without people like that stealing from us.'

'Wow, I never would have guessed she was anything but straight. I can see I am going to have to hone my thief-radar before we get our shop up and running. And to think I thought we saw all of Human Existence in the pubs. Well, I suppose I had better love you and leave you, and go in search of something for myself. This place is so big I am not sure where to start.'

'Why don't you take a walk around the outdoor stalls, and then have a look at the inside ones once the crowds have thinned out a bit more?'

'Good idea, thank you. I'll come back here later, if that's alright?'

'Oh yes please, and tell me all about your adventures too. I'd love to hear what you find.'

'OK, I will, I am very excited about it. I'll bring a tea or a coffee for you with me? Or would you prefer an ice cream?'

'Ah, thank you! I think if the weather forecasters have got it right for a change, then an ice cream will be gratefully received.'

'Alright then, see you later, and be lucky Linda.'

Linda wore a faint smile as she watched Sarah walk away. She was pleased that Sarah had accepted her proposal, and was looking forward to working with her. Linda had lots of ideas about how a small antiques shop would work in Woodford, and knew from observing Sarah in the pub that her new partner would be organised and enthusiastic.

Her thoughts were interrupted by 'Hey, Linda, have you heard what happened to Hugh Jones? It sounds awful! What an idiot, though, to think he could cross the big silver boys for one hundred thousand pounds.'

Linda could feel her tongue bleeding.

Chapter 35

Tuesday 9th August 2016, 8.55am

Lydia walked with a spring in her step through the archway, across the car park, and towards the front door of her new employers. Her first day on the job had been so much more than she could have hoped for. Natasha had met her in the reception area, and taken her on an hour-long tour of the entire building, which covered five floors including a basement. The Victorian building was a mish-mash of nineteenth century large rooms with high ceilings which led off long corridors, and ancient plumbing, and highly varnished one hundred and fifty plus year old wooden flooring, all intermingled with the clean lines of the state of the art auction house technology and office furniture.

Natasha had devised a six-week plan for Lydia to work in one of each of the sections of the business for a week at a time, so that she could follow the processes of valuations and auctions from start to finish. For her first week she was going to be shadowing both Natasha and one of the other auctioneers, Crispin Keogh. After her induction into where to find the toilets, and the strict rules about securely storing and labelling personal food items in the fridge, Lydia then spent the remainder of the day getting to grips with the auction house's computer system, and was given a crash course in cataloguing by Crispin and Jason Chapillon. Lydia thought it was possible she had died and gone to heaven. Jason was *gorgeous*. The sight of his tall muscular frame, and dreamy dark brown eyes, made her pulse race.

Today she was going to be out of the office, travelling in the blue and gold Kemp and Holmes liveried van with Crispin as he went out to people's homes on a combined valuing and buying trip. She liked Crispin, in the way she had once liked her favourite childhood Teletubby toy, Dipsy. With his floppy dirty-blond hair and gently humorous manner, Crispin was patient and kind, and Lydia was glad he was the one she would be spending the most time with. Jason's good looks and his ability to radiate self-confidence was far too distracting if she wanted to learn all about the antiques business.

They had three home visits to complete. The first was to a rambling old house in a state of disrepair, which had been owned by the same family for generations, but after twenty years of only being used occasionally as a country retreat, it was now up for sale. Lydia's mum, Christine, was an estate agent, and over the years Lydia had picked up a fair amount of knowledge from her. Lydia thought it likely the building would be demolished, and several new houses would be built on the sizeable plot of land. It was a shame, because the house was beautiful, and had lots of charm and character.

She was impressed with the way Crispin handled the owners, allowing them to give a brief history of what had clearly been the setting for many happy childhood holidays, but without getting distracted and wasting time. He persuaded them to let him wander all over the

235

house with Lydia, while they stayed downstairs in the kitchen and made them all a cup of coffee.

It wasn't long before Crispin made it clear that he judged the belongings which remained in the house were only fit to be taken to the local tip, and he firmly spelled out his conclusions to the owners. They were disappointed, but not surprised. As he pointed out, if anything was valuable they would have already claimed it for their own homes. While they were drinking coffee and discussing how best to dispose of the last contents of the house, Lydia looked down at herself with dismay; she was absolutely filthy! She couldn't believe how dirty she was after simply looking at neglected belongings.

But it was not all doom and gloom for the owners: Crispin was very interested in two of the garden ornaments and a pair of gates. After a bit of haggling over the price, he and Lydia loaded up the items into the van, something Lydia was not expecting to do. She had dressed for sitting in front of a computer all day, and ended up taking her high wedged red sandals off to help carry the heavy items, adding filthy feet to her general grubby state. She also decided that a top which bared her mid-drift was not ideal everyday workplace clothing. Crispin made a quick telephone call, and arranged for their house clearance team to take away the rest of the belongings before the end of the month.

After a half an hour back at the auction house to unload the ornaments and the gate, or at least watch as the porters did it for them for which Lydia was very grateful, she and Crispin were back in the van and on their way to their next house call.

'Oh God, you can smell the poverty,' muttered Crispin as they walked up the broken pebble dashed path leading to a front door on which they could clearly make out three layers of different coloured paint in amongst the filth, where countless boots had kicked it open over the years.

The door was opened by a woman, whom Lydia guessed was in her middle to late twenties, wearing a filthy dressing gown and with a cigarette hanging out of her mouth.

'Come in, come in,' she stood back to allow them into the dingy hallway, and closed the door behind them, before pushing past to lead them through to the back of the house where the kitchen was located. Lydia tried and failed not to gag as the stench of the body of an unwashed alcoholic filled her nostrils. Crispin pulled a face at her, and motioned for her to stay behind him.

They followed the woman into the kitchen, where she pulled out a plastic carrier bag from inside the washing machine, cleared a space amongst the glasses and bottles on the table, and tipped the contents into it.

Crispin made a show of looking at each piece, but Lydia noticed he made no attempt to touch any of it. On the rare occasions she had seen her father inspect items of jewellery he always used the senses of sight, touch, smell, occasionally sound, and sometimes even taste, in order to ascertain the quality.

'Do you have a receipt for any of this?' The look of disgust on the woman's face told Crispin all he needed to know. 'I am sorry, but in order for us to enter any of these items into one of our auctions we are obliged by law to put a copy of the receipts into our books,' he lied.

The woman had looked unhappy from the moment she opened the front door to them, but now Lydia was worried she was going to burst into tears. For a few moments it was clear the woman was trying to work out how to fake a set of receipts, but the effort of creative thought was clearly too much for her.

Then the woman's face lit up. 'What about this? I've got the receipt for this! And the handbook!' she pointed to the washing machine. It was only then that Lydia noticed it was the single piece of electrical equipment in the room. This was no modern kitchen where every appliance was hidden away behind matching doors, so you needed to start at one end of the room and open every cupboard before you could find the bin or the cooker. Nor was there a utility room next to it, where such items could have been hidden away.

Crispin held up his hands and began to back away. 'I am very sorry, but I think we have wasted your time.'

'No, wait, what about this?' To Lydia's horror the woman pulled open the dressing gown, displaying her naked body. 'I could do the pair of you together for fifty quid' she pleaded.

Calmly Crispin said 'I am sorry, thank you, but no thank you,' and firmly pushed Lydia in front of him down the corridor, reaching around her to open the front door and following her outside.

'Come on, in the van,' he said, pressing the key fob to unlock the doors as they walked back down the path. 'Do not look back.'

He waited until Lydia had fastened her seatbelt before starting the engine, and drove them out onto the main road. 'Fancy a coffee?' he asked, and without waiting for an answer drove the van into the McDonalds Drive-Thru.

'One coffee and one …' he looked at Lydia, waiting for her answer.

'Oh, um, please can I have a strawberry milkshake?' after the shock of what she had just witnessed, Lydia could feel herself reverting to childhood.

Once they had their drinks and were parked up, Crispin said 'I am so sorry you had to witness that. It doesn't happen very often, but every now and then we come across somebody who is desperate to get their hands on some cash.'

Lydia began to giggle. Crispin looked at her in alarm. 'Oh, no, I am not laughing at that poor woman's plight, really I am not. If you hadn't been there I probably would have emptied my purse out onto that filthy table for her. How desperate do you have to be to offer your body to a pair of complete strangers? One of whom is a girl? God, she was a state. What a minger.'

Up until that point Crispin had found it easy to behave professionally. He felt a duty of care towards Lydia, who was only sixteen years old, and through his work he had seen enough human beings in hopeless circumstances to no longer be fazed by them and he knew he had acted appropriately with the woman. But for Lydia to think the scene had been funny was too much.

'Who the hell do you think you are, you privileged, spoilt little bitch,' he snarled, his upper crust accent making the words sound even more harsh than he intended. 'That woman had nothing. Did you notice when you walked past the door into the front room that there was no furniture? No curtains? There was just a disgusting stain-covered carpet. And that kitchen was empty, other than the glasses and bottles, the crappy old table, and the brand new washing machine. How do you think she paid for that? She clearly has children. Not only could we see her C-section scar, but there were children's clothing hanging on the washing line outside in the back garden. But there were no toys out there, nor in the house. You know nothing about her, and yet you sit here and laugh.'

Lydia was stung to tears. 'I promise you, I was not laughing at her, or her situation. I did notice that there was nothing in the kitchen, but I didn't notice the rest. I felt sorry for her, really I did. Look, it isn't funny now, but I was giggling because Dad has this thing about Natasha. He hates her. It is one of the reasons I wanted to work for her, because I hate him. But that all sounds a bit stupid now. Dad doesn't want me to work for Natasha because he is convinced that she is a tart. He says that the only way she has got her hands on this business is by getting her hands on Bertram Kemp. But he is wrong, isn't he? Just by spending that time with her yesterday I could tell how hard she works, and how much respect her staff have for her. I met Bertram this morning too, and I don't think there is anything between them. He was just like a lovely old cuddly teddy bear. I have never met a prostitute in real life before, and for my dad to think that Natasha and that poor woman have anything in common tells me he is even more stupid than I thought he was.'

Crispin was silent for a moment. He was used to hearing rumours about Natasha and Bertram's relationship, and rarely reacted to them anymore because whoever was repeating them was revealing more about the state of their own ignorance and prejudices than about the abilities of either of his employers. But while he was sure there was nothing of a sexual nature between Natasha and Bertram, Natasha's love life was certainly vibrant enough for there to be some truth in a few of the rumours which reached his ears. He suddenly felt awful for his outburst at the young girl sitting next to him.

240

'Looks can be deceiving, but I agree with you about both their relationship, and the reasons for Natasha's success in this business. She works bloody hard, and is one of the most knowledgeable people I know, although Bertram wins that contest. Those rumours your dad has told you about are old news, and I think that she is actually a very lonely soul. I am sorry I shouted at you.'

'That's OK, I understand why you did it. It must have seemed like I was laughing at that poor woman. When he found out the name of my new employer, my dad was being all unpleasant about Natasha, warning me about all the things she will teach me and the sights I will see. But in a funny way he was right, wasn't he? Only he is too stupid to realise that, yes, on my second day I have been introduced to a prostitute, but far from being the glamorous woman in control of her life my dad thinks they are, I have seen first-hand how grim and desolate life is for some people. Do you think she is an addict? Was she trying to get money off you for drink?'

'Probably.' Crispin shrugged. 'But who knows? The bottles could have belonged to someone else. She might have needed money so she could buy food for her kids. Or maybe she had no money to pay the electricity bill, and she had no hot water to wash in. Anyway, we will never know, and if we got sucked in to every sob story we came across in this business we would never earn any money to pay our own bills. Drink up, we are lucky and we do have work in which we can keep our clothes on.'

'Except my shoes,' Lydia laughed, relieved that Crispin had calmed down again.

Their final call was to a bungalow belonging to a couple whom Lydia guessed were in their early sixties.

They were offered ice-cold homemade lemonade on arrival, which Lydia thought was delicious, and perfect to drink on such a hot day. The couple led them through to a beautifully decorated dining room with a huge table laden with various sets of china.

Crispin's heart sank.

'Now,' said the husband, 'we saw this pattern on the *Antiques Roadshow* a few weeks' ago, so we know it is worth a lot of money. And we saw this dinner service on *Bargain Hunt*, but the dealer wanted more money than the contestants would pay, so we know how much this is worth. And …' Crispin listened patiently as the man went around the whole table, listing how the china should be sorted into Lots, and how much he expected Crispin to get for them all in auction.

When he had finished Crispin said 'Well, I can see you have both been doing your research. You do have a fine collection of china and porcelain here. Unfortunately, I do not think we could do it all justice if we put it into one of our general sales. The big buyers won't be expecting to find quality items like these in those sales, and so we will only attract the general dealers who, to be brutally honest, are not going to be excited by them, and won't be willing to pay anything like the prices you are expecting. You see, we are not going to be having another specialist china sale until next year, and even then I am not sure many of these items will be suitable.'

The silence in the room was palpable. Lydia felt slightly sick. The man looked as though he was going to burst into tears.

'Look, do you see this chip on the lip of the cream jug here? And this dinner service is missing quite a few of the bowls and dinner plates. And here, there are more saucers than cups in this tea service. If you have your hearts set on selling all of this in the next few weeks, why don't you try this company?' Crispin wrote the name and telephone number of another auction house on the back of one of his cards, and left it on the table. 'I am sorry, you have gone to all of this effort but I cannot do it all justice,' he indicated the collection which must have totalled over two hundred pieces of china, all freshly washed and arranged in order. 'Thank you for the lemonade, it was absolutely delicious,' and with that he briskly shook first the husband's and then the wife's hands, and again ushered Lydia out of the house before him.

They walked down the path and into the van as quickly as they had when they left the previous house, but this time Crispin didn't wait for Lydia to fasten her seatbelt before he started the engine and drove away, narrowly missing a car being driven by an old lady.

'God, I hate house calls like that.'

Lydia was confused. She had thought the couple were perfectly nice, and wasn't sure why Crispin was in such a hurry to get away from them. He looked over at her and saw her puzzled look.

'Did you see the desperation in their faces? Did you notice the letter on the side in the kitchen about the nursing home fees? The way the lady was clearly confused?'

Lydia shook her head.

'That couple are just as desperate as the woman we saw earlier. The china is worth nothing. They, or I should say he, are clearly trying to scrape together the money to pay for her to go into a home for people with dementia, or something similar. People like that have nothing to sell except their houses, and in this day and age even a well maintained bungalow like theirs isn't likely to sell quickly, or for as much money as they will have been told it is worth. And even if they do manage to sell it and raise the money for the care she needs, where will he live, and on what?'

They were stopped at a red traffic light, and Crispin sighed and rubbed his face with his hands. 'I am sorry Lydia; you are having a baptism of fire into this job today, aren't you? Lugging around heavy ornaments, and getting filthy into the bargain; meeting a real life druggy prozzie who bares all within minutes of meeting us; getting verbally abused by the person who is meant to be looking after you; and ending the day with another sob story of hardship and poverty. It isn't always like this. I do hope you are going to come back tomorrow?'

'Of course I will!' Lydia couldn't wait.

Chapter 36

Friday 12th August 2016, 6.00pm

Closing time at The Woodford Tearooms was flexible, as were the opening times. Either Lisa, Gemma or Caroline were usually in the building by seven o'clock in the morning, because it could take a while to get the woodburner going in the winter, and the pots of soup and the grills to warm up for the numerous bacon sarnies they sold, and in the summer prepping the fresh salads always took long than they anticipated. The end of the day could be as early as three o'clock in the middle of winter when everyone wanted to get home from work or school as quickly as possible, and the thought of stopping for a cuppa and then having to go back outside into the driving rain was unappealing. In the summer, locals and tourists alike were more likely to wander past the sometimes hot and stuffy tearooms, and continue on up the High Street to The Ship Inn, with its all day seasonal opening times, where they could sit out in the pub's beer garden, or inside in the cool conservatory.

Gemma was still struggling to get up in the morning, and by lunchtime she was often exhausted. She had picked up a sickness bug, and so for health and safety food preparation reasons was taking an enforced break from their joint business. Caroline was chomping at the bit to get her own catering business properly up and running: an Aerostream caravan she had already set up on the other side of The Green, at Wellwood Farm. Originally she was going into a new development on the Trailway, but internal wranglings within the committee meant that not only was the start of the project heavily delayed, but Caroline also decided she didn't want to be a part of such an argumentative group. The Wellwood Farm development was moving ahead of schedule, and Caroline was already beginning to establish a strong clientele amongst the builders and other trades people on the site, as well as the prospective business owners who were regularly popping in to see how the build was going.

With both of her fellow workers occupied with other things, Lisa was running the tearooms almost single-handed. In the past she and Gemma had been able to call on the boys in the family, her son Robert, and Gemma's sons Daniel and Nathan, but in what seemed like a very short time they had all grown up and had priorities of their own.

Fortunately the locals were happy to clear away their used cutlery, crockery and glasses, stacking them neatly on the wide shelf in the big open window which separated the kitchen from the tearooms, and one or two of them had become handy with the cleaning spray and cloths. Lisa was becoming adept at maintaining a quick cycle of emptying the dishwasher, and re-stacking it in record times, as well as taking orders and preparing meals. She had reduced their menu to dishes which could be created from a small number of ingredients, so that her stock control and preparation times were minimal. But she was still working much longer hours than she was used to, and finishing later than she would have liked. By the time she had driven home, and then enjoyed a shower, all she wanted to do was snuggle under the duvet and go to sleep.

That Friday had been an exceptionally busy day, because the weather had been alternately rainy and sunny, which meant that the tourists were drawn out of their glamping tents and holiday cottages to enjoy the beautiful local countryside, and then forced to hurry to find somewhere to shelter. Although the last customers had left shortly before half past four, and she had been supported by a number of helpful locals, it had taken Lisa well over an hour to clean and tidy up in preparation for the next day. Finally, she set the alarms and locked the back door, before walking carefully down the steps to her car, which was parked in the yard. Briefly she glimpsed someone behind the wall, but was too tired to go and investigate.

'Lisa?' Robin Morton appeared. 'Please could I have a word with you? I would like to talk to you about something.'

'Can it wait until the morning, Robin? I am exhausted and just want to go home. I don't have the energy for a heart-to-heart with you right now.'

'Oh, er, yes, yes of course. Sorry to bother you. I did just want to have a quick word, but yes, yes, I understand. Sorry. Maybe another time?' He turned and began to walk back out onto the track which ran alongside The Green.

Lisa sighed. He looked so desolate; her heart twinged and made her voice words her brain didn't want to say.

'Robin, come back. Look, I really am very tired. I have more or less been on my own in the tearooms for the last few days, as you know, and I am not capable of any big emotional confrontations, but if your quick word can fit in over a glass of Pimm's, then why don't we go and have a drink in The Ship Inn together?'

Beaming like the Cheshire Cat, Robin marched back and linked her arm through his before she could change her mind. 'Come on then, I am not going to turn down an offer like that one!'

Together they walked in silence up to the pub: Lisa was wondering why on earth she had suggested having a drink in a public place with a man she loathed and despised, although she reflected it was better than being alone with him; Robin could not believe his plan to make Lisa fall in love with him again was exceeding his wildest expectations and had jumped several steps already.

Tom Higston looked from one to the other, and back again, when they walked into the bar together. Deciding that discretion would be the professional way to behave, he asked 'Good evening, what would you like to drink?'

Once they had ordered, Robin carried Lisa's glass of Pimm's and his own half pint of Brackendon Best Bitter through to the snug, where Lisa had already settled her tired body on one of the old velvet-covered benches which ran around the walls.

'Thank you,' she said, as he placed her glass carefully down in front of her on the table. 'So, what is this "quick" word you would like to speak with me about?'

Robin took a long sip of his beer, before answering. 'Firstly, thank you for agreeing to hear me out. I know I do not deserve any of your time, after the way I treated you, and I am truly grateful that you are giving me a chance to speak. I have dreamed of a time when you and I could be sitting back here, in this pub, having a drink together at the end of the day, but I never thought it would happen. Or, at least I certainly didn't expect it this evening.'

'Hold your horses there cowboy. Don't get ahead of yourself. I only suggested meeting for a drink because you wanted to talk to me, and I knew I wouldn't be able to stand up any longer.'

'Understood. Sorry.'

'Well, go on then. This "quick" word has taken almost half an hour already!'

'Right, yes, I'll get on with it. Um …'

The silence between them lasted for more than thirty seconds, giving Lisa the opportunity to study the man she had once thought she would be spending the rest of her life with. It occurred to her that she knew very little about the 'real' Robin Morton, and she wasn't even sure how old he was. She studied his hair, and concluded that even the most skilled hairdresser could not have recreated the flat mousey brown colour with the greying temples. She was pretty sure his eyes were that pale blue, and no coloured contact lenses or dyes had been used. His height was also genuine: she guessed he was probably about six inches taller than her five foot five-inch frame. He was clearly struggling to say whatever it was he was so desperate to tell her, so eventually Lisa took pity on the man she had once enjoyed spending several hours chatting with late into the night. The anger she had felt towards him for months was spent, and she was too tired after the last few days of taking on the burden of the tearooms single-handed to play games.

'Robin, what have you done? Just tell me. I don't imagine it can be any worse than the way you behaved when we were together.'

Lisa's words cut Robin like a knife. While they were romantically involved he had enjoyed every minute of their time together, and when he was working away from her he missed her, even though they were able to contact each other every day, sometimes several times a day. He did not realise how much of a connection they had until he was forced to come clean about his job as an undercover policeman, having told her that he was an engineer for an international company. Lisa made an instant decision to end their relationship; she was not prepared to allow someone into her world who could deceive her about almost every aspect of their life, and whose chosen career was duplicitous by nature. At the time Robin had expected Lisa would be shocked, but it had not occurred to him that she would feel hurt and betrayed to the level where she wanted nothing to do with him.

Over the next few months the extent of the damage his actions had caused to his own happiness became obvious to him. He could have taken another job within the service, and his superior officers were keen not to lose an experienced and competent member of their team. But with all the emotional upheaval, Robin suddenly felt burnt out and wanted a complete change for his future.

He returned to Woodford expecting Lisa to welcome him with open arms because of his life-changing decision, but so far had been unable to make her aware of the good news.

'Lisa, please listen to me.'

'Isn't that what I am doing?' Lisa's tone softened. 'Come on, tell me.'

'Right, here goes. For several days now I have been trying to pluck up the courage to tell you that I have resigned from my job as a member of the police force.'

Lisa said nothing, but waited patiently for him to continue. Robin didn't know what to say next because when he had rehearsed this moment repeatedly in his mind, Lisa had flung her arms around him and forgiven him for everything.

'That's it.' Robin picked up his glass, and drained the rest of the beer.

Lisa was bewildered. She wasn't sure why Robin had made such a fuss about sharing his news with her. If he was to be believed, of course.

'Oh, well, good for you, if that is what you want. So, what will you do now?'

'I'm going to have another, want one?' he gestured towards her empty glass.

'Oh, no, I still have to drive home. If I have any more not only will I fall asleep here where I am sitting, but I will also be over the drink-drive limit. If that is all you wanted to tell me, I had better be going. Good luck in your future endeavours.'

Lisa began to stand up.

'No, you can't go yet!' Robin was beginning to panic. He had finally managed to speak to Lisa, to tell her he was doing what she wanted him to do, and now they could be together, but she was treating him as though he was nobody. 'Look, why don't I get you a coffee? Or something to eat? You are not going to want to cook anything when you get home, so please let me buy you dinner.'

Lisa was shaking her head, and stood up ready to leave.

'Lisa, I have just told you that I am no longer an undercover cop.'

'Yes you have, and I am not sure what it is you want me to say.'

'I want you to say that we can start again.'

Finally the penny dropped, and Lisa had to sit down again, balancing precariously on one of the velvet covered stools.

'You are joking. Why on earth would I put myself through that again?'

Robin sat on a stool next to her, and took hold of both of her hands in his. 'But that's the point, don't you see? You won't be in the same position as last time, because I am no longer a policeman! I love you Lisa, I have given up a job I loved for you. Can't you see that? You have to take me back now!'

'I don't bloody well have to do anything!' Lisa snatched her hands away and was staring at him with fury. 'Who the bloody hell do you think you are? "Oh Lisa, we had something good but I totally screwed it up and now I have made a martyr of myself, so take me back so I can screw everything up again",' she mimicked.

Robin could feel his own temper rising. 'Oh come on. It's not like that and you know it. You and I have something very special. I *did* screw up, I know, and now I am trying to make amends. I promise you that I did not do it deliberately, and once I realised how much you meant to me I tried to put things right. You are vital to my future. It is because of you that I resigned. You have to give me a second chance.'

'No, I don't. I don't *have* to do anything. Particularly not if it involves you!'

'Hey, hey, what's all the shouting for?' Paul appeared in the doorway of the snug, closely followed by Cliff, Nicola and Jennifer.

'Oh, I see you have told her your real name?' Cliff asked, taking in the situation and jumping to the wrong conclusion.

Nicola made a rude noise.

'What? Robin isn't your name?' Lisa couldn't believe what she was hearing.

252

'No, I haven't. Thanks mate,' Robin muttered over his shoulder.

'God you don't believe him do you?' Paul asked Cliff. 'Rebecca told me he tricked you into thinking his name was John Thomas,' and with that he broke off into peals of laughter.

'He did! He believed him!' Nicola joined in.

'No, you wally!' Jennifer pulled a face at Cliff.

'Look, I believe he was telling me the truth, OK?'

'Oh, for goodness sake Cliff, I didn't have you down as someone who was gullible,' Jennifer scoffed.

'Tell them. Tell them what you told me,' Cliff turned to Robin, who was now leaning on the table with his head buried in his hands.

Straightening up, he said 'Yes, my parents, Mr and Mrs Thomas, gave me the first name John. No, wait, better than that, since you are already laughing at my misfortune, they christened me John Orville Thomas.'

'Orville? As in the duck?' Paul fell about with laughter, leaning against the door frame to hold himself up.

'That makes your initials JOT!' Cliff joined in.

'You poor sod,' was all Jennifer could think to say, as she stood staring at him.

'What is going on in here?' Christine appeared in the doorway, with Lydia. 'Sarah said we would find you here in the snug.'

Paul spun around to see them, as all mockery flew from his brain. 'Lydia!'

'We thought you might like to hear about your daughter's first week working for an antiques auctioneer.' Christine was eager to try to get Lydia and Paul talking after several years of estrangement, and as it was possible they would now have some common ground between them she was determined to give them

253

an opportunity to mend their fractured relationship. She guessed that as there was no auction at Black's that evening, Paul and Jennifer would be in the pub. She had managed to persuade Lydia to come with her, and to give her father an opportunity to show an interest in her, by promising to buy her dinner.

'We would all like to hear about it Lydia. Why don't we all have dinner together?' Lisa seized her chance to escape the nightmare she seemed to have fallen into and was glad of the company. She began to rearrange the tables so that everyone had somewhere to sit.

John/Robin knew that any chance he had of renewing his relationship with Lisa that evening was destroyed, thanks to all the people who were now squeezing their way into the snug.

'Good idea Lisa, we all might as well eat here tonight' agreed Paul, thinking that having other people around might help to diffuse the tension between himself and his daughter.

'Here everyone, have a menu,' Cliff leaned through the doorway to pick up a pile from the table outside the snug, and began to pass them around the assembled group.

Chapter 37

Friday 12th August 2016, 7.00pm

Within seconds the room was filled with silence as everyone sat down, either on the benches which lined the wall, or on the stools positioned around one big table, and studied the menu. For some of them, like John/Robin and Lisa, the silence was a welcome shroud to hide behind, but for others, like Lydia and Paul, it formed a barrier. Tom whisked in and took food and drinks orders, and then the group were left alone again.

'Come on then, Lydia, has anything exciting happened this week?' asked Lisa, turning to the girl sitting next to her, and not for a moment thinking there had been. As far as she could tell from observing them in the tearooms, all antiques dealers did was sit around drinking tea and reminiscing about the Good Old Days.

'Yes, lots of things happened. I don't know where to begin. Oh, well probably one of the most exciting things happened before I even started work there. Natasha Holmes' car was vandalised on Saturday morning.'

'Not her beautiful Jaguar XK8!' exclaimed Sarah, who had come in with a tray of drinks. She began to place them on the table, correctly guessing who had ordered which one.

'I thought you were a Mercedes girl?' commented Cliff, who was sitting at right angles to Lydia, on one of the benches.

'Oh, I am, I wouldn't swap it for the world, but I will admit to having car envy for Natasha's Jag. What happened to it?' asked Sarah.

'According to Jason and Crispin, someone scratched all the paintwork, and smashed all the lights. It is going to cost Natasha a fortune to repair it.'

'No! Why would someone do a thing like that?' Sarah was convinced she could feel physical pain at the thought of the damage being inflicted to the car.

'Who would do something like that?' asked Nicola, who was sitting between Cliff and Jennifer.

'I can think of one or two,' muttered Paul from his place on one of the stools, opposite his daughter.

'Oh, for goodness' sake Dad!' exclaimed Lydia.

'Paul,' Christine put a warning hand on his arm, and Sarah glared at him.

'Alright, alright, I'll keep my prejudices to myself.'

'You are so wrong about Natasha, Dad. She is extremely hard-working, and professional at all times. Everyone who works there respects her. All your talk about her being a tart is just horrible.'

Once again the room was plunged into awkward silence. Lydia stared at her father across the table, before a tiny smile began to grow on her face.

'Actually, Dad, I was sent to a brothel on my second day there,' Lydia decided that a little exaggeration would not do any harm. Every pair of eyes stared at her. She waited a few seconds, intending to continue with the elaborate story, but the memory of the woman's distressed state was too serious, and she couldn't keep the joke going. 'If you must know, it was incredibly sad. There was this woman, well a mum, who had a drink problem, and she wanted us, well Crispin, to buy a load of stolen jewellery. At least, we think it must have been stolen because other than the table and a washing machine she didn't have anything else in the kitchen. And get this Dad, she was so desperate for money that she offered to have sex with both of us! Me and Crispin! At the same time!'

Paul shot a furious look at his ex-wife, who was gaping in horror at her sixteen-year-old daughter.

'Lydia! You didn't tell me about that! Honestly Paul, I had no idea about all of this. You should have told me before we left home!' she hissed across the table.

'Why? What would you have done? Banned me from going back the next day? Don't worry, seeing that poor woman was enough to put me off the idea of ever selling my body for sex. Or drinking alcohol' she looked pointedly at the round of alcoholic drinks in front of every adult sitting at the table, except for Lisa who was drinking pomegranate pressé. 'You should have seen that house; it stank! As did she. Crispin said she probably had children, but we didn't see any sign of them. The whole thing was just awful. I can't stop thinking about her, and wondering how she got into that terrible situation, and what is going to happen to her now. I mean, it could have been anyone standing in her kitchen.'

There was a collective sigh of relief when the bell sounded from the kitchen signalling that someone's food order was ready to be delivered to the table, and Sarah went rushing out saying 'That is probably your starters. Don't say anything else until I get back!'

In an effort to change the subject, Nicola turned to Jennifer 'How are you now, after your nasty accident? Are you back at work?'

'Oh yes, I am fully recovered, thanks Nicola. Just the odd twinge from my shoulder when I forget to take the painkillers, but otherwise I am fully functioning again, thank goodness. Madeleine and I had a practise last night for the TREC competition we have entered next month, so I have been back on a horse already, and it felt great.'

'Oh, I saw something about that on facebook. Sarah and I thought we might have a go, if Madeleine can let us hire a couple of horses for it.'

'What's that?' Sarah was back, and together with Tom and Amanda they distributed the plates of pate, seafood and garlic mushrooms amongst the group.

'You know Sarah, we were thinking about entering that TREC competition next month? The one at the Woodford Riding Club? Jennifer is doing it, with Madeleine.'

'Oh yes, that looks like great fun. But we need a bit of coaching, we are not entirely sure what it is all about.'

'Why don't you come with me on Sunday? Madeleine and I are having another practise, and I am sure she could give you some advice.'

'That's a good idea, except I will be working here. Maybe you and I can book a session with Madeleine some time next week, Nicola?'

'Yes, let's do that. It's decided; we are entering our first competition,' said Nicola. 'Thanks Jennifer. I am glad you are almost fully recovered; it sounded like a very nasty accident. Oh, I meant to ask,' she directed her question to include Paul. 'Did you ever find out what that strange note they found next to you when you fell, was all about?'

'What strange note?' asked Christine.

'Oh, that was creepy,' Jennifer shivered. 'Madeleine saw the motorcyclist, you know, the one who caused my accident last Friday, trying to push an envelope down my shirt while I was unconscious on the ground. Fortunately she scared him off before he could do it properly. When the emergency services came to rescue me, they found it on the floor next to me.'

'What did it say?' asked John from the other side of the table. Lisa gave him a look. Somehow they had ended up sitting on either side of one of the corners of the table, but this was the first time she had made eye contact with him. Lisa was still trying to work out if he really had left his career behind him, and his interest in this mystery suggested to her that he had not. John shrugged. She clearly wasn't interested in him, so he didn't need to try to persuade her of his decision anymore.

'It was addressed to me,' said Paul. 'Inside was a piece of paper with the words THINK AGAIN written on them.'

Lydia looked up from her plate of chilli prawns. 'What? That is exactly what was scratched onto Natasha's car!'

Chapter 38

Friday 12th August 2016, 8.00pm

Everyone looked at John, who shook his head.

'Honestly, I know nothing about any of this. Obviously I heard about Jennifer's accident, but I didn't know about the note the madman left at the scene, or about the vandalism to Natasha Holmes' car.'

'Yeah, right,' came the sarcastic comment from his left side.

'Look, Lisa, you can choose to believe me, or not, but it doesn't change the facts. I resigned as a serving police officer four weeks ago, and I have had no contact with any of my colleagues since then. I have no job, and no idea what I am going to do next. I only knew about the note which came with Cliff's flowers because I was there when your daughter brought them round, but that is all.'

Lisa had the grace to blush when she remembered she had assumed the bouquet was for her, from Robin. Catching his eye, she saw he had been told about her assumption.

Nicola looked up in surprise. 'Why was Caroline buying you flowers?' she asked Cliff, with a slight edge to her voice.

'She wasn't. Didn't. Someone left a bunch of white lilies at Lisa's house for me.'

'But that doesn't make any sense. Why would they leave them at Lisa's if they were for you?'

'I don't know!'

'Nor do I,' Lisa interrupted the escalating argument. 'But they came with an anonymous card addressed to Cliff, which had the words THINK AGAIN written on it. Do you really know nothing about this?'

John shook his head. 'I promise you, I do not. But I am sure I can find out who is dealing with this investigation, and ask them to talk to all of you?'

Paul said 'Ian McClure knows all about the attack on Jennifer and her horse, and of course she was riding out with Madeleine Powell so we cannot rule Madeleine's history and that of her parents out of the equation. I suppose the police up in Swanwick would be dealing with the vandalism to Natasha's car?'

He looked at his daughter who shrugged her shoulders. 'I suppose so. I only heard that her car had been vandalised and what was written on it. Kemp and Holmes' staff were full of it on Monday because Natasha asked everybody to be particularly careful about who was allowed in to the building. Apparently she had a bad date one evening last week, and she thought the man attacked her car to get back at her. She was pretty sure she knew who was behind it.'

'No one is dealing with my threatening bunch of flowers!'

Everybody laughed at Cliff's comical face.

'Do you still have the card?' John was serious. 'You need to report them to Ian, as soon as possible. White lilies can be sent to signify a death threat.'

'I hadn't thought of that.' Suddenly the intention behind the bouquet wasn't such a joke.

'I'll do it now.' John pulled his mobile from the inside pocket of his jacket and began to text PC McClure.

'Has anyone else been targeted that any of you are aware of? Have you heard of any other incidents from your customers in the tearooms?' he asked Lisa.

'Not that I can think of. The only strange thing has been that I keep having this strong feeling I am being watched, but I was beginning to suspect it was you.'

'Rebecca was feeling like that too, and I have been catching someone out of the corner of my eye but when I look properly nobody is there.' Cliff said. 'But neither of us thought it was you, John. We suspected it was Simon Maxwell-Lewis.'

John looked up sharply. 'Has anything happened to Rebecca? Or to any of your children?'

'Not that I know about; I will ring her now though, to check everyone is alright. You are beginning to worry me. I can't think why anybody would be targeting us. I am sure she would have told me immediately if anything has happened to them. But, let's not forget, it was Rebecca who Simon Maxwell-Lewis approached last year when he wanted to do me some damage.'

Paul tried to reassure him 'All Simon did was speak to her, and show her a photograph. He didn't attack her.'

'No, but he did cause an immense amount of damage to mine and other people's property in the antiques centre.'

John spoke quietly. 'Simon Maxwell-Lewis also physically assaulted the husband of the woman he was romantically interested in.'

'That's true, I had forgotten about that,' Cliff was looking very worried now as he tried to get in contact with Rebecca. All he could reach was her voicemail, so he left an urgent message, and phoned his oldest son.

'I am sure they are all alright, mate,' Paul tried to reassure him.

Everybody stopped talking and listened while Cliff had a brief conversation with his son.

'It's OK, everyone is alright, they are all sitting outside in the garden having a barbeque together. Rebecca's phone battery has gone dead, which is why it was going straight to voicemail.'

'That is a relief,' he wouldn't admit it to his friend, but Paul had also been worried about the safety of someone he considered to be one of his best friends, as well as a highly valued employee. 'Don't you think that by leaving those flowers at her house, whoever is doing this seems to think you are with Lisa?'

'Or Caroline' interjected Nicola. 'You do go running with her once or twice a week. Maybe the person left them for Caroline to find, and not Lisa?'

'If you think about it, Jennifer was targeted to get to me.' Paul agreed.

'So why was Natasha's car attacked?' asked Lydia. 'She doesn't have anyone else. She is a single, independent woman.'

'Unless they were trying to get to Bertram. Sorry, sorry, I shouldn't have said that.' Paul apologised when everyone in the room began to groan.

'No, you may be right Paul,' John finished texting Ian and rejoined the conversation. 'Ian is on his way over here. He should be with us in about ten minutes. If you think about it, it would only take someone believing that Natasha is involved with Bertram Kemp for them to attack her car, in the same way they attacked Paul's fiancée to get to him, and used one of you to send their threatening message to Cliff,' he nodded to Lisa.

'But Cliff isn't seeing either of them, so we are still left with the question of why were the flowers intended for Cliff left at Caroline and Lisa's house?'

'I have no idea, Nicola. There is nothing going on between you, is there?' There was a slight edge to his voice. Although he was beginning to accept that there was no hope of winning Lisa back, John certainly didn't like the idea of her with Cliff. Impatiently he looked from one to the other waiting for an answer.

'No!' both Cliff and Lisa shouted their denials.

'Or you and Caroline?' Nicola asked, crossing her fingers under the table.

'I promise you, Lisa,' Cliff looked over to Lisa, 'There is nothing between your daughter and me other than being running partners. I am old enough to be her father for goodness' sake!'

'Glad to hear it! But I suppose that could tie in with Robin, sorry John's theory about it only needing someone to believe people are romantically involved with each other for the other person to be dragged into the situation.'

'Evening all! I love saying that.' Ian McClure, Woodford's local policeman, arrived, bringing with him an air of purpose. He was a big dark haired man in his late thirties, and he filled the remaining space in the snug. 'So, is this the sort of official meeting where I can have a pint?'

'Yes, of course, I'll get you one. Anybody else like another drink?' While Paul took a list of names and drinks orders, Lisa made space so that Ian could squeeze around the table too, and sit down next to John.

'I don't know, John, you are only a month into retirement and already you have got yourself mixed up in some dodgy business,' he teased.

Ian and John had known and worked alongside each other for several years. For a while Ian had been tempted to join John and his team of undercover policemen, but he saw the stresses they were under and chose to remain a police constable in the small town of Woodford, where traffic accidents and people driving personal vehicles on red diesel with low fuel duty intended for farming use tended to be as challenging as it got.

John groaned. 'I really haven't, you know, it is just that everyone here began to talk about something, and all of the pieces started to fit together. That is why I called you; I don't want to be involved!'

'Too late!' Ian laughed. 'Ah, good man, thanks Paul, cheers everyone,' he raised his pint of Brackendon Best Bitter, and downed a third of it in one gulp. 'Right, who's going to start?'

'Wait a minute, let's get these out to the right people,' Sarah interrupted him, as she, Tom and Amanda passed the plates of chicken salads, seafood pasta, and sausage and mash to the diners.

For the next thirty minutes, in between mouthfuls of food the assembled group shared the information they knew. With the aid of several pieces of paper, Ian drew a diagram of incidents and coincidences involving some of the people sitting around the table. By the end of the evening there still did not appear to be anything, other than their profession, which connected the three apparent targets: Natasha, Paul and Cliff.

Eventually the individual members of the group decided they had had enough, and said their goodbyes, leaving only John Thomas and Ian McClure behind.

'Right, I am going back to the station for a couple of hours. There are a few things I want to check. Coming with me?' Ian stood up and stretched his tall frame to work out the kinks which had formed while sitting hunched on one of the low stools in the snug.

John groaned. 'I really want to walk away from all of this you know, but I feel as though this is unfinished business. Come on then; one last time.'

Together they left the pub, neither of them acknowledging the presence of the mother and son lurking nearby, but both men aware the pair were there and of their identities.

As they let themselves into Woodford police station a figure rushed in behind them.

'Finally! I have been trying to catch you on your own for days,' the man said to John. 'Hi Ian, come on, I have a lot to tell you. Quick, get that door shut and locked before those people see me.'

Chapter 39

Saturday 13th August 2016, 6.00am

One of the tasks PC Ian McClure completed the evening before was to arrange a meeting in the morning with his colleague, DS Patty Coxon, who was based at the Brackenshire police headquarters, in Swanwick. Together with John and their late night visitor they had pooled all of their information, and Ian was fairly sure he knew what had been going on. The question now was how to prove it.

Bright and early the next morning he kissed his wife, Hannah, and their baby boy, Oliver, and headed off on the hour's car journey from Woodford to Swanwick with John Thomas. Ian and Patty had worked together on a couple of other antiques-related cases in recent years, and he was confident she was somebody he could trust. He had sent her a brief outline of his suspicions by email, and before he and John left the station for the night, she had replied, and suggested they meet in person.

Theirs was a formal relationship, and so when Ian had been granted access to the inner workings of the Brackenshire police HQ, and he had found his way through the warren of corridors to Patty's office, she greeted him with a handshake, and indicated for him to sit down.

Patty and John were close colleagues, and they greeted each other with a hug and an exchange of pleasantries.

'Would you like a cup of tea? Or do you prefer coffee?'

'Nothing for me thanks, Patty.' John was eager to get the meeting over with as soon as possible. He meant it when he said he didn't want to be involved with police work anymore.

'Nothing for me either, thanks Patty.' Ian pulled his laptop from its case, and opened it up. 'Have you had a chance to look at the incident which resulted in the damage to Natasha Holmes's car?'

'Yes I have, and I will try and speak with her later on this morning.'

'Thank you. Poor Hugh has been lurking around Woodford, trying to catch John on his own to speak to him privately for about two weeks, and spooking some of the Woodford residents in the process. He didn't realise John was no longer a member of our police force, because his official police handler failed to pass on that information, and as far as Hugh was aware, John was still his local point of contact. In the end he was getting so desperate he decided to contact me, and it was fortunate he caught both of us at the same time.'

'Stupid man. He should have stayed in the safe house, and not gone running around the countryside. Anyone could have seen him and realised the rumours we were leaking were not true. He could have jeopardised the whole operation, let alone get himself killed, for real this time.' Patty was clearly furious with the way the situation had developed.

'He was lucky not to get caught, because it turns out that other pair were also hanging around at about the same time last night. It was only because John was on the alert for motorcyclists that he happened to notice

268

Veronica Bank in her leathers sitting with her mum eating an ice cream on The Green in Woodford a couple of days ago. I don't think we would have made the connection so quickly without ol' eagle eyes over there.' He pointed at John.

John mockingly bowed his head, accepting the compliment, and then continued 'Because we were already concerned about the Edwards family presence, it meant that when Hugh came in last night with his information we were already eighty percent of the way to working out what was going on. Otherwise neither of us would have believed him.'

Ian nodded his agreement. 'I don't think anyone had realised how much his mother and sister have taken over Adrian's formerly legitimate antiques business. Old Mrs Edwards and Veronica Bank are two women I would not want to tackle on a dark night. Or in broad daylight if recent incidents are any indication of the lengths they will go to.'

'No, nor me,' John was nodding his agreement. 'Veronica has always been a hard woman. Anyone who can shoot someone in cold blood, in a public convenience, and then calmly walk out through the service station and steal his truck, has got to have balls of steel.'

Patty did not like the faint sound of admiration in John's voice. 'Her brother Adrian is squealing like a baby, and thanks to his evidence we can finally link her to Miles Chapillon after all these years. We have always known she was one of his dolly-birds who worked for him, but Adrian was badly shaken by her actions on the Trailway last Friday, and he is giving the interrogating officers evidence of her involvement with Miles. I think until she tried to kill, or at the very least seriously maim Jennifer Isaac with life-changing

269

injuries, Adrian didn't really believe his sister could commit murder. Unfortunately the chances of proving she was the one who pulled the trigger all those years ago will be much harder, and sadly I expect she will get away with shooting dead Miles Chapillon.'

John asked 'What about the Edwards family's connection with the silver Miles Chapillon used to sell? Are we any closer to proving a link there, too?'

'That is going to be much harder, and it is unlikely that Adrian will be the one to give us any conclusive evidence, because it was his mother who was the brains behind that scam. The Edwards family have been benefiting from a very good living from old Mrs Edwards' artistic abilities combined with her business acumen. It is only since her health has started to fail, and Veronica has been able to get her hands on the mountains of faked silver they had stored away, that alarm bells began to ring in the antiques community. Because we suspect that it was Mrs Edwards who was supplying Miles Chapillon with his stock, it is going to be very difficult to prove that the silver items she has stored away were ever on his trailer at the antiques fairs.'

Ian was more concerned with the present, than the past. 'I hope Hugh got home safely? It was good of you to send someone to pick him up so quickly.'

Patty turned her computer screen around so that both Ian and John could see it. 'We couldn't risk his safety any longer, or the knowledge that he was still alive getting out. He was foolish to try and make contact with you, John, like that. He had a chain of communication and he should have used it.'

John shrugged, 'I don't think that was his fault; his handler didn't pass on the necessary information to him about my change of status.'

Patty nodded her agreement and made a note on the pad in front of her. 'So he says. I will look into that. Anyway, in the end it didn't matter, and no one else was hurt. He and his wife and children are now on their way to a new life, and he has more than earned it. I am surprised you haven't taken that option too?'

'Oh believe me, I have thought about it. But there is someone I want to stay for, and I don't think she is ready to start a new life anywhere with me. Yet. Although after last night I may have to accept that is never going to happen, and a ticket to Colorado for one might be a better option for me after all.'

Patty raised her eyebrows but kept her thoughts to herself. She turned back to the computer screen. 'Here we are. A list of some of the crimes we suspect Veronica Bank was guilty of committing. Over the past two years, which incidentally coincides with Mrs Edwards' declining health, there have been seventeen reported incidents where antiques dealers have been targeted by threatening messages either in the form of vandalism to vehicles or property, or who have been sent messages within gifts, all involving the words THINK AGAIN. Colleagues from the other forces where these crimes took place are reviewing those cases to see if the common link you two suspect is there. We should start to have that information any time now.'

Ian smiled. 'I knew you were the right person to come to. Did you go to bed at all last night?'

'I did, but not for long! Ah, here we go, look, the first review has been completed already.'

In silence the three of them read the report which had been added to the open file within the last few minutes. As they were reading them, another two appeared on the computer system.

Patty leaned back in her chair, a wide smile spreading across her features. 'We have got her!'

Chapter 40

Saturday 13th August 2016, 7.00pm

John Thomas, Paul Black, Jennifer Isaac, Lisa Bartlett and Cliff Williamson were gathered together in Paul's tiny cottage. Lisa was not happy about being there, but when Cliff came into the tearooms earlier in the day to ask her to join them, Caroline, who was helping her cope with the lunchtime rush, insisted she attend.

'I know that DS Patty Coxon has spoken to you all, and PC Ian McClure is now your go-to source for information, but they have both asked me to speak to you off the record. Which is, of course, all that I can do, since I am no longer a serving police officer.' He fixed Lisa with a look to make sure she was listening. Grumpily she acknowledged his statement. 'It is going to take several months to compile all of the evidence, but Adrian Edwards, his sister Veronica Bank, and their mother are in police custody, and because of the serious nature of the accident with your horse' John nodded to Jennifer 'combined with an incident involving acid, and another with fire, Veronica will not be granted bail.'

'So it was Veronica who I kept catching a fleeting glimpse of out of the corner of my eye was it?' asked Lisa, hoping that the mystery figure had not been her imagination, but also hoping that the person who had

273

witnessed her disastrous driving incident outside the back of the tearooms was not somebody she was going to bump into on a regular basis.

John hesitated for a second before answering. 'Yes.' he lied. In their late night meeting Hugh Jones had explained that he had been hanging around outside The Woodford Tearooms, The Ship Inn, and Black's Auction House in an attempt to speak to John, whilst also trying to dodge Adrian, Veronica and their mother. But Hugh's innocent involvement in the downfall of one of the biggest silver scandals in the British antiques world had to be kept a secret, for the safety of his family and friends who could not all be put into the witness protection programme. The rumour about his death had been started by the police, and it had grown legs and run, hence the variety of stories which had spread quickly through the antiques trade and beyond.

Cliff looked miserable. 'I never liked the man, but I can't believe that someone as successful in the silver trade as Adrian Edwards would have to stoop to producing all of that faked silver on such a massive scale. I mean, with all of the beautiful genuine items within his reach, why did he have to pollute the market like that?'

'Well, I don't want to defend the man, but I don't think he had much choice.' Lisa made a rude noise. John ignored her and carried on. 'His mother is a nasty piece of work. She comes from a long line of villains, and I truly believe she does not know any other way to live. She brought her daughter up in her own image, although Veronica does not have half the brains her mother has. Adrian was the spoilt baby boy, who never really grew up in his mother's eyes, and so he was spared the worst of her indoctrination. Yes, Adrian developed an amazing eye for genuine antique silver over the years, and he built a legitimate multi-million pound business through using his knowledge and skill. His mother and sister were the ones running the illegal business. But five years ago, when his father died, his mother moved in with him, and that was when she got her claws into him.'

Jennifer asked 'So how did you know where to start looking? I mean, trying to trace the origins of the fake silver must have been like looking for a needle in a haystack. Paul has told me how difficult it can be to detect the genuine from faked silver items.'

John was ready for this question. The true answer was that Hugh Jones had come to them with his suspicions based on the amount of identically flawed silver hallmarks he kept coming across in his working life. Antiques dealers are usually forthcoming about the source of their stock, and time and again the original seller would be Adrian Edwards, with no traceable seller before him. But while the extent of Hugh's involvement had to be kept a secret, John needed to find alternative facts to satisfy their curiosity. This was why neither Patty nor Ian wished to be the ones to meet the group: they had dealings with them before, and knew they would be asked searching questions which could only be answered with a lie. John replied airily 'Oh, like all these people they got greedy.'

He could see that this wasn't going to be enough of an explanation for Cliff or Lisa, and so he shared some more of the genuine facts of the case. 'Veronica Bank made a mistake in targeting Natasha Holmes. It seems that she did not realize who Natasha is now. Natasha is part of the family who run most of the property and food businesses here in the south-west, and Mrs Edwards is related to Natasha's father somewhere in their blood line. But Veronica did not realize that Natasha Holmes, the highly successful antiques auctioneer of today, is no longer the mousy, wouldn't say boo-to-a-goose little girl who attended their big family gatherings. Apparently Natasha has very little to do with her family these days.'

'I don't imagine she has much time,' commented Paul, and then at the collective warning noises made by the assembled group he quickly added 'I mean, because she must be so busy running that business of hers. I wasn't being snide.'

John continued 'However, Natasha recognized the marks Veronica scratched into her car alongside those words, as she was intended to, and then telephoned her parents.'

'What marks? You mean like Masonic marks or something?' Paul was intrigued.

'That's right. These families have their own methods of passing on information. Veronica included severe threats in her artwork on the car's paintwork, expecting quiet little Natasha to do as she was told. Instead, Natasha fought back using her family's connections, and their network swung into action. Within hours her family members had found out who was behind the damage. The family-run protection Adrian, Veronica and their mother have been living within for all of their lives was withdrawn, leaving them open and vulnerable to us. It turns out that as much as those people hate us, their idea of punishment for anybody who breaks their code is to deliver them into our hands. And an integral part of their code is that you do not threaten the life of one of your relatives.'

'I told you she was trouble' muttered Paul to nobody in particular, and everyone in the room ignored him.

'That still doesn't explain why those flowers for Cliff ended up at my front door. I hate to think those people were at my house,' Lisa gave a shudder.

'Yes, Patty asked Mrs Edwards about that because we didn't understand that incident either. Veronica is refusing to talk, and at first Mrs Edwards was not speaking either, but once she realized that none of her family, including her son, were going to protect her then we couldn't shut her up! We now have enough evidence in the form of the silver hallmarking punch with the identical flaws to the ones on the faked silver candlesticks and bowls and so on, to send her to prison for several years. Although it is unlikely she will live that long. Old Mrs Edwards is making the most of having people to talk to since she changed her mind about keeping silent, and is filling our case files with boasts about her life of crime, and how proud she is that her daughter is following in her footsteps. She feels that she has nothing to lose now.'

'Typical, she always was a loud-mouth' commented Cliff. 'I can't believe I didn't recognize her when I saw Adrian walking down the High Street with her last week? She literally looks like a shadow of her former self.'

'That is probably because she has cancer and is dying. She is very frail, and has lost a tremendous amount of weight in the past few weeks. The doctors do not hold out much hope for the latest treatments to be successful, and it is unlikely she will live long enough to be sentenced.'

'Oh, I don't like the woman for what she has done to us, especially to you via her daughter, Jennifer, but I wouldn't wish that on anyone,' Lisa voiced the thoughts of most of the group.

John continued 'She explained that all of you who were specifically targeted had rejected one or more pieces of their faked silver, and it had got to the stage where Mrs Edwards was having more of her stock rejected than accepted into auctions and antiques centres. It turns out she had been following Cliff, because she couldn't work out who, if anyone, he was romantically involved with, and over the years she had found that the most effective way of forcing people to do as she wanted was to threaten the ones they love. She knew he and Rebecca used to be married, but said that they seemed to spend a lot of time together for a couple who are meant to be separated.'

'Divorced.' Now it was Cliff's turn to mutter his correction of the situation.

'Sorry, divorced. Then she thought he and Nicola Stacey might be an item, but it seems that you two' John looked at both Lisa and Cliff questioningly 'had what Mrs Edwards described as a Lovers' Tiff in the middle of Woodford High Street last week, so she figured that you were seeing each other romantically.'

For a few seconds both Cliff and Lisa looked quizzically at each other before the memory of that excruciating encounter over Lisa's new hairstyle came back to them simultaneously, and they began to laugh. Long after Cliff had stopped, Lisa was still going, tears pouring down her face.

'Oh, I am sorry. Do you know, I can't remember the last time I laughed like that!'

Jennifer rubbed her arm. 'I think you have been under a lot of stress recently,' she said. 'I have noticed you are nearly always on your own in the tearooms at the moment. You must be hoping that Gemma recovers from her sickness bug very quickly?'

'Tell me about it. And it is about to get worse. I don't know if your father has told you, and I am sorry to break the news if he hasn't, but my sister isn't ill; she is having another baby!' Lisa complained.

'I told you so!' Cliff tried to High Five with Paul, but his friend was looking at Jennifer, whose mouth had dropped open.

'She is what?' Jennifer's tone brought the room to a frozen silence. Even Lisa picked up on the effect her casual moan had produced. 'What did you say, Lisa?'

'Ah. I guess that means your dad has not broken the good news to you? Sorry, I probably shouldn't have opened my mouth.'

'Good news? Is that what you call good news? Tell me, what, exactly, is good about it?'

Lisa decided, too late, that keeping quiet was the best decision, and simply shook her head at Jennifer.

'Darling…' Paul put his hand out to touch Jennifer's arm, but quickly withdrew it when she turned on him.

'Don't you "darling" me' she snarled, before leaping up from the sofa and storming out of the cottage, slamming the front door with as much force as she could manage.

Everyone in the room waited for the sound of smashing glass, but Paul's builders had made a good job of fixing the windows into their frames when they built his house.

'Maybe it would have been kinder to let her find out from Peter and Gemma?' Paul was furious with Lisa for upsetting Jennifer, but kept his tone even. 'That was not your news to share.'

'She's my sister, and it is our livelihood which is already being affected, so I have every right to tell whomever I choose about it!' Even though she knew she was in the wrong, Lisa was not going to give in without a fight.

'Believe it or not, this is not all about you' Paul was indignant.

Lisa threw her hands up in the air and yelled 'I give up!' before following in Jennifer's footsteps, but aware that she was already unpopular with the home owner, Lisa closed the door more gently.

'Pub, anyone?' asked John.

Chapter 41

Sunday 14th August 2016, 6.15am

Lisa was exhausted. Despite being run off her feet while she tried to manage the tearooms almost single-handed, she had spent the night wide awake, going over and over her behaviour towards both Gemma and Jennifer. Lisa kept replaying the way she broke the news of a future brother or sister to Jennifer, and how the rest of the people in the room had reacted to her. She wished she could go back and, this time, keep her mouth shut.

Lisa had been taken by surprise when Gemma came bouncing in to the tearooms and enthusiastically shared her news. Lisa was finally closing up for the day, after a very busy Friday afternoon when she had not stopped serving customers, clearing tables, stacking and emptying the dishwasher, and producing plates of food and drinks. She was exhausted, her feet and her back ached, and she was fed up with producing a second rate service for the customers by leaving them waiting longer than usual for their orders. The moans and whinging about the delays from ordering their food to finally receiving it were on the increase, and Lisa was at a loss as to how to rectify the situation until Gemma was feeling well enough to come back to work.

When Gemma appeared with a huge grin on her face and gleefully announced that she was expecting her third child in six months' time, and seemed to think Lisa would be as pleased as she was, Lisa could not believe how thoughtless her sister was behaving. Lisa had snapped at Gemma, and stormed out of the tearooms leaving Gemma to finish clearing up, while she went for a walk around The Green in an effort to calm down.

She was hurt that Gemma had kept it a secret from her. She was jealous that Gemma, who already had a happy experience when her first two children were born, was having a second chance. And she was lonely. She forced herself to go along to the meeting at Paul's cottage, but the last thing she wanted to do was sit and listen to someone else who had kept secrets from her. While John Thomas was talking, she barely listened to him, choosing instead to seethe at how unfair the world was to her. When Jennifer had offered her a word of comfort, Lisa responded by blurting out something she knew would have repercussions. By the end of Saturday evening Lisa had been on the receiving end of Caroline's, Gemma's and Peter's thoughts on her recent behaviour. Their disgust with her, combined with the realisation that she had deliberately attempted to make Jennifer as miserable as she was, kept her awake.

Today was going to be another busy day in the tearooms, and as she was awake Lisa decided to capitalize on the early start of a town event. The second of the Woodford Flea Markets was already underway as the sellers queued up on the High Street in preparation for driving down the small access road to Wellwood Farm, and turning left onto The Green before the farm's entrance. Lisa unlocked the front door from the inside, and started to go back to the kitchen before the sound of the cow bell made her turn to see who was coming into the tearooms.

'Robin' she sighed.

'John, please,' John Thomas closed and locked the front door behind him.

'What the hell do you think you are doing?'

Holding his hands up in surrender, John pleaded 'Please, Lisa, just listen to me.'

Before she could draw breath to start shouting at him, he took her by the arm and pushed her in front of him, into the kitchen and away from the windows which looked out onto the High Street.

Turning her to face him, and taking a firm hold of her other arm too, John said 'Look, you don't owe me anything, but please, just listen to what I have to say. Whether you like it or not, I love you. Whether you believe me or not, I am no longer a serving police officer. And whether you want me or not, I am determined to persuade you to give me a second chance.'

The sound of someone rattling the handle on the front door interrupted the moment, and Lisa seized her opportunity and pulled away from John, before hurrying back out to unlock the front door again.

For the next five hours the tearooms were filled with a steady stream of hungry antiques dealers and buyers, all desperate for some sustenance. To Lisa's annoyance, John got stuck in with the business of taking orders and clearing tables, leaving her free to prepare and deliver the food and drinks to her customers. The news of Gemma's pregnancy had already spread through the town, and Lisa had to face a number of questions about exactly how old Gemma was, and what the sisters were going to do with the tearooms. Time and again John rescued her by calling her back to the kitchen, and giving her the excuse to leave the gossiping customers, and rush back to save burning bacon, or prepare another plate of scrambled eggs.

Nicola Stacey popped in to buy a couple of bacon rolls to take back round to Williamson Antiques, for herself and Barry. She took in the scene of Lisa and John working alongside each other, but made no comment.

A short while later, Caroline let herself into the kitchen to check whether her mother had any spare cakes, because even though she thought she had plenty, the early start had meant that she had already sold out from her little café-caravan. She took one look at the busy tearooms and knew the answer to the cake situation without investigating further, and left before anyone noticed her, smiling at the teamwork she witnessed.

Cliff came in, pretending he wanted a couple of takeaway cappuccinos for himself and Sarah, but admitted to John that he had only come in because Nicola told him what was happening and he wanted to see for himself. He left empty handed.

All of a sudden the tearooms were empty of customers, and Lisa and John were alone.

'Thank you for your help this morning; I really don't know how I would have coped without you.' Lisa was surprised to find she felt grateful to John for his support.

'Well, thank you for letting me stay. I really enjoyed myself.'

Lisa tilted her head to one side while she thought about how to phrase the idea which sprung unbidden into her head. Tentatively, she said 'If you really are unemployed at the moment, do you fancy working here for a few weeks, until Gemma and I can decide what we are going to do with the business?'

John beamed 'Yes please, I can't think of anything I would rather do.'

Please leave a review on Amazon or Goodreads, or with your favourite retailer. Every review helps to promote these books to a wider audience, and therefore assist me to produce the next one!

For more information about me, please join us on the Kathy Morgan Facebook page, and @KathyM2016 on Twitter. #thelimnersart #thebronzelady #deathbyetui #silversalver

Kathy

Printed in Great Britain
by Amazon